Charmed AND Dangerous

Charmed and Dangerous

Shelly Page

joy revolution

Joy Revolution
An imprint of Random House Children's Books
A division of Penguin Random House LLC
1745 Broadway, New York, NY 10019
penguinrandomhouse.com
getunderlined.com

Library of Congress Cataloging-in-Publication Data is available upon request.
ISBN 978-0-593-89764-5 (trade pbk.) — ISBN 978-0-593-89765-2 (ebook)

Sparkles by SunnyScrap/stock.adobe.com, film reel icon by vladvm50/stock.adobe.com, book icon by alekseyvanin/stock.adobe.com.

The text of this book is set in 11-point Adobe Garamond Pro.
Interior design by Megan Shortt

Manufactured in the United States of America
1st Printing

The authorized representative in the EU for product safety and compliance is Penguin Random House Ireland, Morrison Chambers, 32 Nassau Street, Dublin D02 YH68, Ireland, https://eu-contact.penguin.ie.

Random House Children's Books supports the First Amendment and celebrates the right to read.

FOR QUEER GIRLS
AND '90S ROM-COM LOVERS

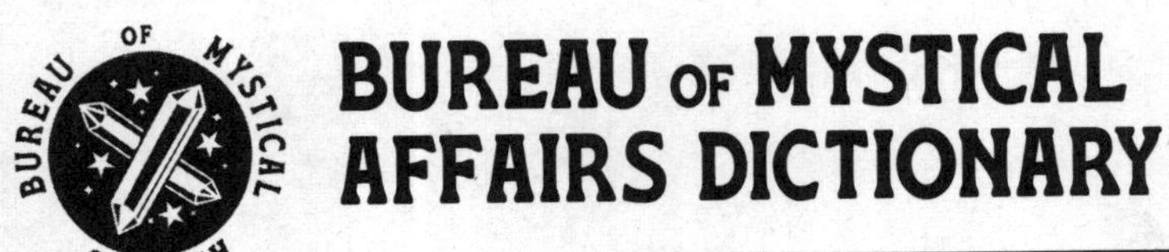

CHARM DUST—magic that can be sprinkled on a human or an object; once bottled or bagged, it is called a charm.

CHARMED—when a human or object comes in contact with charm dust

COLLECTIONS—a subdepartment of R&D that stores charms

COLLECTOR—a glass jar lined with quartz crystals used to neutralize charm dust

DISSOLVER—a counteragent that can remove charm dust from human skin

DISTRIBUTION—a department of the Bureau of Mystical Affairs that approves charms for sale

MUNDANE—a person who cannot see charms or their dust; most people in Fair Glen

MYSTIC—a person who can see charms and their dust

OPERATIONS—a department of the Bureau of Mystical Affairs that investigates contraband charms

RESEARCH AND DEVELOPMENT (R&D)—a department of the Bureau of Mystical Affairs that studies, categorizes, and houses charms, charmed objects, and their residual dust

RESIDUE—the remains of a charm, present after a charm is removed from an object or human

LOCAL RULES AND REGULATIONS OF MAGIC

TO BE ENFORCED BY THE BUREAU OF MYSTICAL AFFAIRS

1. The sale of all charmed objects must be vetted by the Bureau of Mystical Affairs.
2. Charmed objects deemed unsuitable for public use are considered contraband.
3. Charm dust meant for humans is considered contraband and must be turned in to the Bureau.
4. Charmed individuals are subject to investigation.
5. Anyone in possession of contraband will be in violation of Bureau law.

NOTE: Breaking any of these rules or regulations could result in criminal consequences.

Charmed and Dangerous

One

Of all the days to get stuck in traffic, why does it have to be on the most important day of my life? The clock on the car's dashboard reads 6:56. Having a meeting at seven in the morning is bad enough, but for there to be this much traffic at seven in the morning is the devil's doing. I've got four minutes to drive half a mile, which would be doable under normal circumstances, except the roads are completely gridlocked.

I can't be late for my first debrief as a junior recruit for the Bureau. Making a good impression is key, especially if I'm ever going to fill Dad's very big shoes.

Sweat dampens the collar of my suit jacket as I try to maneuver around the cars blocking the intersection. Lying on the horn does nothing. Every minute lost feels like an eternity. I make a sharp left around an SUV, hoping to cut through the alley.

A garden gnome darts in front of me.

I slam on the brakes and watch as the little green-and-red terracotta statue hobbles past my car. I squint. Am I hallucinating?

Two more gnomes race past. Nope. Not me. There are now three garden gnomes running through the intersection of Rosewood Avenue and Juniper Lane. Most cars swerve to avoid them.

One driver is too busy trying to take a picture to notice that a car's stopped in front of them. The crash happens in seconds. The loud crunch of plastic bumpers colliding is enough to make me pull over completely and climb out of the car.

The gnomes aren't close enough for me to see the charm dust animating them, but I know it's there. As a Mystic, I can help. As a junior recruit for the Bureau of Mystical Affairs, it's my duty to.

As I jog after the gnomes, I spot a vaguely familiar boy around my age who's built like a linebacker and has brown, disheveled hair. He jumps out of a dark green Volkswagen and runs over. The quartz crystal in his hands is already pulsating, faint filaments of magic ready to suck up the charm dust that has these gnomes causing chaos. The similar crystal I keep around my neck warms, activating. Together, we chase after the gnomes while carefully avoiding oncoming traffic.

I swerve around someone on a scooter, hop over part of a car's hood, and reach for a gnome in a green hat. The little minx slips right through my fingers.

The boy helping me is having a much easier time. His quartz crystal glows when he grabs the leg of a gnome just as it's trying to nosedive through a man's open window. The driver swears, and the boy grunts as he snatches the gnome before it can escape again. Its flailing limbs immediately still. Some of the residue from the charm spills to the ground, while the rest dissipates into the air.

Movement to my left catches my attention. The second gnome slides underneath a van in front of me. I race around the front and dive for it, seizing it by its pointed red hat. It stiffens into a lifeless piece of clay and pink charm dust falls to the pavement, as fine as grains of sand. I grab my collector, a glass jar lined with quartz crystals I keep in my bag, and scoop the dust inside. As long as most of the residue is contained, there shouldn't be any future mishaps.

The boy captures the last gnome and collects all the remaining dust on the pavement. I can hear clapping coming from people in their cars and the crowd on the sidewalk. The boy gives me a thumbs-up, tosses the two gnomes he caught—now lifeless—onto a grassy bank, and heads back to his car. I do the same with the one I captured and then jog to my old sedan. The time on the dashboard reads 7:06. Ugh.

I shift the car into drive and cut through the alley as planned. While I close in on my destination, I try to work out a good way to explain my tardiness.

A bunch of fairies decided to have a block party this morning.

Rosewood Avenue was closed for the annual lawn-gnome parade.

Never a dull moment as a Mystic, am I right?

Cringe.

Fair Glen, Illinois, is full of charms, vials of magic dust meant for people, and charmed objects that were leftover from a time when Mystics could create magic. Fifty years ago, Mirror Lake, the source of Fair Glen's magic, dried up from a drought. With it gone, there's no magic for Mystics to draw from. Mystics can still see magic but can't make new magic. We're stuck with the charms made during the time before the lake dried up. Since charmed objects are old, they sometimes degrade, causing mishaps like with the garden gnomes. What was likely a simple charm to make the gnomes wave or dance expired, resulting in them running through traffic like a herd of wild deer.

That's where the Bureau comes in. We stop the mishap and clean up the leftover dust so it doesn't cause trouble. Bureau agents also investigate contraband—mainly charms given to people illegally, which often have unpredictable and dangerous consequences, but also charms that are used as weapons. Contraband is the reason I was awake before seven today.

I turn into the parking lot and pull into the first spot I can find. I give myself a millisecond to admire the metal building in front of me, small white lettering at the front reading:

BUREAU OF MYSTICAL AFFAIRS
FAIR GLEN FIELD OFFICE

The Bureau has field offices around the country, each with the aim to study magic, approve charm usage, and investigate and prevent mishaps. I've been to the Fair Glen office countless times between visiting Dad at work and taking tours during school field trips. I spent my first semester of senior year as a trainee. On the weekends and after school, I shadowed agents and basically did grunt work like cleaning crystals and organizing reports filed on contraband. In the interim, like all trainees hoping to be promoted to junior recruit, I studied for the written exam on charms and crystals, passed the endurance test, secured recommendations, and successfully deactivated a charmed object in under sixty seconds. All that hard work paid off.

When I walk through those doors, it will be as a junior recruit. I'm finally getting assigned a case. No way am I blowing this opportunity.

Inside, Larry, the security guard who sits at the front desk, is nursing a large cup of coffee and listening to something on his phone. He's been working the desk since I was in diapers and has always seen me here wearing a visitor pass. Today, I flash him my official badge with a wide grin.

He takes out an earbud. "Nice job, Monroe! I knew you'd follow in your dad's footsteps. Head up to Operations. Seventh floor. And be quick. They've already started."

"Thanks, Larry!" I call over my shoulder as I sprint toward the elevator.

I tap my foot on the tile while I wait for the doors to open.

Dad's picture hangs on the wall across from me, along with other honored Bureau agents. I've traced his name on the plaque countless times since it was installed ten years ago. I've imagined my own name beside his for just as long. I grew up thinking he was a superhero. I saw how happy working at the Bureau made him. So when I was old enough, I didn't even think twice about applying to be a trainee. Getting into the Bureau last month was a huge life accomplishment, but I'm not done yet. There's a whole ladder to climb. And I want to leave behind a legacy like Dad did.

Just as I'm about to bite the bullet and take the stairs, the elevator arrives, and I dash inside. I check the time on my phone: 7:12.

The elevator dings, and the doors creep apart to reveal the dark-carpeted flooring and plain white walls of the seventh floor. Voices drift through an open door halfway down the hall. I bolt toward the sound, checking that my shirt didn't get too wrinkled during the gnome incident. Then I smack into something hard.

A muffled yelp sounds as pain erupts in my forehead and shoulder. I step back, holding my head, and someone gasps.

Once the dizzying haze clears, I realize I'm staring like a deer in headlights at the heart-shaped face and round dark eyes of Iris James, the Director's daughter. I know her from school and the random Bureau functions Dad would bring me to over the years. Her hair is styled in brown boho braids that fall in waves to her waist. Her white crop top looks good with the flowers she's drawn on her loose jeans. She's stylishly put together as usual, although I don't think I've ever seen that expression on her face before.

I follow her line of sight. The white button-down shirt I'm wearing under my navy suit for today's meeting—ironed perfectly, exactly like Dad taught me—is now covered in some kind of pink, glittery smoothie. As soon as I see the mess, I feel the cold seeping into my skin.

"Monroe, I am so—"

"It's fine," I say, more sharply than I mean to. "Do you have a napkin or something?" I manage to keep my tone even this time, but panic is seeping in faster than the smoothie.

"No, but I think there are sweats in the maintenance closet on this floor. Fair warning: They've probably been in there for a while."

An old sweatshirt is better than a shirt soaked with smoothie. Besides, I'm pretty sure you can see the outline of my sports bra now.

Taking off my blazer, I sidestep Iris without another word. Not only am I late, but I'm also going to be underdressed.

I find the closet, then grab the first sweatshirt I see. I do what I can with a few paper towels in the bathroom, and by the time I've changed and head to the conference room, it's 7:20. I glide inside the room silently and creep toward an open chair while Director James points at something on a PowerPoint slide.

I'm hoping not to draw too much attention to myself, but since I've been saddled with the worst luck today, I trip on a power cord. My hand juts out, catching on the edge of a swivel chair, which bangs into the table and jostles everyone's coffee cups and tablets. All eyes snap to me, including the Director's. Fantastic.

"Ms. Bennett, is there a reason you're late and out of dress code?" the Director asks. She's a stern-faced woman in her mid-forties with black hair styled in large finger waves and wire-frame glasses. She stuffs her hands into the pockets of her tailored blue pants and frowns. Her doubts about my competence are basically written on her face while she waits for my reply.

"Um . . . There were garden gnomes in the road."

A few snickers erupt around the room. I glance at my peers. There are four other junior recruits this spring, three I recognize from Fair Glen High, the public high school in our town, and one who must be from St. Mary's, the tiny local K–12 Catholic school.

The Director inclines her head. "Garden gnomes?"

I nod, grabbing the contained magic from my bag and carefully sliding the jar across the table. "I collected the residue."

The Director scrutinizes the swirling pink dust. The properties of magic make charms appear as pink dust on objects, and gold dust on people. The Director glances back at me.

"It's admirable that you helped to contain and gather degraded charm dust, but you missed the icebreaker and introductions. I was just about to start the debrief. Are you aware of the charm making its rounds at Fair Glen High?"

Everyone looks at me. Suddenly, my throat is desert dry. "Um . . . no."

"You haven't noticed the mishaps around school?" asks Taylor Evans, a dark-haired girl in my grade who has a sharp jaw and piercing blue eyes. She arches her brows challengingly. Sitting next to her is Jude Featherstone, her best friend. She's enviably tall with a stunning number of freckles and a curly brown afro.

The Director seems to be curious about my response. I don't want to get caught in a lie, so I reply honestly. "I haven't."

I've been a little busy trying to become a junior recruit. I may not have known about the charm at my high school, but I do know that, as a recruit, it's my job to figure out who is using or dealing the charm dust and stop them because it's strictly prohibited. Unlike charmed *objects*, which sometimes degrade and can cause minor accidents, charmed people almost always lead to mishaps because the conditions for the magic to work on them must be perfect. It's hard to know exactly what those conditions are.

The Director hums before turning back to the smart board in the front of the room. She probably thinks I'm inattentive now too.

Great. I'm trying to make a name for myself. All I've managed to do today is arrive late, underdressed, and unprepared. I plop into an open seat with a heavy sigh.

"Well, someone has gotten a hold of contraband and is using it on the students at your high school," the Director says. "A love charm, to be exact."

She clicks to the next slide: a bullet-point list about what the Bureau knows so far.

"The charm was first spotted three weeks ago at the Illusion Salon & Spa. A few of you were present during the event, but for those who weren't, interviews were conducted and outlined in the case notes, which you can access on our database. Essentially, a delivery boy was injured while conversing with the spa owner's daughter. Based on analysis provided by Research and Development, we believe the intent of the charm is to find the perfect love match."

She clicks to the next slide: a photo of the softball team next to a dozen balls lodged into a chain-link fence. I remember my best friend mentioning something weird happening with the team, but I didn't realize it was magic-related and, therefore, the Bureau's business.

"Charmed students keep having accidents when they try to pursue someone romantically. Flirting, hand-holding, asking someone on a date, you get the gist. Aside from the incident at the spa, the situation is presently contained to Fair Glen High, but we're concerned it could spread. We're under pressure from the mayor to figure this out before someone gets seriously hurt. As this has only hit teenagers so far, we want our junior recruits leading the investigation. With my direct oversight, of course," the Director says.

"Are we sure it's only one charm causing problems?" Taylor asks.

The Director moves to the following slide. Two pictures side by side show a girl in a softball uniform and a boy in a delivery uniform, both with flakes of gold dust beneath their skin. "We tested the dust. It's the same."

"Has the charm worked for anyone?" I ask. *Or is everyone just shooting their shot with the wrong person?*

"Good question. Mishaps stop once the charm's intent comes to fruition. In this case, the person charmed should be cured once they find a true romantic match. We haven't seen this happen in real time yet. It's very possible that other people, besides those we have recorded, were charmed but their feelings were reciprocated and thus no mishaps occurred.

"Research and Development is trying to find a dissolver that will dispel the charm dust from persons affected. In the meantime, you five need to find out who's behind its distribution."

A phone number appears on the next slide. "Save my number. I have all of yours from your applications. Don't hesitate to reach out if you need advice or run into trouble. Don't try to contain a situation if it seems too big to handle alone. Call it in. Remember your training. Look at this as a test of your skills, not only to analyze charms and theorize suspects, but to communicate and problem solve. We'll have regular check-ins to go over your findings. Any other questions?"

I look around the room, taking in the rest of the recruits. Around the table are rapid nods and eager smiles. Taylor and Jude look giddy as they furiously scribble down notes. Am I the only person who's terrified? This is all I've ever wanted, and now that the opportunity is here, I'm afraid I'm going to mess up.

"Okay," the Director says. "Meeting adjourned."

I gather my things as quickly as I can, hoping to have a word with the Director before she leaves, but Taylor blocks my path.

"Cute shirt. Is that the nicest one you own?" Taylor asks and Jude snickers.

I roll my eyes. "Very original."

"Don't think you're getting special treatment just because you're a legacy kid," Taylor says. "Some of us actually had to work hard to get this."

"Me included," I grit out.

I knew facing nepo-baby hostility was a possibility. Dad was one of the Bureau's shining stars until last year, when he retired to start his own private magic-cleaning business and to spend more time with me. Dust-B-Gone is doing great, and he travels way less. Still, his legacy here remains. I don't want to be treated differently because of it. In fact, his acclaim is more of a reason for me to prove myself.

I brush past Taylor and her amused expression, beelining for Director James. She's tapping on the glass window of the break room to get Iris's attention.

"Excuse me, Director. I'm sorry for being late to the debrief. I did leave on time, but the gnomes caused a huge traffic jam and, well, I also needed to change after my shirt got ruined." I know I'm rambling, and the truth sounds like a bad excuse.

The Director turns to me. "Tardiness is not something you want to make a habit of, Monroe." She peers over the rim of her glasses. "Your dad was an excellent agent. I've been looking forward to seeing how you do as a junior recruit. This was not the first impression I expected. This first assignment will not be easy, and I was a bit surprised you were out of touch with what's happening in your school."

Shame floods me. Iris, who has slunk out of the break room with her hands tucked into the front pockets of her jeans and purple headphones covering her ears, gives me a curious look.

"I'm not as social as Taylor," I reply, "but it won't stop me from doing my best to solve this case."

"Good. No more showing up late and unprepared. Do you need a ride to school? I'm dropping off Iris."

"No thank you, ma'am. I drove," I say.

"Okay. Don't forget to take the residue from your morning collection to R&D before you leave," the Director reminds me as we walk out.

She jabs a manicured nail at the elevator call button and turns her attention to her phone. The other recruits waiting to go downstairs are chatting quietly among themselves. I feel very awkward standing here doing nothing. As I head for the stairs, my shoulder brushes Iris. She trails her gaze from my windswept hair to my loafers, and I suddenly forget what I'm doing. She smirks.

The elevator dings, and everyone piles inside but me. By the time the doors close, I've managed to come back to earth. I shove the whole encounter with Iris from my mind and take the stairs down to the fifth floor.

Research and Development, aka R&D, is a row of labs and storage lockers where the Bureau studies, categorizes, and houses charms, charmed objects, and their residual dust. Once an agent collects residue, it's processed, then archived.

I shuffle down the tiled hallway, aware that school starts in ten minutes. Enormous glass windows reveal blocks of tables lined with microscopes, beakers, droppers, and bins full of crystals.

Researchers in lab coats and gloves run about, pushing bins full of random charmed objects ranging from rugs to doorbells.

Inside one of the rooms, microscopic views of magic are displayed on flat monitors docked at each station, appearing as pink or gold strings. On a shelf, I spy glittering pink swirls of charm dust in glass vials.

In another room, a technician sprays a silver substance onto a dish. The gold dust in the container disintegrates before my eyes. Although no one can make new magic, R&D uses different counteragents like that silver substance, aka the dissolver, to dispel charms from human skin. Crystals work on a small scale to fix wonky charmed objects, but charms given to people, which are contraband, need much stronger magic to undo. Depending on the charm's anatomical properties, dissolvers can be anything that fights the original charm's intentions—from witch bells to sage sticks to other charms. While it's amazing to see the scientific side of magic, I love being in the field more—seeing magic in action.

"Um, excuse me. Where can I drop off a collection?" I ask the first person who passes me, a boy with his head down moving in long and quick strides.

He looks up. "End of the hall. I'll be there in a minute."

With a start, I realize that it's the same familiar-looking boy who helped me with the mishap this morning. I must've seen him around the Bureau. "Hey! You work here?"

Recognition washes over him slowly. "Gnome girl. Yeah, I'm an R&D recruit. I handle collections during this time. What's your name?"

"Monroe Bennett."

"Bennett. Like Jeffrey Bennett?"

"Yep. He's my dad."

"That's awesome! I'm Noah Cham. Good work this morning," he says with a grin.

We step aside as a woman in a white lab coat passes by carrying vials of charm dust.

"Thanks," I reply. "I'm still new to all of this."

"You don't adjust overnight, but keep at it."

I rub my hands together, thinking of my disastrous start today. "I have some pretty big shoes to fill."

Noah's expression softens. "Are the other field recruits already giving you trouble?" When I don't reply, he nods to himself. "Figures. They're intimidated. Want to exchange phone numbers? You can text me if you need anything. I don't know if I'll be much help, but I'm a good listener."

A smile breaks across my face. "Likewise." I give him my phone, and he plugs in his number before handing it back to me.

"I need to run a quick errand, but I'll be back up shortly if you want to leave the dust in the bin," he tells me before heading toward the elevators.

Did I just make a new friend? Maybe today isn't a total dud after all.

The drop-off bin is a plastic container poking out the bottom half of a Dutch door. It's full to the brim with glass vials of charm dust. It reminds me of the book-return bins at Fair Glen High's library. How does anyone go through all of this?

Once I deposit the dust from the gnomes, it will be sorted—probably by Noah—then archived since it's evidently degraded and has caused mishaps in town. When new charms are found, usually in the unlikeliest of places, like someone's attic or shed, the Bureau determines whether they are stable enough to redistribute. Since Mystics can't make more magic, people reuse leftover charms or buy charmed objects from independent vendors. Stores can sell charmed goods, like infinite bodywash, announcing doors, singing welcome mats, or mood-changing nail polish, only if they're approved by the Bureau. Charms meant for humans can never be sold. Way too risky. Whoever is giving the love charm to my classmates didn't get it from a reseller. So where did it come from?

I drop off the residue I collected from the gnomes and head straight to school, feeling determined and excited to crack this case wide open.

BUREAU OF MYSTICAL AFFAIRS
RECORD OF INCIDENT

DATE: Monday, March 2

RESPONDING OFFICER: Junior Recruit Monroe Bennett

CASE NUMBER: 26-311880

LOCATION: Rosewood Avenue and Juniper Lane

SUMMARY: Around seven a.m., three charmed garden gnomes escaped their yard and ran through an intersection, causing an accident and a massive traffic jam.

ACTIONS TAKEN: Noah Cham and I caught the garden gnomes, removed the charm dust that brought them to life, and collected what remained.

RECOMMENDATION: This charm should not be approved for redistribution unless the goal is more escape-artist lawn ornaments.

Two

The sun is high in the sky, casting lemon-colored rays of light over the endless, flat terrain surrounding me. If it weren't for the Bureau, Fair Glen would be a boring place to live. There's nothing but stalks of corn, one-lane roads, and short brick buildings. It's a town of only five thousand people but happens to have the largest collection of magic outside of Chicago. Working with magic and solving cases is exactly what I want to do after college. Luckily, the Bureau office hires high school recruits. So for me, Fair Glen is perfect.

Most students are already at school when I arrive. Some go straight inside while others hang out on the blacktop behind the building, enjoying every minute they can before the first bell rings. On my right, Taylor Evans and Jude Featherstone climb out of a green car, and whoever is behind the wheel drives off a second later. They both ignore me and promptly head inside.

I take a beat to stare at the redbrick building in front of me, which seems somehow both the same and different knowing I'll be looking into my teachers and classmates. Someone is dealing a love charm to students. Part of the reason the Bureau assigns this kind of case to junior recruits is because it's less daunting talking to a peer than a Bureau agent. As Dad would say, you catch more flies with honey. The problem is, how am I supposed to find this person when I'm not exactly Miss Popular?

Anyone could be behind this, but a Mystic makes the most sense because Mundanes can't see magic. Once I find a clue or even the barest hint of a lead, I can start building a suspect list.

My collector clangs against my books and crystals as I sling my bag over my shoulders and head inside. Crystals, like quartz, tourmaline, and even selenite, are good at removing energies, which is essentially what magic is—old intentions, good and bad. Charm dust on objects can be removed using crystals, but charm dust on a person can be removed only by using a dissolver because the magic seeps into their system and is driven by their actions.

Take the love charm, for example. It activates when the person charmed tries to romance someone who isn't a match with them. In this case, the only way to stop the charm from causing mayhem is to find a match for the charmed person or hope R&D finds the right dissolver to remove the dust.

A slow-moving line of sleepy faces and smudged eyeliner passes me. I don't make it to the main hall before a slip of paper is shoved in my face.

"Vote for me for prom queen!"

Chloe Nguyen smiles like a politician, all white teeth and wide eyes, which tracks since she's our class president. Her dark hair is tied up with a blue ribbon that sways as she waves her flyer in my face. I take it reflexively.

"And don't forget to grab a latte!" she tells me before moving on to the next unsuspecting victim of her campaign.

There's a table set up next to me with cups of steaming liquid and a huge cardboard sign that reads:

VOTE CHLOE FOR PROM QUEEN!

Considering I had to wake up early for the debrief this morning, caffeine might be the only way to stay functional the rest of the day. I grab a cup and trudge on.

Someone drapes their arm around my shoulders as I head for my homeroom.

"So how was it?" Andie Rivera, my best friend, asks. He's wearing his signature jet-black eyeliner and a purple pimple patch in the shape of a star below his eye. His blue hair falls into his face as he navigates us through a crowd of students.

"It was a mess," I reply. "For starters, I was late. Garden gnomes caused a huge traffic jam between Rosewood Avenue and Juniper Lane. I caught one, and someone who works at the Bureau caught the other two. But man, the Director was not pleased after I missed the first half of the meeting and showed up clueless."

"And your shirt?" Andie asks, gesturing toward the musty sweatshirt I'm still wearing.

"Ugh. Courtesy of Iris James and one large smoothie."

"Yikes. Well, that Good Samaritan stuff is what got you into the Bureau in the first place, right? I'm sure the Director will understand."

"I had to train, get a letter of recommendation, and pass a written and physical exam. Junior recruits aren't guaranteed agent status once we turn eighteen, so basically, this is just a trial period, one I can't mess up."

Andie waves me off. "You won't." He holds the classroom door open for me, and we step inside. The door announces our arrival.

"Monroe Bennett! Andres Rivera!"

"It's *Andie,*" he corrects, releasing an annoyed grunt.

The door is charmed to announce us from a list of names our homeroom teacher reads to it at the start of the semester. Saves the teacher time on taking attendance. But Mr. Patterson has yet to make corrections to the list despite the regular reminders. He genuinely seems forgetful, but it still feels personal to me and Andie. Maybe because we're gay and preferred names are important.

There are only a few people here, including Mr. Patterson, who's wrestling with our charmed chalkboard at the front of the room. Today it seems to have a mind of its own, immediately erasing all the words he writes when it's supposed to shift his atrocious handwriting into more legible, larger text, especially for the kids in the back. Mr. Patterson mumbles to himself about needing a raise. Most of the time, charmed objects are well behaved, doing exactly what they're supposed to do without much fuss. But sometimes, very old magic, like from the nineties, degrades. The chalkboard is definitely old.

Andie and I find seats in the last row of the classroom as usual. As soon as we sit down, Andie's phone lights up with a text. He ducks his head and smiles softly.

"Who are you texting?" I ask while leaning over and trying to read the name.

"No one," Andie singsongs.

"That's a weird name. I hope he's cute, at least," I reply.

Andie grins. "He is. He paid for my donut at Bewitched Buns last month. We've been talking ever since. I'm pretty sure he's the golden retriever boyfriend all the girls, gays, and theys want." Andie fans himself and pretends to swoon.

"Sounds like a catch. What's his real name, and when do I get to meet him?" I ask.

"He goes by Neo. He's a senior at St. Mary's. And prom? I've been charging the freshmen ten dollars for makeup tutorials, so I can splurge on a cute outfit," Andie says.

Here we go again. Prom. The event of the year. Good thing I've completely sworn it off. "Nice try."

"I wish you'd go," Andie whines. "You don't have to ask anyone or be asked, you know. Just come with me and Neo. Or take Liz." He gestures to our mutual best friend, Liz, who's strolling into homeroom just as the bell rings.

"Elizabeth Palomino!" the door announces.

Dad always says having a couple of good friends is better than a lot of mediocre ones. Liz and Andie are as good as they come. I've known Liz since pre-K, and when Andie moved to Fair Glen two years ago, he melded into our crew like he'd been with us for years. They always have my back and stepped up when my parents broke the news about their divorce. My friends came straight over, with Andie streaming *Pose* and *RuPaul's Drag Race* and Liz keeping my plate full of her homemade chocolate cupcakes.

"I'm not going to prom. And I don't want to be a third wheel," I reply.

"You wouldn't be if you go with Liz," Andie insists.

"Don't bring me into this. I'm going to be out of town, remember? My brother's wedding." Liz takes the open seat next to me. She keeps her curly brown hair cut short to show off an impressive collection of ear piercings.

"Okay, fine. It looks like you have to bring a date, Roe." Andie folds his hands on his desk. "Who are you crushing on?"

I ignore the uncomfortable tug in my chest at even the mention of crushes. "I'm focused on the Bureau right now. Not girls. And after my disastrous morning, I can't get distracted by dating."

Andie and Liz share a look but don't say anything, at least not while I'm sitting here. Announcements blare over the speaker, Chloe's staticky voice filling the room. Andie starts texting his new boo while Liz draws trees in her sketchbook.

They don't understand why dating is the last thing on my mind right now. Even if I weren't in the Bureau, romance seems pointless when I'm not even sure that kind of love exists. What *is* real is the

Bureau. Even during the divorce, Dad found happiness working there. Being able to help people plagued by magical misfortunes is the thing that makes my heart race. Romantic love only reminds me of hard times and broken promises. I'm good without it, and nothing's changing my mind.

The gym smells like armpits, wet socks, and tears. The lights need to be replaced, so it's unnecessarily dark in here. Perfect mood-setter. You'd think being in the Bureau means a free pass from gym class since part of the requirements for recruitment is a physical exam. But no. I'm still required to complete whatever torture Mr. Kowalski invents twice a week for the rest of the school year. (I guess the Bureau higher-ups want to make sure you're always able to run after garden gnomes.)

Today, there are different stations for us to use: hoops, sit-ups, planks, sprints, rope climbing, and some adaptive strength training exercises for those who need them. Mr. Kowalski divides the class into five groups of four. Andie pouts in my direction when he's put into a group with Taylor and Jude.

I'm stuck with Dante Morelli, a boy in my homeroom who's on his phone; Iris, my boss's daughter; and Anita Patel, Iris's girlfriend. Iris has changed out of the clothes she was wearing this morning at Bureau headquarters and into a long-sleeve FGH shirt and yoga pants.

None of us say a single word to each other. Our first station is rope climbing. To get a break from the awkward silence, I go first.

My upper body strength is decent, yet the skin on my hands tugs as I hoist myself up the rope. I lock my feet around the knot at the bottom and repeat the process, my arms burning with each inch I gain. The rope sways. I look down at the others in my group. Dante is still on his phone, and Iris and Anita are too busy staring at each other to notice me struggling.

"Hey!" I yell. "Can one of y'all hold the rope?"

Iris jerks her head up. She grabs the swaying rope, but asking for help was hardly worth the trouble. I'm sweating, and my arms are shaking when I attempt to resume my ascent. It's no use. I make it halfway to the top before realizing going any farther is impossible.

I ease myself down and catch my breath while Iris starts to climb, and Anita steadies the rope. Iris looks over her shoulder at Anita and winks. Anita rolls her eyes and sighs.

That's when the rope begins to move on its own. It yanks itself out of Anita's grasp and thrashes to the other side of the room. Iris makes a startled noise, drawing everyone's attention. Mr. Kowalski is frozen in shock, looking paler than a ghost. Dante has finally stopped texting, but only so he can point his phone at Iris. Anita's hands shake as she looks around for help.

I move closer. Shimmery gold dust seeps from Iris's palms onto the rope. Even though the dust is stuck to Iris's skin, it can transfer to objects she touches. If she's been covered in the love dust, the charm's goal is to keep her away from a mismatch . . . Anita?

The smoky quartz and black tourmaline crystals around my neck warm, signaling that I can dispel the dust from the rope. I jut out my hand and the wriggling cable stills. Unfortunately, Iris is unprepared for the sudden stop. She loses her hold, and her body falls.

Everything slows to the pace of poured molasses. I race forward on instinct, but this isn't a Marvel movie. I can't catch her out of thin air and walk off like nothing happened. What does happen is Iris lands on top of me, the two of us plummeting onto the sticky blue mat in a pile of limbs.

All the air in my lungs whooshes out. My vision is obstructed by hair; my nose invaded by the sweet scent of lavender perfume. I brush Iris's braids out of my face with my free hand, the other one trapped somewhere underneath her back. Our eyes lock, my breath catches, and I'm surprised to find that looking away is harder than it should be.

The fear in her deep brown eyes slowly recedes, replaced with something closer to surprise. Our classmates' murmurs only distantly register. All my focus is on Iris. Up close, I notice her lilac eyeshadow and the gentle dimple on her right cheek, but more importantly, the faint sparkle of charm dust that makes her skin shine like freshly mined gold.

I wriggle out from underneath her, straighten my glasses, and tug Iris to her feet, holding her hand until she can steady herself.

Mr. Kowalski is next to us a moment later. His brown mustache twitches as he asks, "Are you two good? What happened?"

"I—I don't know. One minute I was climbing the rope, and the next it was trying to fling me into the cosmos!" Iris exclaims.

"It sure did appear that way," Mr. Kowalski replies with a frown so deep it looks comical.

Taylor rushes over, slightly out of breath, her eyes the size of saucers. "Iris, are you okay? There's charm dust . . ." She trails off, glancing at me.

We both know the rest of that sentence. The magic on Iris shimmers like glitter. Is this the same charm as the one we were debriefed on this morning at the Bureau? Iris stares at us like we've grown extra heads.

"Iris, Monroe, the two of you should go to the nurse. I'll have Mx. Michaelson come and check the rope."

Mx. Michaelson, aside from being an awesome librarian, is a Mystic and our school's go-to inspector for the occasional magical occurrence. They don't work for the Bureau, preferring to educate and organize rather than be in the field; they simply volunteer to keep FGH as safe as possible.

"It's not the rope," I reply to Mr. Kowalski. Not anymore. I can remove charm dust from objects Iris touches so they're no longer hazardous, but mishaps will keep happening whenever she flirts with the wrong person until R&D can find a dissolver. Until then, Iris and everyone else who's charmed are spreading their magic germs whenever they attempt even a smidge of romance.

"You need to see the nurse," Mr. Kowalski insists. He's a nervous man already, always checking his watch, drumming his hands, and casing the area. He looks more shaken than me and Iris. "Have her make sure you aren't injured."

"I'll write up a Bureau report during my free period after this. Go and talk to the nurse. Make sure you're both good," Taylor says, gesturing toward the exit.

Mr. Kowalski nudges Iris and me out the door. In the empty hallway, the faint sounds of students typing and teachers lecturing filters through the quiet between us.

Iris appears torn on where to begin and settles on, "Thanks for breaking my fall."

I rub the arm that took most of her weight. "I'm pretty sure I'm going to have a bruise the size of Texas tomorrow."

"You're supposed to say you're welcome," she huffs, sweeping her boho braids out of her face. The silver cuffs on the front strands twinkle.

"You're welcome." I shuffle my feet and stare at her some more, trying to figure out how I didn't know she was charmed until she was halfway up the rope. The gym's lighting is shot, but also the gold charm dust blends so perfectly with her complexion it almost looks like part of her makeup.

"Why are you staring at me? It's creepy," Iris says, snapping me back to the moment.

"Oh. Um. I think you're charmed," I say, gesturing to the dust that has seeped beneath her skin.

Iris's eyes widen. She rubs her hands over her skin as if that will do anything. It won't. Since magic can be found anywhere, lots of people experience the effects of a wayward charm at least once in their lives. Iris just has the misfortune of being intentionally charmed.

"Charmed? Are you sure?" Iris asks.

I nod slowly. "You have dust all over you."

"So what happened in the gym . . ." Iris trails off.

"Will keep happening until the Bureau finds a way to remove it permanently."

"Jesus." Iris scrubs a hand down her face, slightly smearing her makeup. "How did this happen? *When?* No one has said anything." She looks around. There's no one else in the hallway with us. "Do you think it's the love charm the Bureau's investigating?"

Surprise jolts through me. "You know about that?"

Iris shrugs. "My mom regularly falls asleep on top of her case files. I might've peeked at the one labeled 'Fair Glen High.' "

Somehow, I can't picture the Director with her stern expression and ramrod spine slumped over casework. Then again, I would sometimes find Dad asleep on the couch with a case file on his stomach. "You need to tell your mom," I say. "She can have the residue on you tested to be sure."

I'm pretty positive this is the love charm, though. Charms aren't so common that there would be two of them hitting our school at the same time.

Iris rubs her temples. "This is the last thing I need right now. I'm trying to get back with Anita before prom."

I didn't know she and Anita broke up, although again, I'm embarrassingly out of touch with the school gossip.

"Has anything like that happened before?" I ask as we make our way down the hallway. I'm certain I didn't see any gold dust on her this morning at the Bureau. We were standing as close as we are now. Plus, her mom would've clocked the shimmery substance clinging to Iris immediately. She must've been recently charmed. Sometime between our run-in at the BMA and gym class.

"Definitely not," Iris confirms.

Iris comes to a stop outside the nurse's office. "Are you going in?" she asks, a single eyebrow raised in challenge.

"I've got better things to do than hold a lukewarm ice pack against my arm." Like figure out *how* Iris was charmed. She just might be my first lead. "Can you think of anyone who would want to charm you?"

"What does this charm do exactly? I didn't make it far into snooping before my mom woke up," Iris says.

"It's supposed to prevent mismatched love," I reply.

Iris's mouth opens. "I was literally flirting with Anita when that rope tried to loveblock me! A mismatch? Fake. We're perfect for each other."

I wince. "Maybe the relationship *seemed* perfect?"

"Nope. It was. *Is*." She crosses her arms. "I'll prove it. Aside from our astrological signs being aligned—I'm a Cancer, she's a Taurus—the fortune teller at the mall said we'd be together forever."

"A fortune teller?" I snort. "Come on, Iris."

She steps closer to me. "The charm could be defective. Who knows how old it is. It might've started to degrade or was bad from the jump. It's possible."

"True. But—"

"I don't trust it."

"Fine. Don't. I only want to know who would charm you."

Iris deflates a little. "No one I can think of." She glances at the clock on the wall. "Anything else? Because I have fifteen minutes of freedom, and I don't want to waste them."

"We're good for now," I reply.

"Cool. Thanks again for the assist."

She brushes past me, heading away from the nurse's office and toward the exit. She throws a dazzling smile over her shoulder that's inching toward the line between friendly and flirty, and then steps outside into the waiting sun.

Iris and I have talked more today than in the past four years. We don't travel in the same social circles or have many classes together. At Bureau functions, she's always hanging out with Taylor and Jude. But I've got a gut feeling, considering she's charmed, that we'll be talking a lot more now.

I use *my* fifteen minutes of freedom to work the case before my next class. I spin on my heel and head toward the girls' locker room. I scan the floor for evidence, as well as the benches, and then open all the lockers. I find nothing but regular dust, a soggy sock, and some hair ties. I even check the trash bins and the mildewy showers. No sign of charm dust. Whoever charmed Iris didn't do it here, or if they did, they were strategic. Could a Mundane have charmed Iris with such precision when they can't even see magic? Maybe they had help?

I head to my next class, wondering whether the culprit is a Mystic from Fair Glen High. That certainly would narrow down suspects.

When I get home from school, the scent of spicy baked mac and cheese and the sound of smooth jazz lure me toward the kitchen. Dad's set up at the table with a stack of crystals and his cleanser—a narrow container charmed to trap sunlight and moonlight, which are the best methods for cleaning all crystals. It was a retirement gift from Director James. Only a handful even exist in Fair Glen. Other Mystics charge their crystals the old-fashioned way: on the windowsill.

Like snowflakes, every crystal is unique. Some have cracks, ridges, and bumps from being unearthed. Others have different levels of clarity and even subtle changes in colors depending on how the light hits. They also come in different shapes and even feel different when you hold them in your palm, ranging from warm and pleasant to prickly and cold. Dad's crystals have very few imperfections, and they serve him well on his cleaning jobs.

Dad glances up from his work and notices me. I look more like my mom than him with my short stature and round face, but we do have the same smile.

"Hi, Roe!" He crosses the room and hugs me. "How was school?"

"It was fine," I say, once we part.

"And your first day as a junior recruit? Are they still making you trek to the seventh floor for debriefs?" Dad chuckles to himself.

Do I tell him what a mess my first day was? Nah. "Also fine."

Dad pauses, reading my face. He tosses a towel into the sink, and when he lifts it, the dishes that were previously dirty are clean and sparkling. As is the case with most Mystics, many objects in our house are charmed. The charmed rag is one of our favorites because neither of us likes doing the dishes.

Dad grabs two clean bowls from the drying rack. "Did something happen? Was Laura too hard on you kids? I can talk to her—"

"No! It wasn't that. I was just late and a little out of the loop."

Dad scoops three heaps of spicy mac into each bowl and hands one to me. "How'd you wind up late? You had three alarms blaring so loud this morning, you nearly woke the neighbors."

"Garden gnomes," I start, and then relay how I wrangled them with the help of another recruit.

Dad's eyes crinkle at the corners when he smiles. "You did good. The Director will see that," Dad replies, easing some of my worry that I've already blown this. "Have you talked to your mom today?"

The cheesy goodness I'm currently downing turns sour. "Nope."

"You should give her a call."

I shake my head. "I don't have anything to say to her."

"Tell her how your first day went."

"Our conversations always feel forced and awkward because all I can think about is how she left."

Dad winces. "She *moved out* because we separated, and you opted to stay here."

"This is our *home*." I cross my arms and focus my attention on the table. "She's the one who stopped seeing it that way."

Dad sighs. "You can't keep punishing her for the divorce, Roe."

"I'm not." The response doesn't ring true, so I add, "I'll text her."

He nods more to himself than to me. "Good, because she wants to see you. It's been a month since your last visit. She's your mother. Give her another chance to explain her side of things. Don't avoid her forever, okay?"

I stir the macaroni in my bowl, watching the cheese mush together. "Fine."

Dad pats my shoulder before taking his seat across from me. The house feels bigger than ever since Mom left, like it's stretching and adding all this empty space I don't know what to do with. Mom and I love each other, but she doesn't love Dad anymore, and that's the part I'm trying to understand. Dad's a great cook and an even better listener. He's supportive and has dedicated his life to helping others. I don't see how Mom couldn't love him anymore. Love can't be this great, life-altering thing everyone thinks it is if after twenty years it can vanish. It's got to be a sham. I'm better off staying as far away from it as possible.

Three

Everyone is staring at me. Seriously, there are at least twenty pairs of eyes on me as I walk toward my locker the next morning. Students nod in my direction or whisper my name as I pass them.

"What?" I ask of no one in particular. "Do I have slobber on my face or something?"

No one replies, although a few people snicker. None of these people have given me the time of day since freshman year. Why the interest now?

I practically sprint the rest of the way to my locker, rubbing my mouth as I go. I twist out the combination and yank open the metal door. I check the mirror hanging on the side, scrutinizing my face. Thick eyebrows, a gently sloping nose, full lips, and curious dark eyes framed by glasses stare back at me. There's no drool in sight.

I take a moment to hide my face in the dark recess of my locker while I swap out the books I took home for the ones I'll need for first period. When I close the door, Andie's face pops into view, a single pierced eyebrow curiously peaked.

I jump. "Don't sneak up on me like that!"

"Girl, do you not check your phone? I've been texting you all morning!" He flails his arms in my direction. Behind him, Liz frowns deeply.

"It's on Do Not Disturb. What's going on?" I ask, fishing my phone out of my back pocket and going to my messages.

There are a dozen unread texts—most from Andie and Liz, but also a few other random people I forgot had my phone number.

Andie points to a text he sent with a link to an Instagram reel. I'm almost afraid to look, but if it will explain the stares, then I've got no choice. I click the link.

The gym comes into view. I'm standing there in my sweatpants and FGH T-shirt, watching Iris climb the rope. She looks over her shoulder and winks at Anita, who's on the ground frowning. A second later, the rope flies out of Anita's hands, taking Iris with it.

I remember this, though it's so much weirder watching it play out on a screen. It happens so fast. One minute Iris is holding on to the rope, and the next, I'm diffusing the magic and gracelessly breaking her fall.

The camera zooms in on the two of us. Our faces are a hair's width apart, and our eyes are locked on each other's like we're in a stare-off or worse, *in love.*

Andie clicks to another video where someone has remixed my clumsy save to music; the thump Iris and I make when hitting the ground perfectly syncs up to the beat of "Hollaback Girl" by Gwen Stefani.

And worst of all, the video has gone viral. The original has fifty thousand likes, and the remix is inching closer to sixty thousand.

Holy shit. No wonder everyone is staring at me. I have the sudden urge to hide inside my locker and never come out.

"Check out the comments," Liz says.

As I begin reading them, my heart rate kicks into high gear.

The internet's takeaway from the original video is clear: Iris and I would make a great couple.

"Who posted this?" I ask, although I already have an idea of who it might be. Dante, the only other person in our group, was on his phone like his life depended on it.

"Dante Morelli," Liz confirms.

I spin on my heel. "I'm going to strangle that little sh—"

"Monroe, wait!" Andie calls after me.

I'm power walking down the hallway before they can stop me. He recorded me and posted the video online without my consent! Now people are shipping me and Iris like a *Love Island* couple.

I search for Dante in the crowd of students, some of whom are nodding in my direction while others huddle together to watch the video. I find Dante near a cluster of lockers by the stairs. He's on his phone, of course.

"Dante!" His head jerks up, and his eyes widen. "You need to take down the video."

"What? No way, it's got like a million views! It's my best video yet."

"I don't care. You shouldn't have posted it to begin with!" I snap.

Dante shakes his head. "Taking down the original video won't do much at this point. There are too many remixes."

"I don't know what that means. Just delete it."

Dante pinches the bridge of his nose. "It means other people have made commentary on the video. It's still going to be floating around somewhere. What's the big deal? That save was amazing, dude. I bet news outlets are gonna reach out. You know how good this will be for my account? I've already got over two hundred new followers!"

"The whole internet is shipping me and Iris!"

Dante raises his hands. "That's not on me. I just documented the facts."

"That's the issue. Iris and I—" Someone grabs my arm before I can finish the sentence and tugs me in the opposite direction. "Hey!" I yell.

"*Shh!*" Iris tugs me down the hallway with a determined gleam in her eyes.

"What are you doing?" I ask, trying not to stumble over backpacks left on the floor of the hall while their owners grab books from their lockers.

I try to pull away, but Iris's grip is ironclad. She doesn't stop walking, not even for Anita, who's openly ogling her. Iris yanks me through a doorway on my left. The chatter in the hallway dims as the door clicks shut behind us. We're in an empty classroom. The lights are off, but the window shades are raised, letting in enough cold blue light to get a better look at my kidnapper.

Iris has her braids piled on the top of her head, a few strands framing her face. Her low-riding jeans and crop top covered in tiny black flowers are giving a 2000s vibe that she pulls off well with her figure. The bangles on her wrists clang together as she lifts herself onto the teacher's desk. It's easier to see now, without her gym clothes on, the magic making her skin sparkle.

I lean against an empty desk, trying to match her chill posture despite not knowing what we're doing in here. "I'm guessing that you've seen the video?"

She nods. "And the comments. Apparently, we make quite the pair. That's why I pulled you in here." She toys with her perfect braids. "It really did look like we were having a moment."

My stomach tightens. She's not implying that I like her, is she? Because that would be ridiculous. I mean, she's gorgeous. Objectively, one of the prettiest girls in school. And she's smart, if memory serves from the few classes we've had together over the past three and a half years, but I hardly know her. "I thought you wanted Anita."

"I do. *She* broke up with *me* two weeks ago after we dated for four months. She said I wasn't into her, only the idea of being with her. Whatever that means." She shakes her head. "I've been trying to win her back. Then this video drops, and Anita's paid more attention to me in the last two hours than she has in the last two weeks. I think seeing me interested in someone else has her realizing she still likes me."

"What's that got to do with me?" I ask.

Iris leaves her perch on the desk and walks over to me. "I want us to date."

I choke on my own saliva. *"What?!"*

"Fake date. Just until prom so I can go with Anita like we planned," Iris clarifies.

"What are you talking about? Maybe the nurse should've checked you out after all."

Iris rolls her eyes. "I'm fine. Great, actually. I finally have a way to get Anita back." I stare at her. She levels me with a pointed look. "By fake dating you."

"People don't fake date."

"Yes, they do. Haven't you seen a rom-com? It would be just like that. I want to make Anita jealous. If she gets bitter after seeing us together, that means she still has feelings for me."

"That . . . doesn't make sense. Wouldn't moving on only prove her right—that you're looking for *anyone* to love, and not her in particular?"

"Nope." Iris smiles knowingly, like she's already thought about that, which makes one of us. "If I show her that I've moved on and have a real connection with the person, Anita will realize I can have genuine relationships. Maybe she'll believe me when I tell her ours was real. Maybe she'll realize she made a mistake."

"Sounds manipulative. Also, our connection is not real."

Iris leans forward, an inch shy of being too close. I can smell her sweet perfume and nearly get lost in those deep brown eyes. My breath hitches. "Isn't it, though?"

"Um . . ."

Iris rocks back on her heels with a smirk. "I'm not trying to manipulate her. I'm trying to get her to realize she's not over me. If she truly has moved on and doesn't care that I'm seeing someone else, then I'll move on too."

I swallow and force myself to focus on this conversation and not how close Iris is standing to me. "Why can't you just talk to her? Aren't you still friends?"

Iris laughs. "Not every queer person stays friends with their ex. Anita would rather avoid me, which is making it hard to win her back." Iris turns her attention to her nails and twists her lips like there's more she wants to say. "So are you down?"

"Am I down to partake in your horrible plan to win back your ex? Hard pass."

Iris pouts. "Why not? You don't have to stand outside my bedroom window with a boom box or climb my fire escape with roses in your mouth. Just act interested in me."

I have no idea what she's talking about.

"Are you not allowed to date or something?" she asks.

"No, I can date. I think. It's just . . ." Telling her the truth feels like I'm giving away a secret. It isn't one, but it feels like too much information to give to someone I don't know well.

"Just what?" Iris raises her chin and tightens her brow. "Are you uncomfortable with it because I'm a girl?"

"No." I rub my hands together. "I like girls. I—I only like girls."

Iris's expression softens. "Oh. Cool. Same. So what is it, then?"

I sigh, feeling a pressure come off my chest. "I don't date, real or fake. I don't believe in love, so I'd never be able to convince people we're in a relationship."

"Wait. Run that back. You don't believe in love? Don't you know love is, like, the most popular feeling ever? So much so that rom-coms make about one hundred million dollars at the box office every year. And romance books generate over one billion in yearly revenue. Seriously, people love love."

"Yeah, well, not me," I grumble. "And how do you even know that?"

"Because I'm obsessed with romance novels and movies. An important fact you're going to need to know when we start fake dating."

I roll my eyes. "Sounds like Anita might be onto something."

"Rude!" Iris nudges my shoulder playfully. "Anyway, you don't need to believe in love to help me. You wouldn't even need to do much, besides sit with me at lunch and laugh at my jokes. Anita will notice."

I fold my arms. "No thanks. I have a lot of work to do as a new recruit for the Bureau. I can't afford to be distracted right now. My first day was kind of a disaster."

Iris dips her head. "Yeah, sorry again about the smoothie. Look, you're perfect for this, romance-hater or not. My mom threatened to send a Bureau agent to school with me today after she saw the gold dust on me. You can't even imagine what that would do to my social life."

"Has she seen the video?"

"God, I hope not. She'll only worry more," Iris replies.

The bell rings, signaling the start of classes. I hop off the desk and make for the door. Iris grabs my arm, and I pause.

"I meant what I said about you being perfect for this. You're one of the few people in school with the skills to prevent magic-related accidents. Reconnecting with Anita will be impossible with this love charm ruining the moment. And without you helping me with the mishaps, I won't be able to gauge Anita's true feelings for me."

Iris pouts and bats her naturally long lashes at me. I pretend not to be as amused as I am by the performance.

"Sorry. You're on your own," I say. "Oh, and some advice? We know the mishaps are caused by romantic advances of any kind. So if you think the charm is faulty, stay away from Anita unless you want whatever object you're touching to loveblock you again. That climbing rope was trying to get you as far away from Anita as possible." I open the door and pause. "In fact, stay away from love in general."

I am certainly doing the same.

The stares lessen throughout the day, but only because people have gotten bold and started to approach me.

"Do you have a crush on Iris?" Taylor asks while I head to lunch. "Because she likes Anita."

"Yeah, I know," I reply, not stopping to talk.

Taylor jogs to catch up. She looks like she's considering saying more. She probably thinks I want to be with Iris, like everyone else. I don't have an explanation for the so-called heart eyes I have in the video. Adrenaline? Relief? Maybe I temporarily lost touch with reality and thought I was gazing at an ice-cold glass of Diet Coke.

Whatever the reason, it isn't enough to give in to the gossip or make me agree to fake date her.

"I'd steer clear of her if I were you," Taylor warns, side-stepping a student holding a sign that reads: "PROM?"

I lower my voice. "Because she's charmed? Iris was flirting with Anita right before she fell."

Taylor nods. "I interviewed Iris."

I stop. The lunchroom doors are only yards away, teasing me with the promise of food, but this is important. "Shouldn't we work together on this?"

Taylor rolls her eyes. "You know as well as I do that of the five recruits this year, only one or two of us are getting promoted to junior agent next year. That's how recruitment works. You best believe I'm becoming an agent in the fall. I'm not taking my chances on a group project."

She's not wrong. Two years ago, my older cousin, Nora, made the mistake of thinking working for the Bureau as a junior recruit meant automatically staying on once she turned eighteen. She didn't, and even though she's now the head baker at Bewitched Buns, I still haven't heard the end of it. I'm on my own.

"Suit yourself," I reply, shrugging and heading toward the cafeteria.

I open the doors, and the noise swallows Taylor's huff. We go our separate ways—Taylor sitting at her usual table with Iris, Jude, and a few other popular kids while I slide in next to Liz and Andie three tables down.

"What was that about?" Andie asks, pushing his basket of fries toward me.

"Bureau stuff. If you had applied to be a junior recruit you could be helping me right now." Andie is a Mystic, too, but unlike me, he's never been interested in joining the Bureau.

Andie shakes his head. "You know I'm not as altruistic as you. Plus, you like solving puzzles and studying. I like listening to music and watching reality TV. I'm rooting for you, though."

"I'd help if I could," Liz tells me, popping a fry into her mouth. She turns to Andie. "Now tell me more about *Love Island*."

As she and Andie go over a "recoupling" that happened on the show, my gaze drifts to Iris. She tucks her hair behind her ears and playfully shoves the boy next to her, who grins, his cheeks tinting red. Across from her sits Taylor and her boyfriend, Sean Ashton, who's got one arm slung around her shoulder and the other holding his phone while he swipes. His baseball cap is on backward, perfectly holding back his blond hair.

The boy next to Iris grabs a teddy bear from his backpack. It's covered in shiny pink, legal charm dust. He hands it to Iris, whose eyes double in size. The bear cracks open its mouth and speaks loud enough to be heard over the chatter in the cafeteria. "Iris James, I think you're *beary* cute. Will you go to prom with me?"

Everyone at the table and even the tables surrounding them stares. There's at least one promposal a day this semester, and I'm assuming this isn't Iris's first one.

"Um . . ." Iris toys with her braids and rests a hand on his shoulder. "I'm flattered, Jaxon," she starts. She looks around, her gaze finding Anita, who is poking at her lunch. "This is so sweet. You're great." She bats her eyelashes at him. "But—"

Iris's tray of spaghetti flips into her face. Pasta sauce slides down her top. She yelps while the table erupts in laughter. The mishap was subtle enough that it could easily have been Iris herself knocking her fork, but the knowing look on Taylor's face is a dead giveaway. She grabs the tray, and the crystal rings on her fingers begin to glow. The residue lifts away in a plume of gold before it can do any more damage.

Iris appears defeated. Taylor says something to her I can't hear over the noise. Iris shakes her head and jumps to her feet, her mouth tugging down at the corners as she examines her shirt. When she jogs past me, we lock eyes.

Before I can think twice about it, I'm on my feet following her. "Be right back," I tell Andie and Liz.

"Iris, wait!" I yell.

She slows but doesn't stop. She ducks into the girls' bathroom, and I follow a second later. Iris pulls her shirt over her head, and I drop my gaze, my well-loved Air Force 1s suddenly becoming the most interesting things in the room. The sink turns on, and the sound of running water is drowned out by diligent scrubbing.

"Reconsidered my proposal?" Iris asks.

"No. I—uh—wanted to ask what happened," I reply without looking up, ignoring how my heart is suddenly beating too fast.

"I'm assuming another mishap. Taylor had to suction out the magic."

I glance up at Iris. Her side profile doesn't give away her feelings on the situation. She's concentrating on cleaning her shirt.

"Were you expecting the promposal?" I ask.

"I guess I shouldn't have been surprised."

"Flirt with him often?"

Iris scoffs. "Not intentionally. It's like . . . a nervous habit. Jaxon is nice, but as I said before, I'm not into guys." She moves to the hand dryer, and while the noise drowns out any response I would have, it does nothing to quell my thoughts.

Once the dryer stops, I say, "He seems to like you."

"Did the talking teddy bear give it away?" She sighs, the frustration clear in the way she tugs on her shirt. "Sorry. It's just, that was the third promposal in two weeks. Meanwhile, I can't even get Anita to talk to me for more than five minutes."

"She'll come around," I reply, because it seems like the right thing to say.

Iris walks over to where I'm leaning against the sink. Her shirt is still damp, but the stain is much less noticeable now. She smells a little like tomato sauce. "Any more questions, recruit?"

I shake my head. The Bureau knows the charm is meant to help you find a perfect love match. From observing Iris for all of five minutes, I'm pretty sure I can add "activates mishaps even if the charmed person doesn't have feelings for the person they're flirting with" to its profile. Iris was nervously flirting with Jaxon, and that was enough to spark a reaction.

Iris fixes her hair in the mirror behind me. "I don't want people to know I'm charmed. You have to keep that a secret, right? Bureau rules or something." Iris raises her eyebrow in challenge.

"Um, sure." I actually don't know the answer to that. "But any Mystic can see you're charmed, and I can't stop them from telling other people."

Iris leans against the sink with a groan. "How am I supposed to prevent the mishaps until the right remedy is found? You said to stay away from love. I haven't talked to Anita all day, and yet my lunch acted like I told it a dirty joke. I'm naturally flirty—at least that's what Taylor, Anita, and Jude always say—but that's not enough to cause a mishap, is it?"

"Clearly it is," I reply. "The charm is triggered between people who don't have mutual feelings for each other. You said Jaxon likes you, but you don't like him. You like Anita, even though she no longer has feelings for you." Iris winces. "Sorry. I'm trying to explain."

"We don't know if she has feelings for me or not," Iris replies. "She doesn't want to be with me right now, but she could still like me. Feelings don't disappear overnight." Iris grabs a tube of lipstick from her pocket and applies it with practiced perfection.

If Anita doesn't have feelings for Iris, then my theory holds. Mishaps occur only with unrequited love. It doesn't matter who rejects whom. The person charmed is going to experience the consequences. "Look. You need to stop flirting. Avoid promposals. Don't even hug someone for too long. Actually, don't even smile at anyone."

Iris snorts. "I can't *smile*?"

"It's flirty!"

Iris quirks her lips and I narrow my eyes. "That's the one. You know what you're doing."

Iris grins. She runs a hand through her braids, which flow around her shoulders in waves. "How am I—" Her eyes flash as an idea seemingly overcomes her. "All the more reason to fake date you."

She's persistent as hell. Iris does seem to be a magnet for mishaps—some more dangerous than others. And observing her today has helped me learn more about the charm. But there are reasons why this won't work: 1) Fake dating is a distraction, and I need to be focused on my first assignment for the Bureau. 2) Iris is the Director's daughter. If this goes sideways, my future at the Bureau could be on the line. 3) How am I supposed to sell being in a relationship when I don't even believe in love? Bottom line: Fake dating Iris won't work.

"Sorry, it's still a no. Why do you want to win Anita back after she dumped you, anyway?" I ask.

Iris tips her head back, seemingly in thought. The light in the bathroom catches on her silver hoops and the specks of gold beneath her skin. Her plum-colored lipstick is impeccable.

"Imagine you're walking down the hallways at school, one body in a mass of hundreds, a thousand different stimuli threatening to overwhelm you. You're unassuming—"

"You are not," I cut her off without thinking.

Iris tilts her head. "I'm flattered, but that's not where I'm going with this. Anyway, you're unassuming and counting down the days until you're free of your tiny, boring town. And then you bump into her. The prettiest girl you've ever seen, and she smiles at you, and she knows your name, and all the noise dims. You know in that moment, you can't be without her."

"That sounds . . . intense," I reply honestly. "Is that how it was with you and Anita?"

Iris snorts. "No, that's the vibe of the movie *The Half of It*, but I *do* feel like I need to be with her, you know? We were so perfect together. She listened to me and made me laugh. She read my fan fiction and didn't make fun of my romance obsession like my first girlfriend."

"That all sounds like the bare minimum," I mumble.

"I felt *seen*, okay? I want that back. I want *her* back." Iris grabs her phone from her bag and holds it out. "Let me at least get your number in case I'm having a mishap and Taylor isn't around to help me."

"Fine." I plug my number into her phone and then hand it back to her.

Iris grins, flips her hair over her shoulder, and brushes past me. Beneath the tomato smell is that enticing scent of lavender. Iris pauses at the door and winks. "See you around, Monroe." She slips out of the bathroom, leaving me both confused and a little intrigued.

Four

"Dust-B-Gone? Oh, thank goodness you're here! I'm Madeline Knight. We spoke on the phone."

Madeline, Dad's latest client, is a tall woman in her forties who looks like she's been through the rinse cycle. Her hair and clothes are sopping wet, and water puddles at her feet. She's vaguely familiar, like most people in Fair Glen are to each other.

"Hi, Madeline," Dad replies, shaking the woman's hand. "You're the owner of Charmed Spotless, right? We took our laundry there a few times when our washer was on the fritz."

"Yes! I've been the owner for about four years now. Took over after my pop got sick. You'd think being in the laundry business means knowing not to cut corners when it comes to getting something clean. Some things are better done the old-fashioned way." She shakes her head. "Please follow me and excuse my appearance. It was either this or start itching from all the soap." She briskly ushers us around the side of her house.

"That's quite all right. Your call sounded urgent. What's going on?" Dad asks. He's wearing his tool belt stuffed with ropes and crystals, and his collector is tucked beneath his arm. I jog to keep up, holding my own collector.

I love doing jobs with Dad. We get to spend more time together, and I receive valuable insight into all the ways magic can go wrong.

As we approach the backyard, I can already see the problem. Pink bubbles cover the entire lawn and are climbing the side of the house. Suds envelop the wooden swing set and have practically swallowed what must be the family van. A fluffy white dog is barking from the porch, the only portion of the backyard currently safe from the frothy assault.

"I bought this new charmed sponge from Conjurer's Corner. One swipe is supposed to leave a trail of soap suds, and the second pass dries and polishes. Only when I started to clean the outdoor kitchen, the sponge leaked suds everywhere! It hasn't stopped for *hours*," Madeline says.

"Okay, we'll take care of it. Where's the sponge?" Dad asks.

"On the counter, if you can find it."

There's too much soap to make out anything but the shape of her pizza oven.

"I'll find the sponge and vacuum up the charm dust," Dad says. "Monroe, collect some more information from her." Dad wades into the sea of soap, leaving me with the customer.

"You said you bought the sponge from Conjurer's Corner, correct? Have you used it at all before now?" I ask.

"No. This was my first time," Madeline says distractedly. She grabs the dog as soap creeps toward the porch. "It's okay, Toby," she tells him before turning back to me. "How am I supposed to clean this up?"

"My dad and I can try to find a similarly charmed object to reverse the damage, like a towel or a brush, though that might take some time. Your water hose is probably the safest and fastest option once my dad gets the sponge to stop producing soap."

Madeline nods. "The hose is on the side of the house. I was able to spray myself off before you came."

I wade through pink foam that smells vaguely of strawberry bubble gum. I drop to my knees and feel around for a rubber hose. When I find it, I trail the line back to the faucet and turn it on. I don't know if there's enough water to wash away all the soap. Her grass is definitely gonna be dead after this.

"Got it!" Dad calls from under a pile of pink fizz. He shoves the entire sponge, which isn't much bigger than his hand, into his collector and then trudges toward us wearing a grin.

I spray as much water as I can over the suds, watching them slowly fizzle and pop out of existence.

"I'll grab my nozzle."

Dad has a spray nozzle that's charmed to spray water without being connected to anything. The water never runs out. There are several in existence, making the nozzle a fan favorite with Fair Glen's fire department.

"You can call this into the fire department as well. They'll be helpful in cleaning up. The most important thing is that the sponge is now soapless," Dad says.

"You did that so fast!" Madeline exclaims. "I called two other companies before yours, but one was busy and the other was plain confused."

Dad smiles. "Always happy to help. Do you happen to have white vinegar by any chance? It will help break down the suds."

While Madeline dashes back into her house to find the vinegar, I follow Dad over to his truck. "She's right. You're so fast at getting a situation under control," I tell him.

"Eh, it takes time and practice. How's your Bureau case going?" he asks.

"Honestly, I'm not sure where to start. I'm trying to find a good lead."

Dad grabs his spray nozzle from the truck bed. "Always start at the beginning. Where was the first sighting of the charm?"

"Illusion Salon & Spa," I reply.

"Might be worth paying them a visit, then."

As we start toward Madeline's backyard, my phone rings.

Incoming Call: Director James

The spike of panic that lances through me at the sight of the Director's name popping up on my phone stops me in my tracks. Could she have seen the video of me and Iris? Or did I do something wrong as a recruit? I honestly don't know which one would be worse.

"Everything okay?" Dad asks.

"It's the Director. I should take this."

Dad gives me a proud smile. "Do your thing. I'll finish up with Madeline."

I nod and answer on the last ring. "Hello?"

"Monroe? This is Director James."

"Hi, Director."

Please don't ask if I had a moment with your daughter.

Please don't ask if I had a moment with your daughter.

There's some shuffling of papers on the other end of the phone and a pause before she speaks again. "I apologize for calling out of the blue, but there's been a development. Iris is charmed, though I think you know that already. There's a video. Have you seen it?" she asks.

My initial response is to play dumb, but being a junior recruit is basically one giant test. A good recruit would know of the video by now. "Yes."

"I saw what you did. Your quick thinking might've saved Iris's life. She could've broken her neck if it weren't for you," she says.

I exhale. "Thank you, ma'am."

"Iris claims she doesn't know why or how she was charmed, but the fact of the matter is, the charm is there, and it's not going away until we crack this case. I've been putting in the hours myself, but I'm not on the ground like you and the other recruits."

"I understand," I reply, although I'm not sure where she's going with this. "So you want me to keep you updated on my findings?" I ask.

"Yes, but I also want to ask a personal favor of you, if you're willing. It would alleviate some of my concerns for Iris while she's at school if she had someone looking out for her until we can find a solution. I don't know your schedule, but if you can check on her between classes and at lunch, I'd greatly appreciate it. I'd ask Taylor Evans or Jude Featherstone, but I don't trust Iris's friends to keep the task to themselves. Iris hates it when I meddle in her business, but I'm worried, especially after seeing that video. Pulling her from school isn't feasible without an estimate of how long it'll take for R&D to get a suitable dissolver."

"You want me to be a protection detail for Iris?" I ask warily.

"Nothing so official. But as a Mystic and junior recruit, I trust you to keep any potential mishaps at bay when you can." She pauses for a beat, and then adds, "I'm putting together an investigative task force of junior agents in the fall who would handle lower-level mishaps like the ones with the garden gnomes and the gym rope, freeing up senior agents' time. Since you're willing to do extra fieldwork outside of your assignments, and assuming you do well on this current investigation, I'd love to have you on board."

To be recommended to stay on after this case, and go into the field no less, is all I could ask for. Thus my answer is out of my mouth a second later. "Yes!"

The Director releases a relieved sigh. I imagine her now on the other end of the line, like Iris described, at home at a table, papers stacked everywhere. Or maybe she's still working hard at Bureau headquarters.

"Excellent," she replies. "And I'd appreciate it if you watching Iris's back stays between us. Iris is on my case enough as it is about hovering."

"She'll know I'm helping her. We aren't exactly friends," I admit.

"If there is another mishap, tell her you were in the right place at the right time. I just want her to have a sense of normalcy."

I don't want to lie to Iris, but I also want to stay on with the Bureau next year, and this could ensure that happens.

Iris's proposal comes crashing back to me. Keeping her safe would be a lot easier if we were together as often as possible. Fake dating might be my way in. It also gives me a chance to learn more about the charm and our school's social scene. Since I don't believe in love, there's no way I'd fall for Iris, ensuring she remains safe and earning me points with the Director. We all win.

After the Director and I hang up, I find Iris's name in my phone. I laugh when I see she's saved it as "Iris James (TEXT ME!)." I change it to "Iris" and type out a message.

Hey, it's Monroe. I thought more about what we talked about and I'm down. Meet me in the library during lunch tomorrow?

Iris: i knew you'd come around 😉

Five

The staring has died down significantly by Wednesday. They say the average attention span of a teen is thirty minutes, but I'm blessed that it's more like thirty seconds at FGH. I can at least walk to class without feeling like a B-list celebrity sneaking into an award show.

The library is on the second floor of the main building above the cafeteria. Dust motes are suspended in the shafts of light streaming through the dingy glass windows. The bookshelves are grimy and smell like aging paper while the carpet is basically one large dust bunny. It's perfect. I've been volunteering here for a couple of hours a week since sophomore year, helping Mx. Michaelson, the librarian, do things like stop charmed books from reciting text in unintelligible voices and extinct languages. Fair Glen High has a whole section of the library dedicated to charmed books. It makes for an interesting tour for prospective students.

I knew the library would be empty of seniors since it's our lunch period, which means it's the best place for me and Iris to hash out our fake dating scheme.

Mx. Michaelson is sitting at the checkout desk typing on the computer. They wave when they see me. "How are you, Monroe? I heard about the rescue in gym the other day."

"Oh, I'm fine. Just trying to help get this charm under control."

Mx. Michaelson nods. "I sent a sample of the dust to the Bureau. That should help. In the meantime, there's a fresh stack of books for you." They point to a bin of books ready to be shelved. A few of them flap their pages at me. I reach for the first book on the pile, a thick hardcover with silver foil edges. It flips open and starts reading rapidly in what sounds like German, a language not taught here.

I close the book, and it snaps at my fingers, apparently annoyed I interrupted its recitation. I grab the rest of the books and head over to the metal winding stairs just as Iris arrives.

Today, she's wearing a fitted white top with orange cuffed corduroys that complement her brown skin. She searches the space with a puzzled look, her broad nose and perfectly shaped eyebrows scrunching. I remember myself and wave.

She grins slowly, an expression that doesn't falter when she joins me at the base of the stairs. Up close, I notice her signature plum-colored lipstick matches her eyeshadow.

"What made you change your mind?" she asks.

I look around, even though nothing has changed in the past minute. The library is still empty save for a few freshmen using AirPods while studying, and Mx. Michaelson, who's now on the phone. My mind jumps to the conversation I had with the Director last night, but I think I do a pretty good job of keeping my face neutral when I reply, "It's no secret I'm not super popular around school. I'm not clued in to what's going on around here. You know a lot more people than I do, and I need your help to ensure I'm put in the field next year."

That's not . . . totally a lie. I *do* need to keep working this assignment, and since Iris is a flirty mishap magnet, she's great to stay connected to. She just doesn't know that I'm also fake dating her to keep her safe per her mom's request.

"What kind of help?" Iris asks. "Information?"

I nod and climb the stairs. My muscles burn from the weight of the books, but in a good way. Iris follows close behind me, openly staring at my arms. I try not to smirk.

"Can you tell me if you hear anyone talking about having strange accidents or any chatter about a love charm being sold or passed around? That kind of info will give me a leg up," I reply.

Iris clears her throat. "Isn't that cheating? If I help."

I drop the books and start separating them by category. The balcony on the second floor overlooks the library's entrance and a half dozen wooden tables where students can study during open periods.

"It's not the SATs," I reply. "You'd be helping me research, which will keep students safe. Don't they have informants or sources in the rom-coms you consume?"

"Not really. No." Iris studies me, her gaze heavy and subduing like a weighted blanket. "But I guess it's a fair ask." She slides closer, leaning her arm on the bookshelf behind me. The air thins, and she raises an amused eyebrow. "Lucky for you, I know all of Fair Glen's most romantic spots. I bet there will be mishaps and intel to gather at those places."

"Places like what?" I ask.

"Like the drive-in movie theater," she replies, and then jabs her finger in my direction. "But you need me because you're only going to stand out if you're there by yourself, flashing your badge and doing the whole Bureau bit. You'll scare everyone off."

I scoff. She grabs the book I'm holding, and it snaps at her fingers while swearing in French. "Ouch!"

I can't contain my laugh. "They bite."

She cradles her hand to her chest. "Noted."

I take the book from her and slide it onto the shelf. It jostles around before settling down. "So how would this work? Anita knows you're still into her. She won't believe you're dating me," I say.

"We tell everyone that we shared a moment on that smelly gym mat and are trying it out. Instant connection."

"And people believe in that kind of stuff?"

Something flickers in her expression, tugging her lips into the barest hint of a frown. She turns her attention to the shelves behind us and trails her sparkly blue nails over the spines of the books. "Why not? I pretty much started crushing on Anita after talking to her for like five minutes."

Love clearly melts the brain. I'm glad I'm not bothered with it, although pretending to be into Iris romantically will require my best acting skills. "If you're sure we can sell it, then fine."

She turns to me. "Trust me, I can sell it."

"So smug."

She grins like it's a compliment. "I guess all that's left is establishing some rules."

I grab another book from the pile and find its home on the shelf. "Rules?"

"Yep, guidelines to follow. Like no one can know our relationship is fake. I forgot you don't watch or read a lot of romances."

"Try any."

She shakes her head. "We're gonna have to fix that ASAP. The first thing you need to know about me is that I love romance."

"I got that much."

She nods. "So you can't tell your friends we aren't truly dating. Having certain people know but not others would get confusing."

It will be hard not telling Liz and Andie the truth. They know I don't date. But this is my chance to be promoted to junior agent in the fall. Securing that position is what I want more than anything. That goal is worth keeping this secret.

"Okay, but can you maybe not tell your mom we're dating? I don't want her looking at me differently," I say.

Iris shrugs. "She's too busy to take the time to ask about my dating life." A hint of bitterness laces her words, like she wishes her mom *would* ask. "What about PDA? What are you comfortable with? Kissing?"

"Oh, um . . ." My gaze drops to her lips automatically. I snap my eyes up before my mind can wander. Thankfully, she can't see the heat flooding my cheeks.

I've never kissed anyone before, so I'm probably horrible at it. Before I realized I was a lesbian, I used to think something was wrong with me. I didn't like any of the boys Andie was always gushing over. I didn't like boys.

And then one day, a girl at the mall smiled at me. When I waved, she blushed, and from that moment on, I knew. I was no longer standing on the sidelines; I was in the game. And I felt so relieved to finally know this part of myself. But before I could even think about dating, Mom moved out, and the idea of pursuing romance was yanked out from under me. She ruined love for me.

"Better not," I say.

"Okay," Iris replies easily. "How about hand-holding, hugging, and cuddling?"

"Y-yeah. That's fine."

"Cool. I think we should break up at least a week before prom. I want to take Anita."

"That should work," I reply. Prom is next month. Hopefully, we'll have a solution to the mishaps before then.

"Are we sure the fake dating won't cause any accidents?" Iris asks.

I grab the rest of the books from the bin and move down the hallway to find their spots on the shelves. "I'm sure. The love charm is only triggered by real romantic advances, not fake ones."

She studies me. "That means you can't fall in love with me."

I choke on my saliva. "That is *not* going to happen. I refuse to fall in love. *You* can't fall in love with *me*, Miss Romance-Is-My-Middle-Name."

"I never said that! And I won't. In almost every fake dating romance, the characters fall in love. But we won't, because I've got a foolproof plan on how we'll stay platonic."

"I'm on the edge of my seat," I deadpan.

Iris laughs. It's a bright, airy sound, different from the snort of surprised laughter in the bathroom yesterday. I like both.

"We do things that annoy each other so we don't fall in love. For instance, I hate pet names. Honey. Baby. Sugar. *Yuck*. Call me one of those, and I'll immediately get the ick. I also don't like being walked to class. I'm an independent woman. I don't need an escort."

"So let me guess; you want me to walk you to class."

She grins. "Bingo."

"Won't Anita be suspicious knowing you hate those things?"

"I'm glad you asked. Anita always wanted to call me pet names and pick me up for dates and hold my hand. She'll be jealous if I do that with you," Iris replies.

I shrug. "If you're sure. How about we also try to keep our conversations light? Nothing too deep. Only basic stuff. Better yet, let's talk mostly about the case or how to make Anita jealous."

"Deal. Are you sure you're cut out for this? This may be your toughest assignment yet, recruit," Iris asks.

"Well, it'd only be my second."

Still, it's a valid question, though her quirked brow and purple-painted smirk tell me it's also a challenge. Flirting is so not my thing, but I want this arrangement to work. I need Iris's social status at FGH to get answers about the charm. If proving I'm up for faking dating is how I do that, so be it.

I step closer to Iris. She's two or three inches taller than me, so I have to raise my chin to look her in the eyes. It's oddly intimate in this quiet fold of the library's stacks. I'm pretty sure people come here to make out, which makes my heart race.

Act confident, I tell myself.

I drape my arm along the shelf next to her and tuck a braid behind her ear. Iris's eyes widen, and I lower my voice. "But yes. Are you?"

A slow grin spreads across her mouth. "That was good. I almost believed you."

I step back and take a bow, willing my heart rate to slow down. Maybe this could be a way to practice being undercover.

Iris holds out her hand. "Ready to make our debut as a couple?"

Right, we're actually doing this. I slip my hand in hers. Heat radiates across my palm. "Let's do this," I say with confidence I don't feel.

What have I gotten myself into?

Six

By the time Iris and I leave the library, there are about ten minutes left of lunch, just enough time "to debut our relationship." The thought of doing so locks me in place outside the cafeteria doors.

Iris grabs my hand again, and this time I flinch. "Sorry."

"It's okay. All good?" she asks with an easy smile that seems to quell some of my doubts.

"I'm nervous," I admit.

"Just follow my lead."

We step inside the cafeteria, and I expect everyone's heads to turn or a mishap to sweep me off my feet. Nothing so dramatic happens. In fact, walking through the rows of lunch tables isn't ceremonious at all. Most people are too busy talking and scarfing down the remains of their lunch to notice us. The few heads that do turn don't kick up much of a fuss, only raise some eyebrows.

It dawns on me that I don't know where to sit. We hadn't talked through the logistics of whose friends we'd be hanging out with, or anything beyond the rules we set. Panic slowly seeps in as I realize we've come to a stop at my lunch table.

Liz looks up midbite of pasta. On instinct, I drop Iris's hand as if burned. Iris is smoother than me. Without missing a beat, she loops her arm through mine.

Liz frowns. "What's this?"

Andie, who's been texting, finally notices us. His eyes bug out, and his eyebrows jump to his hairline. His phone is all but forgotten. "Monroe Presley Bennett, you've been holding out on me."

Iris mouths my middle name amusedly. "Introduce me, babe," she says.

"Babe?" Liz and Andie say at the same time.

Iris nudges my shoulder. I better say something before Liz has an aneurysm or Andie falls into the fourth dimension. "Iris and I are . . . dating." *Wow, that sounded weird.*

"Is this a joke?" Andie looks between me and Iris expectantly.

"No. We're together," I reply, ineloquently and unconvincingly.

Liz and Andie stare at me with blank faces. They're not buying it, and why should they? My friends know me better than anyone. I don't date, and yet suddenly, Iris is hanging on my arm and calling me "babe"? Getting them to believe me likely won't happen in one lunch period, but today is good practice for everyone else.

"We all saw the video." I look at Iris and try to find a way to sell this. "There was chemistry."

Liz folds her arms across her chest. "You told us on Monday you didn't want to date, because it was a distraction."

Iris raises her eyebrows at me. I do my best not to visibly react. "Yeah, well . . . I changed my mind."

"Must've been one hell of a moment between the two of you," Liz mutters.

Iris hesitates. "Seems like y'all need a moment. I'm going to grab a drink from the vending machine. Be right back." She lets her hand trail down the outside of my arm before turning away.

It takes everything in me not to startle at her touch. Pretending to flirt with her in the library was different. We didn't have an audience. My friends' suspicions would totally throw me off my game—if I had any.

Liz and Andie pounce the second she's out of earshot.

"Okay, spill. What's really going on?" Andie asks, pushing his food aside. "Is she blackmailing you or something?"

"What? No." I pinch the bridge of my nose. "We both felt something that day in gym class. We talked it over and decided to give it a go."

Liz rests her forearms on the table. "Give *what* a go?"

"Us. Together. Honestly, I thought you'd be happy for me. Y'all were bugging me yesterday about dating." I plop into an empty chair with a sigh.

"We are happy for you. Right, Andie?" Liz jams her elbow into his ribs.

"Ow! Yes. Happy as clowns." He rubs his side with a grimace.

Liz picks at her food. "It's just . . . have y'all ever hung out before?"

"We've known each other for years from all the Bureau events our parents have dragged us to," I reply, which is true to an extent. I leave out that Iris mostly ignored me.

"Actually," Iris says from behind me, holding a Sprite. "I've had a little crush on Monroe since the Bureau's Fourth of July cookout last summer." She sits in the chair next to mine. We're so close our arms touch. The whiff of her perfume is almost distracting. "Remember the softball game?"

"I remember losing."

"You hit a home run," Iris says with a lopsided grin that appears genuine. She holds my gaze and says, "You knocked the ball right over the fence. It was smooth as hell." She turns back to Liz and Andie while I'm stunned that she remembers my one good play. "I'm glad she finally gave me a chance."

Andie raises an eyebrow. Liz nods slowly. "Sounds like you made an impression, Roe," Liz says.

"I guess I did." Why does Iris remember that? It seemed like she was too busy with Taylor and Jude to notice me.

The table quiets. It's not exactly a comfortable silence, but it isn't unbearably awkward either. Iris and I eat as much as we can in the five minutes we have left before the bell rings.

I keep a watchful eye on the plastic silverware, lunch containers, and food wrappers to make sure there aren't any impending mishaps. I can't help but be overly cautious, even if only true romantic advances activate the charm. The last thing we need is for charm dust to bring the silverware to life or eject us from our seats.

The bell rings, and the noise level rises as students begin scraping their chairs on the floor. I deflate with an audible sigh. Longest ten minutes of my life, but I made it. I'm not sure how well we sold the relationship, though. It's going to be a long month until prom.

Everyone shuffles over to the garbage and recycle bins before heading out. Iris tosses her trash and asks, "Walk me to class?"

"Oh, right. Okay. *Baby*."

Iris cringes. She takes my hand and squeezes it as we follow the crowd out into the hallway. "Your friends seem surprised you're with me. You really don't date, huh?" she asks as we slowly walk toward the east wing.

"I told you I didn't."

"Well, I'm glad to be the exception, even if it's all a ruse." Iris glances around, likely looking for Anita. I give her a nudge and hope that helps keep her present. If we're going to sell this, she can't look preoccupied. "Anyway," she continues seamlessly. "Anyone who knows me will expect me to be at Electric Dust tonight."

"The drive-in movie theater you mentioned?" I ask.

She nods, her hair flowing around her shoulders with the movement. "They play classics on Wednesday nights, usually romances. Anita and I went a good number of times. I basically drag everyone I date to a movie there at least once a month, so we have to go. And you're in luck; *Pretty Woman* is playing."

"Hm, another romance movie I should know?" I ask.

"Precisely. It'll be just like in *Grease*, minus the funny business." She winks. "Pick me up at seven?"

Iris comes to a stop in front of an open classroom door. I glance inside and spot Anita sitting near the front of the room with Taylor and Chloe Nguyen. Anita is not so subtly watching us.

"I was planning on doing recon tonight. The first mishap documented was at Illusion Salon & Spa. The Bureau report could've been more thorough. I want to visit the owner to see if the responding agent missed anything."

"I got a manicure there with Taylor and Jude a few weeks ago. I knew *something* happened because my mom grilled me about the visit. I didn't realize the mishap was related to the love charm."

"Did you—" The final bell rings. *Damn*. "I'll call you."

"No. I'll see you tonight at seven. We're watching a movie," Iris presses.

I groan. "I'm not getting out of this, am I?"

Iris shakes her head, smirking.

"Fine," I reply. "Seven." I guess I'll dig up information there instead, if it's a romantic hot spot like she said.

"Perfect." Iris hesitates a moment and then leans in.

My heart leaps into my throat, and my limbs lock into place. For a second, I think she's going to kiss me. And then Iris presses her lips to my cheek. It's a quick peck, nothing more than you'd give your grandma, and yet my whole body is on fire afterward.

"Was that okay?" she whispers.

I nod dumbly, finding it hard to think about anything other than the spot where her lips were. It tingles.

"Good. See you tonight, recruit."

Seven

Illusion Salon & Spa is nestled between the laundromat Charmed Spotless and the bakery with the tastiest cakes and cookies in Fair Glen, Bewitched Buns. My cousin Nora has been working there for years, climbing her way up the bake chain. The block is populated by quaint brick storefronts with fairy lights in the windows. The peonies along the sidewalk have just started to bloom, the pops of pink brightening the street.

As I climb out of my car, the heavenly scents of sugar and butter with a bit of fresh detergent fill the air. Madeline waves from the doorway of Charmed Spotless and yells, "The yard is completely soap-free! Thanks again!"

I grin and give her a thumbs-up.

The door to Bewitched Buns swings open, and the floor mat flaps one of its corners to beckon me inside. I can never resist the invitation.

"Hey, Roe. The usual?" my cousin asks when I approach the counter.

"Actually, I'll take two cookies today."

"Oh? Celebrating? Did you crack a Bureau case? You know, I could've been an agent, but—"

"You slacked off while you were a recruit. Yes. Please let me live."

Nora chuckles. "Just making sure you don't make the same mistake as me, girl." She hands me two chocolate chip cookies on the house. I plan to save them for me and Iris to eat during the movie tonight.

After I leave Bewitched Buns, I walk next door to Illusion. Taylor and Jude are exiting the salon when I arrive.

"Well, well, well," Taylor says. "Following us?"

I cross my arms. "Great minds, and all that."

Taylor snorts. "There's nothing here."

"I'll find out for myself. This isn't a group project, remember?"

Taylor grins, but her eyes remain cold. She brushes past me and Jude follows, which I'm noticing is typical of their friendship.

I enter Illusion, and the shop bell dings in welcome. The dim lights, the faint smell of acetone and jasmine lotion, and the gurgling sounds of water promise a relaxing self-care experience. I'm not into getting my nails painted, my eyebrows waxed, or my face scrubbed, but my mom is a regular customer here and she raves about their services. They even offer a charmed nail polish that changes color with your mood.

"Hi, Monroe. Long time no see. Are you here for yourself? Your mom was here just last week," Mrs. Le, the owner, says.

"No, I'm actually here to ask a few questions." I show her my Bureau badge.

"Your friends just did," she says with a frown.

"I know, but I'd like to gather information for myself. To be as thorough as possible. I'll be quick. I promise."

"Okay," Mrs. Le replies with a sigh. She leads me to an office in the back of the salon. She draws the blinds to keep out prying customers and then sits at her desk.

"Can you tell me about the incident?" I ask, taking the seat across from her. I grab my tablet from my bag so I can take detailed notes.

"It happened a few weeks ago. We got a delivery, and then the fans started whirling and blew the delivery driver, Diego Narvaez, into a table. The fans kept going even after I unplugged them. Thankfully, Diego wasn't hurt. Just a few scrapes and bruises."

"That is good. Did you have many customers that day?"

"Our only customers that morning were regulars. Teens. Two of them just left." Mrs. Le pulls out a notepad of receipts and flips back several pages. "Iris James, Anita Patel, Taylor Evans, and Jude Featherstone got manicures. Taylor also got a facial, and a boy named Noah Cham got his brows waxed. The accident happened after they left. Then we closed for the rest of the day so the Bureau could question us and dispel the magic."

I nod. So far, that aligns with what was in the report. "Was there anyone else working with you?"

"My daughter, Luna."

"Is she here?"

Mrs. Le shakes her head. "She's out of town for two more weeks. Short-term exchange program."

I make a note to return once Luna is back to see if she knows anything. "And the victim?"

"Diego. He's been delivering our supplies from Conjurer's Corner since last year. He's a smart kid. Always timely. I asked him the day of the accident if he did anything different or if our moody nail polish could be to blame. He said no. The Bureau verified this and noted that the polish seemed fine. The agents think he was charmed *here*."

"It's possible. I'll need to follow up with Diego."

“You could try calling Conjurer’s Corner. He works there most days after school,” Mrs. Le suggests. “I’d like to get this resolved. Nothing like this has ever happened before. We are so careful with our charmed products, only buying ones that have been sold for years and with a low-risk rating from the Bureau.”

“The cause of the mishap wasn’t a product, but a love charm made for people. Do you know if any customers or even your daughter might have charmed Diego? Were any of them checking him out?” I ask.

Mrs. Le balks. “Not Luna. She would never do that. She knows better. And the regulars paid him no mind. They all seem like good kids, but I guess you never really know.”

The shop bell chimes, and chatter filters in from the front room. “Excuse me. I need to attend to my customers,” Mrs. Le says.

I dial the number for Conjurer’s Corner as soon as she leaves. The phone rings and rings and rings. I glance at the clock on the wall. I have twenty minutes before I need to meet Iris, which should be enough time to pop over to Conjurer’s Corner and try to get a statement from Diego. I want to talk to him today while my conversation with Mrs. Le is still fresh in my mind.

I take my leave and drive west into downtown. Giant bur oak trees stretch across the street and catch rays of golden sunlight in their branches. Chittering squirrels scramble up their trunks carrying mouthfuls of acorns.

There are no parking spots outside Conjurer’s Corner, so I’m forced to park a block away, near the Bureau headquarters. It must be happy hour at Toil & Trouble because people wearing suits and pencil skirts crowd the bar’s entrance while the bouncer checks IDs. I spot Larry, one of the Bureau security guards, and wave.

The gentle breeze promises a warm spring as I head inside the shop. Customers crowd every corner, picking up products like immovable hair gel and trying on all-weather jackets that morph from fleece to wool to coated nylon.

The store is owned by the Patels, so I'm not surprised to see Anita behind the counter ringing up a customer. If I need to question her, I can do that another time. Right now, finding Diego is priority number one.

Since I don't have Instagram, I search his name online along with "Fair Glen." An article about St. Mary's mathletes populates. Diego's name is listed beneath a picture of a shaggy-haired boy wearing glasses and a blue blazer.

I wander the aisles, searching the faces until I spot a boy with tousled brown hair carrying a cardboard box. He's got his head down like he doesn't want to be seen. His skin twinkles gold beneath the fluorescent light.

"Diego!" I call out. The boy looks up, and I rush over to him. I flash my badge. "Got a minute to talk?"

"One minute," he confirms. "I'm preparing some deliveries."

"This won't take long. I can see that gold dust on you. Do you know if anyone would want to give you a love charm?"

"Not really." He rests the box on the ground. Inside are charmed stuffed animals that bark, meow, and moo at me, their mouths moving. "I keep looking over my shoulder, afraid someone is going to hit on me, and I'll have another accident, so I wish I did. My parents don't even want me to work, but we need the money."

"I understand. Take precautions where you can. Stay away from anyone who might ask you out or flirt with you," I reply.

He nods. "I have. Like I told the Bureau back in February, nothing out of the ordinary happened before I arrived at Illusion. I loaded my van with deliveries, and then I drove straight to the nail salon. I didn't talk to anyone before I got there."

"What happened after you entered Illusion?" I ask.

"I dropped off the supplies and said hello to Mrs. Le and Luna. After that, the fans started blowing like crazy. It felt like I was inside of a tornado."

"I'm glad you were okay. What happened right before the fans started blowing? Did you maybe wink at Luna or ask her out?"

Diego's face pinks. He rubs the back of his neck. "No. I didn't tell the Bureau agent this because I didn't know it was important, but Luna has a crush on me. She was subtly checking me out and then randomly gave me one of those generic Valentine's Day cards. I kind of stumbled back in surprise, knocked into a fan, and that's when things popped off."

Huh. Maybe Mrs. Le doesn't know what her daughter is truly capable of. Luna likely sprinkled the charm onto the card. "Any chance you still have the card she gave you?" I ask.

Diego lifts the box and nudges the door to the back of the store open with his foot. "Nah, sorry."

"Okay, thanks."

Diego disappears into the back room, and I leave Conjurer's Corner with a working theory that he was charmed at Illusion by touching a card covered in charm dust. That means someone there had the dust on them that day. Luna is a prime suspect since she flirted with Diego before the mishap. But that doesn't mean she's the one selling or sharing the charm.

And I can't rule out the other people there, namely Mrs. Le, who could want to see her daughter's crush reciprocated, or the customers: Iris, Anita, Taylor, Jude, and Noah. Iris seemed genuinely shocked about being charmed. I don't think she'd charm herself or Diego when she's so smitten with Anita. Anita can't see magic, but she could've used the charm blindly. Taylor and Jude are Mystics, but why would they give out a love charm? Taylor has a long-term boyfriend, so I doubt she's looking elsewhere. I can't say the same for Jude.

My phone buzzes, drawing me out of my thoughts.

Mom: Hi honey. It's Mom. Give me a call when you can. I'd love to hear how your semester is going and maybe grab dinner this week.

I clear the notification. I'll reply later. Maybe.

It's not that I don't want to see her, but rather, I don't want to be reminded of everything that's been lost in the divorce.

My phone vibrates again. I almost don't check it, but another text comes in right after.

Iris: where r u?

we're missing the previews!

Damn. It's past seven. I race back to my car and hurry toward Iris's house.

BUREAU OF MYSTICAL AFFAIRS
RECORD OF INCIDENT

DATE: Sunday, February 8

RESPONDING OFFICER: Senior Agent Stephanie Rudd

CASE NUMBER: 26-292085

LOCATION: Illusion Salon & Spa

SUMMARY: The nail salon received several customers that day, including Bureau recruits Taylor Evans, Jude Featherstone, and Noah Cham along with two Mundanes: Iris James and Anita Patel. Delivery driver Diego Narvaez was knocked into a wall by fans.

ACTIONS TAKEN: Interviewed the customers, victim, and employees at the salon. Cleaned up charm residue.

RECOMMENDATION: Forward to Director James for case assignment.

UPDATE: Luna Le, an Illusion employee, handed Diego a Valentine's Day card right before the mishap. She's currently out of the country. I, Monroe Bennett, plan to interview her when she returns.

The Jameses live in a blue Victorian with a perfectly mowed lawn and charmed rosebushes that bloom all year—at least I think that's the type of charm I see shimmering on the petals.

I send off a quick text to Iris.

Here. Sorry!

I drum my fingers against my leg while I wait, fiddling with the music until I settle on a Kehlani song. It's ten past seven. So much for getting to the drive-in early to scope out any charmed students and gather intel. Maybe we can stay after.

Iris exits her house and practically runs toward my car. She climbs inside, and the sweet, alluring scent of her perfume envelops me. She looks great in her wool skirt, black tights, and a red sweater. Under her arm, she carries a denim jacket with a pride flag pinned to the pocket and a huge silver purse.

"Hey!" She gives me a once-over with a frown. "Why do you look like you're going on a stakeout?"

I glance down at myself. I'm wearing black cords, my usual

hoodie, and my favorite black beanie. "We're seeing a movie, not going to a fashion show."

Iris rolls her eyes. "I thought you'd try to look like you're going on a date."

"Rude. I was doing recon. I didn't have time to go home and change."

"So that's why you're late." Iris tugs on my hoodie. "What's under here?"

With a sigh, I pull the sweatshirt over my head to reveal my thrifted oversize rugby polo.

"How gay of you," she comments, but it's affectionate. "Can I?" she asks, pointing at my beanie. I nod slowly, and she adjusts it a little so it's sitting better on my head. The back of her hand grazes the skin on my face. I swallow as she fixes my shirt collar, suddenly very warm.

"Shouldn't I look like I don't care so you won't fall in love with me?" I ask.

Iris scoffs. "I have standards, Monroe."

She pulls one of her three silver necklaces off and hands it to me. It's the shortest one, basically a chain, but delicate. I put it on and touch the cool metal.

"Better. Let's go before we miss the entire movie." She straps on her seat belt and leans back. She almost seems unfazed by our fake date, except her forefinger tap, tap, tapping against her knee, gives her away.

"Nervous?" I ask as I drive east toward the outskirts of town. I've been to Electric Dust a few times as a kid on Halloween and Christmas for their holiday-themed movies. I had no idea they played classic romances on Wednesday nights too.

"That obvious? I want our scheme to work," Iris says. "When

Anita sees how I've let you in, she'll want to give us a second chance. Even though we were only together for four months, what we had felt more real than any other relationship I've been in." Iris pouts. I absolutely do not find the expression adorable. "I worked really hard on coming up with cute dates for us, like making cider from apples we picked. I made a custom playlist while we stargazed just before winter break and even registered a star in her name! A romcom could never. I mean, maybe *A Walk to Remember*, but that's like the saddest romance ever and I don't think Anita has seen it."

"Do you think that your relationship with her felt different because you put in a lot of effort, whereas you didn't before? I'm not an expert, but it sounds like anything you work hard at would feel important," I reply.

"No. It felt different because we were in love," she says stubbornly.

I shrug. "You're the expert."

The sunset dips below the horizon; orange and purple rays glimmer through the trees and gaps between buildings. I turn off the road, follow the signs, and drive along a gravel road. There's nothing but cornfields out here, the stalks stretching on for miles and miles. There are at least thirty other cars parked in the lot tonight. A giant screen stands on the far side of the field. The previews have already started, but there are cars still arriving, so we aren't too late. One perk of living in a small town is that it doesn't take long to get most places.

I stop at the booth where an attendant a little older than us is dressed in all black. He steps out, and I roll down my window.

"Here for the movie?" he asks. "Oh! Hi, Iris. I didn't recognize the car."

Iris leans over the center console. "Hey, Jimmy. Two tickets."

Jimmy types something into the tablet he's holding and then

holds it out for Iris. She leans farther across me to pay with her phone. I stiffen at the soft press of her body against mine.

"Have fun," he tells us, and gestures for the next car to pull up.

"I could've gotten my own ticket," I say as I drive forward.

"It's ten bucks. You can get the next date." Iris directs me to a spot not too close to the screen, and not too far back. It's also the perfect location to be seen.

"Okay, so you have to turn the radio to FM 101.1 to hear the movie, but there's no need to leave the engine running." She hauls her purse onto her lap and unzips it.

The sun practically shines out of the bag when I look inside. Popcorn, Sour Patch Kids, and two cans of Sprite greet me.

"Whoa."

Iris grins. "Let's take a pic to commemorate your first time seeing this classic before it starts."

I don't usually take pictures. Since I don't have social media, there's rarely a reason to. Whenever I do take a photo of myself, I always end up looking goofy.

Iris tugs me to her side and nuzzles against me before I can say as much. The scent of lavender, the cotton-candy sweetness of magic, and something just Iris fills my nose. She takes the selfie before I can even smile.

She sits back and examines the photo. Her brows dip together, and the corners of her mouth tug down. "Can you pretend to be enjoying yourself?"

I roll my eyes but lean in, the console between us digging into my ribs. Because Iris is taller than me, my face is basically in the crook of her neck. The heat of her skin rivals a similar warmth radiating from my crystal charms as our heads touch. The quiet comfort I get from the position pulls my lips into an easy, natural smile. The camera flashes.

"Better?" I ask.

Iris grins when she sees the result. "Much."

"I brought snacks too." I take the two chocolate chip cookies I got from Bewitched Buns out of my pocket. One is a little crumbly, and some of the chocolate has wiped off on the napkin. I smile sheepishly.

"Thoughtful, but I don't eat chocolate. Snickerdoodles are my favorite," Iris replies.

"Oh." I ignore the twinge of disappointment in my chest. We're supposed to be doing things we hate so we don't fall for each other. So bringing her a chocolate chip cookie is actually a good thing. Right?

The speakers set up in the corners of the parking lot crackle to life, and a voice that I'm pretty sure belongs to Jimmy, the guy who sold us our tickets, filters through. "Movie-lovers, the show is about to begin. Please silence your cell phones and tune into FM station 101.1 for audio and 101.2 for audio description. Subtitles are turned on. In the event of an emergency, the rows closest to the exit will be evacuated first. If you need to leave before the movie ends, let an attendant know. No drinking, smoking, or using charmed objects during the show. Enjoy the movie."

Pretty Woman starts, and Iris grins. She slides her seat back, kicks off her shoes, and tucks her feet under herself. She drapes her jacket over her legs and passes me the popcorn.

"Tell me about Illusion," I whisper to Iris as the male lead speeds through the Hollywood Hills in a silver car. "Was anyone acting weird?"

Iris groans. "Would watching the movie kill you?"

"No, but you promised to help."

Iris throws her head back. "No one was being weird. We all got cute wintry nails and then we left."

"No one seemed distracted or nervous?" I asked. "What about Jude or Luna, Mrs. Le's daughter?"

Iris twists her lips in thought. "Luna did pause halfway through my set to reapply her lipstick and put on perfume. I only noticed because she usually doesn't wear any makeup."

She was getting ready to give Diego the card.

"Now pay attention!"

I lean back in my seat and try to focus on the movie instead of the case. It doesn't take long before I'm locked in. I'm still not a believer, but watching Julia Roberts tell off that judgmental store clerk on Rodeo Drive was amazing.

The earsplitting sound of a blaring car alarm slashes through the dialogue and turns heads. Flashing lights draw my gaze to the car across from us. Inside, Dante Morelli, the boy who posted the video of me and Iris, is frantically clicking the car key while the girl in the passenger seat, Chloe Nguyen, tries to help. In the back seat is another girl with curly brown hair, whom I recognize from Spanish class. Daisy Guzman.

Everyone covers their ears. The car's doors fly open. Chloe screeches as she's thrown out the side of the car, her body flailing before it hits the pavement. The movie stops, and attendants and curious moviegoers rush over.

Iris grabs my arm. "What's going on, Monroe?" she asks over the commotion.

Even from here, I can see all the gold charm dust on Chloe twinkling in the moonlight as Daisy helps her to her feet.

"Stay here," I tell Iris. I'm out of the car a second later, rushing over to Chloe.

"What's happening?" she asks, rubbing the angry red spot on her arm where it hit the ground.

I show her my Bureau badge. "You've been charmed."

Residual dust covers the seat where Chloe sat. It's the only part of the car that's shimmering with magic.

It's pretty hard to sprinkle charm dust on someone in a parked car full of people without them noticing, so it's likely the dusting happened earlier and only now has someone made a move on her. When I saw her yesterday passing out flyers for prom queen, Chloe was magic-free. The only person here, that I know of, who was also at the nail salon is Iris, and she's been with me the entire movie. Someone other than my initial suspects charmed Chloe. How many people have this charm?

A small crowd has gathered. Attendants hold people back, but that doesn't stop them from pointing their phones at us. Iris pushes to the front, a concerned divot surfacing between her eyebrows. So much for staying in the car.

"Can you hand me my bag?" I ask.

Iris rushes back while I brush my hands across the charm dust on Chloe's seat. My crystal bracelet warms against my wrist. I close my eyes and try to tune out the crowd and focus. Sometimes I wish magic was something I could *create*, rather than just collect.

The dust lifts from the seat. I wave my hand over the particles hovering in the air. Passing my hand through them feels like grabbing a golden spiderweb. At night, charm dust is the brightest thing around.

A second later, Iris kneels beside me with my bag strung over her shoulder. "Need help?" she asks.

"Take out my collector, it's a—"

"A container full of neutralizing crystals, I know. Bureau kid, remember?" She grabs the tool, opens the lid, and holds it out for me. Although she can't see the magic, I'm grateful for the assist.

Once I have as much of the dust as possible in my palm, I dump it inside the collector and close the lid.

"Is it contained?" an attendant holding back the audience asks.

"It is. It's safe to resume the movie," I say.

A few audience members linger to ask me questions about how this happened and whether the charm is dangerous. I'm not good around a lot of people. The crowd pressing in to get a better look at what I'm doing makes my throat tighten.

Iris seems to sense my discomfort. She throws her shoulders back and projects her voice. "Everyone, the Bureau is handling it. Please give us some space."

Her tone leaves no room for discussion and melts away some of my worry about the situation. "You three, I need to talk to you," I say to Dante, Chloe, and Daisy.

"I need to call my dad first. He's going to flip out if the car is charmed," Dante mumbles, moving off to the side.

"Is the car charmed?" Chloe asks.

"Not the car. You," I reply.

"But . . ." Chloe brushes at her arms and legs as if it will remove the charm.

"That won't help. The only way to get rid of it is for the Bureau to find a suitable dissolver or to let the intent of the charm come to fruition. And in this case, that means finding your perfect love match," I explain. "Until then, stay away from anything you'd consider romantic: flirting, holding hands, kissing, slow dancing—"

"That's literally half the point of going to prom and running for queen! Who would do this to me?"

"Someone who's into you but doesn't know if you feel the same," I reply.

Daisy, who's standing next to her and chewing on her lip, seems to debate what to do with her hands. She reaches for Chloe and pulls her into a tight hug.

"Did anything weird happen today?" I ask once it seems like Chloe has calmed down a bit.

She shakes her head. "Everything was normal. I tried to get signatures for prom queen, had a meeting with a few teachers about a fundraiser the student council is having this week, went to class . . ."

"You didn't have any mishaps before now?" I ask.

"Nothing," Chloe replies while Daisy rubs circles on her back.

"Have you flirted with anyone recently? Like your date tonight?" I ask.

Chloe tenses. "Dante? He's not my date. He's a friend. The three of us are on student council together."

"Okay, did *he* flirt with *you*?" I ask. "The charm is triggered by romantic advances, so something must have set it off."

"When does he not?" Daisy mutters.

Chloe drops her gaze. "I mean he tried to, like, put his arm around me, but I shrugged him off. I don't like him in that way." She rubs her hands together. "I think I'm—" She cuts herself off and shakes her head. She glances at Daisy, who's watching her curiously. "Never mind. Are we done? I want to go home."

"Yeah, but I'll need your number in case I have to follow up with questions."

"Right. Sure." We exchange numbers while Daisy watches with a furrowed brow.

"Can I check your bag? I need to make sure you don't have any contraband." Daisy grinds her jaw but hands me her purse. "What do you think of all this?" I ask while I examine the contents of her bag. She has a wallet, lipstick, a single playing card, and a pack of gum. Nothing sparkles like charm dust.

Daisy furrows her dark eyebrows. "I don't know. It's scary. I kind of thought Sasha was exaggerating, but this does feel like a *Final Destination* movie. You can't escape your fate."

"Sasha?" I ask.

"Sasha Gordon. A softball pitcher at our school who was charmed," Daisy replies.

I'll need to talk to Sasha to see if I can make any connections. I hand Daisy her purse, and she promptly loops her arm around Chloe and steers her away. "Come on. I'll call us a ride home."

When Dante returns, I waste no time asking him questions. "What happened in the car?"

"Nothing. We were watching the movie, and then suddenly, the car alarm went off and Chloe went flying."

"You didn't try to put your arm around her shoulder?" I ask.

He balks. "I mean I—I—"

"Do you like Chloe?" Iris asks, coming to stand beside me. "Because I've seen you making heart eyes at her in stats."

"What? No!" Dante scoffs, and yet the red splotches blooming on his cheeks give him away.

"Very convincing," I reply.

Dante steps closer and keeps his voice low. "Look, I had nothing to do with this, all right? Why don't you figure out how to fix it instead of interrogating innocent people?"

I can't tell if he's trying to be intimidating or sincere. "That's not my field of expertise. I'm trying to find out who's sharing illegal charm dust because clearly more than one person is in possession of the contraband," I reply.

Dante shakes his head. "Can't help you there." He runs a stiff hand through his wavy hair. "My car is safe to drive, right? I don't have to turn it in to the Bureau, do I?"

I shake my head. "The car is free of charm dust, but any romantic advances toward Chloe will cause another mishap. Sorry, bud. Her flying out of the car means she is not into you."

"Her loss," he says, then shrugs.

"Right. I need to check your pockets for contraband."

"Seriously?" Dante rolls his eyes but turns his pockets inside out. The only things in them are his wallet and car keys, both of which are charm-free.

The speakers set up in the parking lot crackle to life as the movie attendant makes another announcement, this time offering a discount on the next film to the audience because of the disruption and then promising to resume the movie shortly.

Dante uses the interruption to slink off. Hopefully, he remembers my warning and doesn't try to make another move on Chloe. But, you know, some people can't take a hint.

I text the Director about the incident like she requested all the recruits to do while Iris leans against my car and tosses popcorn into her mouth.

"You were helpful back there," I tell her.

Thanks to Iris, I was in the right place at the right time tonight. She was spot on about Electric Dust being a good location for romance. Maybe we *should* go to places where our classmates or the kids at St. Mary's will be on dates so I can catch another lead.

She says, "Gotta keep up my end of the bargain and make sure you're put in the field next year. Do you want to finish the movie?"

My stomach twists when I remember the deal I made with her mom. I'm lying to Iris about why we're spending time together. While she *is* more popular than me and knows where to go and whom to talk to, I'm not pretending to date her solely for those reasons.

"Actually, I should write up the mishap and get this charm dust to the Bureau," I reply.

"Oh. Yeah. Okay." The slight dip in her brow almost looks like disappointment.

“Rain check?” I ask before I can think twice about it. “I was getting into the movie.”

Iris brightens. “Really? All right. I’m holding you to that.” She pokes me in the shoulder before rounding the car and opening the passenger-side door.

I grin. “I’m counting on it.”

BUREAU OF MYSTICAL AFFAIRS
RECORD OF INCIDENT

DATE: Wednesday, March 4

RESPONDING OFFICER: Junior Recruit Monroe Bennett

CASE NUMBER: 26-292085

LOCATION: Electric Dust Drive-In Movie Theatre

SUMMARY: The mishap occurred during the showing of *Pretty Woman*. Dante Morelli tried putting his arm around Chloe Nguyen, who happened to be charmed. Chloe was thrown from the car but uninjured. Key witness Daisy Guzman was in the back seat.

ACTIONS TAKEN: Dispelled the charm from the car and questioned then searched suspects.

RECOMMENDATION: Narrow down when Chloe was charmed and follow up with Daisy. She seemed jealous?

Nine

I arrive at school early Thursday morning so I can talk to the softball team before class. Sasha Gordon isn't here yet, so I drop my stuff on a metal bench and check the database for an update from R&D. They should be making progress on finding a suitable dissolver for the love charm. But nothing comes up. Maybe they haven't gotten around to it yet, or the database is lagging.

A Jeep blasting Taylor Swift pulls up, and a group of girls climb out wearing warm-up clothes. I shove my notebook into my bag and scan the faces for Sasha Gordon. She was the tallest girl in the team photo and thus is easy to spot. The platinum blond hair also helps.

"Hey, Sasha," I say, trying to keep my voice casual. I flash my Bureau badge. "I need to ask you a couple questions."

"Ugh. Fine." Sasha turns to her teammates. "Tell Coach I'll be there in a minute." Once the girls have walked onto the field, she shifts her attention back to me. It's then I notice that her skin is absent of gold charm dust.

"You're no longer charmed," I murmur.

Sasha looks down. "The mishaps stopped last week after Dana asked me to prom." She glances across the field at her teammate wistfully.

A flurry of excitement shoots down my spine. Sasha Gordon and Dana Reeve are a love match! Not that I'm starting to believe in love, but the charm sure does.

"Start at the beginning," I say, my voice shaky with excitement. "When did you notice you were charmed?"

"I noticed a few weeks ago. We were warming up before a game, and it was my turn to pitch. I grabbed a ball from the bin, and then all the balls flew at me *Final Destination*–style. I thought it was a prank until Mx. Michaelson mentioned the magic. Thank God they were in the stands."

"Who all was there?" I ask.

"My teammates, a few teachers, and students. Oh, and my slimy ex-boyfriend, who winked at me."

"The charm hit you in the face to tell you he was never your perfect match."

She snorts.

"But that doesn't mean he was the one who charmed you. Did anyone stand out to you? Anyone acting suspicious?" I ask.

"No one, but honestly, I wasn't paying that much attention. I was thinking about the season and whether scouts would be at our next game. I want a softball scholarship."

"Sasha!" the coach yells from across the field.

"I've gotta go." Sasha turns on her heel.

"Wait! One more question. Where does the team store the softballs?" If Sasha was pitching, someone could've covered a ball in dust from the love charm knowing she'd be the first to touch it.

"In the gym," she calls over her shoulder. "But Mx. Michaelson checked them. They're clean."

Of course they did. How is our suspect targeting people? So far, there's nothing that connects Diego, Sasha, and Chloe.

As I'm heading toward class, my pocket vibrates. For a second, I worry it's Mom again, finally putting her foot down and making me visit her, but it's just Andie in our group chat with Liz.

Andie: girl, is this you?

A sinking feeling floods my chest as I click the link he sent. It takes me to a post on Iris's Instagram. I recognize the picture immediately as the one we took at Electric Dust. The caption reads Movie night with my fav ♥. It's simple enough, but with the addition of the cheesy film quote she's added and the hearts she's drawn in the corners, it looks like we're a real couple. Iris posted this late last night, and already the photo has over three hundred likes and dozens of comments.

Cuties!

#couplegoals!

wish I had a gf . . .

where'd you get that top?

I should've known that picture was for social media rather than to document my first time seeing *Pretty Woman*. It makes sense that she'd want to post "proof" of our relationship online. No doubt Anita is still following her. I stare at the photo, transfixed by how natural and good Iris and I look together.

Another text comes in.

Liz: You're an IT couple now, Roe

Ngl seeing you with Iris is still kinda weird . . . I need more than 10 mins during lunch to get her vibe!

Andie: yaaas let's all hang out!! xx

Idk . . .

Liz: Don't get so lovesick you leave us behind!

I would literally never.

Andie: prove it lol

Ugh fine! I'll ask Iris when she's free.

Iris hanging out with Liz and Andie was bound to happen again, but I'm still hesitant to keep involving my friends in this charade. It'll only be harder for us to bounce back when the arrangement inevitably ends.

Director James drives a sleek black SUV that pulls into the school parking lot and stops right in front of me. She gives me a curt nod when she sees me waiting against my dusty old sedan with my ankles crossed and my hands in my pockets. I wrangle my expression into indifference, despite the spike in my heart rate as Iris climbs out of the car wearing a long floral skirt with a daring slit up the side and combat boots. Her braids are tied back with a purple ribbon that matches her lipstick. Her mouth curves when she notices me. She waves goodbye to her mom, who drives off, and then skips to my side.

"Your picture worked," I tell Iris as we cross the parking lot.

"You saw it?" she asks, raising an eyebrow. "I thought you didn't have Instagram."

"Everyone saw. Andie sent it to me this morning. It got hundreds of likes," I reply as we pass a boy setting up silver balloons that read "Prom?" in a parking spot.

"Anita most definitely saw it too. She still follows me," Iris says.

"I figured. Is that why you posted it?"

Iris twists her lips in thought. "Partly. But I also thought the photo was super cute. Are you mad?"

"I mean, posting pictures of us together on social media wasn't one of the ground rules," I say.

Her eyes roam across my face, as if trying to decide how I feel about this. "I'm sorry. I can take it down right now if you want."

She grabs her phone from her back pocket, and I still her hand. Her skin is warm to the touch. "No. It is a cute pic," I tell her quickly. Iris relaxes, her shoulders dropping from around her ears. "Your mom doesn't follow you, right?"

Iris laughs. "No. I doubt she'd care we're dating, though. She thinks too highly of those chosen for the Bureau to dislike me dating a recruit."

I doubt the Director would think highly of me if she knew I was dating Iris when I'm supposed to be protecting her.

After a moment of hesitation, Iris loops her arm through mine and steers us inside. Her presence is surprisingly comforting. I try not to dwell on that.

In the hallway, someone hands me a flyer. Large letters scroll across the charmed sheet of paper that reads:

PROMRAISER: ANNUAL PROM FUNDRAISER
SATURDAY, 7 P.M., AT HEXED HOLLOW MUSIC HALL

And then the illustration of a band playing for a crowd of people comes to life.

"Another prime location for mishaps," Iris says as she guides us toward the auditorium for our weekly assembly.

"Monroe Bennett and Iris James," the door announces when we enter, taking attendance.

The few people sitting on the aisles look up. I focus on the warmth of Iris's hand instead of their stares, unused to this kind of attention.

"Y'all are so cute together," a girl from my AP government class, Nikka Parker, says as Iris and I walk by.

"Uh, thanks," I mutter.

We're one of four other out couples at school. Freshman year, I told my friends and my parents that I'm a lesbian, and while I don't hide it, I've also never made a public announcement. Who does? It's weird being visible to everyone at school, only for my queer relationship to be a sham. I feel seen in a way I never have before. It's gonna take some getting used to.

"Are you going to couples' night at Spellcast Roller tomorrow?" Nikka asks. "A bunch of us will be there."

Iris glances at me and subtly nudges my arm. Couples' night is exactly the type of event I wouldn't know about if Iris and I weren't fake dating. It's also the perfect opportunity to scope out suspects. And as I'm sure Taylor will be there with her boyfriend, she won't be able to beat me to this lead.

"We'll be there. Right, sugarplum?" I ask.

Iris makes a muffled, pained sound at the pet name. "Right," she replies.

As we head down the aisle, she exclaims, " 'Sugarplum'?! Only my grandma calls me that!"

"I'm doing my part to make sure you don't fall in love with me!" I hiss.

She rolls her eyes. "You're a little too committed. We should take more photos at the rink. I think it will help sell our relationship and get Anita's attention. I won't post them without asking first unless you call me 'sugarplum' again; then all bets are off."

I laugh. "I'll stick to 'babe,' but you have to promise to get my good side."

"What's your good side?" Iris takes my chin and turns my head from side to side. The warmth of her palm seeps into my skin and draws me up short. She watches me curiously, her dark brown eyes pinging across my face. My lungs burn for air. I inhale audibly, and Iris smiles, a delicate, encouraging little thing. "Both sides look perfect to me."

" 'Babe' is the best you're going to get. Flirting will get you nowhere," I say breathily.

She winks. "Oh, you'd be surprised how far it gets me."

I usually sit in the back of the auditorium with Liz and Andie, but today Iris guides me toward her row near the front. Taylor's already here, her brown hair pulled into a sleek bun while Sean fidgets with a baseball. Taylor stares like I've grown a second head as Iris and I take our seats, but it's nothing compared to the daggers Anita shoots at me from across the aisle. The weight of her gaze lingers as the principal calls for quiet.

When I lock eyes with Taylor again, she's scowling openly.

"Is it me, or does Taylor have a problem with us?" I ask, keeping my voice low.

Iris looks around me to view Taylor a few seats down. "She's just watching out for me. She saw how hurt I was when Anita dumped me."

"Are you still hurt?" I ask, finding I'm truly curious.

"I'm . . . better. I mostly need her to understand my side of things, you know? If she did, she'd see that I've been sincere this whole time. Just because I love the idea of love doesn't mean I'm not interested in her."

"You don't need to convince me. I believe you."

Iris's expression softens. "Thanks. Anyway, I think we should up our romance at couples' night to squash any lasting suspicion and make her überjealous. Think you can handle it?"

"I can handle it," I reply. A sudden, inexplicable draw has me leaning in until my mouth hovers near her ear. Her jasmine body lotion and lavender perfume make my head spin. "Can you handle scoping out anyone suspicious?"

Iris's arm twitches, and her voice is a little shaky when she replies, "Oh, I can definitely handle that. Like mother, like daughter."

That immediately sets my mind right.

I lean back and turn my attention to Principal Walters, who's talking about precautions to take while there's an active investigation. "I know half of you won't listen, but please no romancing on school grounds unless you're positive that feelings are mutual. Immediately report potential incidents to Bureau recruits Monroe Bennett, Jude Featherstone, or Taylor Evans. If they aren't available, tell Mx. Michaelson. While we're on the topic, sports teams must have a Mystic present during practice in light of yesterday's baseball game against St. Mary's."

"What happened at yesterday's game?" I ask Iris.

She shrugs. "I was with you, remember?"

I peer down the aisle and try to get Taylor's attention. Now she's ignoring me. Great. I check my phone, but there are no alerts from the Bureau. I wasn't on call yesterday, but I think Taylor might've been.

"Taylor!" I whisper-shout.

Slowly, she slides her gaze to me. "What?"

"Were you at the baseball game?"

"Yes."

"Well, what happened?" I ask.

Taylor sighs. "Nothing serious. Some girl was in the stands flirting with Zeke Hart. And he wasn't into it. St. Mary's recruit, Reggie Murphy, submitted the Bureau report this morning."

"He did? I didn't—"

"*Shh!*" Mr. Patterson, my homeroom teacher, who's sitting at the end of our row, leans over and snaps his fingers at me. He points at Principal Walters, who's listing events for the remainder of this week and the next one, including Promraiser.

I stifle a groan. Iris's eyes shine brightly. Zeke Hart is a popular baseball player at St. Mary's whose rivalry with Taylor's boyfriend, Sean Ashton, is well known. I'll read Reggie's report later.

Once the assembly ends, I walk Iris to class. She laughs at my dumb jokes, and during AP government, she texts me a list of romantic films I have to watch that includes *Love Don't Cost a Thing*, *Love & Basketball*, and *But I'm a Cheerleader*, along with links to romances I need to read, like every book by Jenny Han. During lunch, Iris and Andie recap the latest drama on *Love Island* while Liz sketches them on her tablet. I don't know when, but sometime during the week, Iris has melded perfectly into my crew like she's always been there. She's becoming somewhat of a friend.

"Let's get some fresh air," Iris says during our free period.

"There's a park across the street. Want to go?" I ask.

Iris nods vigorously. "I haven't been there in years!"

One of our fake dating rules was not talking about anything

too deep, and yet I find myself telling her the story regardless. "My mom used to take me here. I'd make her spin me as fast as she could on the merry-go-round, and then I'd jump off."

"That's so dangerous," Iris scolds with a small laugh.

"Wanna play?" I ask, half joking.

Iris surprises me when she says, "I'm game," with a mischievous little lift at the corner of her mouth.

We race to the park and spend the next forty minutes spinning each other until we're dizzy, the trees in the park blurring by and the wind rushing in our ears. Iris leaps from the wheel and rolls across the wood chips grinning madly. The sun catches on the dark strands of her braids and highlights the gold charm dust freckling her skin. My heart stutters at the sight. I'm breathless for the rest of the day.

BUREAU OF MYSTICAL AFFAIRS
RECORD OF INCIDENT

DATE: Wednesday, March 4

RESPONDING OFFICER: Junior Recruit Reginald "Reggie" Murphy

CASE NUMBER: 26-292085

LOCATION: St. Mary's baseball field

SUMMARY: Zeke Hart, a senior baseball player at St. Mary's, had a mishap during a baseball game against Fair Glen High. His bat started tugging him around the field midgame after a fangirl tried to flirt. Yesenia Rodriguez, a junior at St. Mary's, was at the game with her boyfriend when the bench she was on collapsed.

ACTIONS TAKEN: Fellow recruit Taylor Evans, who was there supporting FGH, and I disarmed the magic, and the game resumed.

RECOMMENDATION: Discuss at the next debrief. Is it a coincidence that two St. Mary's students were charmed during an event with Fair Glen High students? So far, Diego Narvaez, Zeke Hart, and Yesenia Rodriguez are St. Mary's victims. It's spreading.

Ten

By Friday afternoon, I'm actually looking forward to couples' night at Spellcast Roller. Iris had a prom committee meeting after school, so we decided to link up at the rink, and I'll drive her home. I fret over what to wear before finally settling on plaid trousers, a white Henley, and a black jacket. It's basic, but a step up from what she referred to as my stakeout clothes. I even put on a silver chain, grinning as I picture Iris admiring my fit.

Spellcast Roller has been around since my parents were my age. They said it was one of the main hangouts in Fair Glen because the DJ played the best music, and the concession stand sold slushies that were to die for. Now the owner has added special events to bring in more customers, like VR night, where you can skate through time and space. Spellcast Roller also hosts a roller-skating competition twice a year where the rink, with monitoring from the Bureau, is dusted with a charm to turn the lanes into a winding obstacle course.

I arrive at six like we planned and step through the slightly sticky doors. A sign is posted near the entrance prohibiting the use of charmed objects inside the rink. Multicolored disco lights illuminate the red-green-and-white geometric carpet. Waxy wooden benches are arranged around the rink's edge. The dueling scents of frying oil, sugar, and ammonia make my head hurt.

Most people here at this time of day are elementary and middle schoolers with their parents, although a few people my age loiter near an old *Pac-Man* machine. The locker area is empty with no sign of Iris, so I go to the skate rental.

"What size?" the boy asks. He's got a round, cherubic face, his braces gleaming every time the disco light falls on him. I've seen him around FGH but am blanking on his name.

"Eight."

He hands me a pair of skates and then taps the tip jar next to him.

Dad would call this tipflation at its finest. I drop a couple of quarters collecting grime at the bottom of my bag into the jar and find a bench to put on my skates. They somehow feel both too big and too small when I slowly stand to test them. Embarrassing fact: I can't skate. I plan to sit on one of these benches and cheer on Iris. Then we can take pictures for her Instagram, and I can question a few students.

"Monroe!"

I whip around a little too fast for someone with wheels on their feet. My body pitches forward, but Iris glides toward me and steadies me with firm hands on my shoulders.

For a moment, I'm so far off balance, all I can do to stay upright is rely on Iris. She seems happy to see me, a gleam in her eyes and a grin brightening her face. The red ribbon tying back her hair matches her red lipstick. She's wearing a white crop top, wide-leg jeans, and chic flowery skates.

"Are you okay?" she asks with a frown.

"Yeah. Perfect."

Iris watches me for a beat before tugging me back down to the safety of the bench. "You look nice," she says.

I touch my necklace and smile. "Someone told me to try to dress like I'm going on a date."

"She sounds wise," Iris jokes.

I nod. "I have a reputation to uphold, even if it's all for show."

Iris rolls her eyes playfully. "What reputation? You don't date. Unless fake dating me is changing your mind?"

"You wish." It must be the fluorescent lights overheating my brain because I swear her cheeks color. "Anyway, what's the game plan for tonight? I need to do recon."

"Let's stay low key. We can hold hands and maybe do a few slow skates so you can scope out the couples to see if you learn anything helpful." She stands and holds out her hand for me to take.

"Uh, about that . . ." As soon as I stand, I tilt dangerously to the left. I latch on to the side of the rink with a frustrated sigh.

"Please tell me you know how to roller-skate?" Iris asks.

"It's not exactly the world's most popular pastime."

Iris flashes me a bemused glare. "Popular pastime? It's not like you're on social media, which *is* a common activity. I'll argue, *the* most common." She skates back and forth in front of me, her braids swaying around her. I feel unsteady just watching her. "What *do* you do for fun?"

I glance around the rink and notice Taylor and Sean. Taylor's slipping on a pair of cool silver skates while Sean's are a shiny midnight black. I look at the rented skates I'm wearing. Cracked and brown as dirt. Cute.

Iris pokes my shoulder. "Don't you dodge the question. Fun, remember?"

"Fun. I . . . um, like helping my dad with his cleaning business and watching *Pose* with Liz and Andie." I concentrate very hard on keeping my feet underneath me and my body upright. Iris gingerly guides me onto the rink. How does she manage to make this seem easy? She links her arm through mine to steady me. "Mostly, I've been focused on getting recruited by the Bureau."

"Which paid off. So you deserve to let loose." Iris shakes her hips in demonstration while crossing her feet over each other to the rhythm of "Beat It," an eighties banger I recognize only because Dad plays it during Saturday-morning housework. Iris is impressively smooth on those skates. "We'll start by teaching you how to roller-skate," she announces.

"You don't have to teach me—"

"I want to."

Iris falls back until she's standing behind me. Notes of lavender and vanilla replace the funky sweat stench of the rink. She rests her hands on my hips and gently glides me forward. I'm a shaky mess the entire trip around the rink, but Iris doesn't let me go, and by the second pass, I feel steadier.

"See, it's not so hard!" Iris exclaims. She spins around so that she's in front of me skating backward.

"Show-off."

Iris laughs. As the rink begins to turn, she starts to release me.

"No, don't! I'll fall!" I exclaim.

Iris tugs me closer to her as we round the bend. "I'm not gonna let you fall," she says with a smile. "You're doing great."

I probably look like a newborn fawn, but Iris's praise warms me. The song changes to one with a slower beat. Around us, people pair off. Some do complex footwork I'm jealous of, their moves fluid and effortless. A few more kids from FGH have arrived, and some from St. Mary's are still in uniform. I spot Noah Cham with a group of girls in plaid skirts and white polos.

Iris moves to my side, and I snake my arm around her waist to keep myself upright. I don't even realize how close we are until she tenses. Panic bubbles to the surface, and I'm about to start apologizing until my face turns blue, but then I feel her shift nearer to me in return. She finds my gaze with a pleased grin. I'm surprised until Taylor and Sean round the corner.

Of course. Showtime.

Sean drapes an arm around Taylor's shoulder and high-fives another boy in our grade. So far, there's no sign of Anita or anyone charmed.

"Who taught you how to skate?" I ask. Iris hesitates. "Too personal? Sorry, I forgot the rules."

Iris shakes her head. "It's fine. My mom taught me. Before she became the Director, we went skating, went to concerts, and watched the best rom-coms." Iris smiles, but it doesn't reach her eyes. "We did all the things she enjoyed when she was my age. Now she works nonstop."

"I'm sorry," I say. "My relationship with my mom isn't the best right now either."

Iris raises her eyebrows. She nods slowly, and a quiet understanding fills the space between us. It's nice. Noah rolls up next to us a second later.

"Hey, y'all!" he says.

"Hey, Noah," I reply.

Iris smiles and waves. "Did Taylor put you on carpool duty today?" she asks.

"Not today. Sean's driving our passenger princess," Noah replies. "I'm with some people from school."

"You have a green Volkswagen, right?" I ask. I've seen Taylor and Jude getting out of the car on a few occasions.

"Yep. I'm neighbors with Taylor, Jude, and Daisy. We live in the same cul-de-sac. Since St. Mary's starts later than FGH, I drive them to school." Noah skates around me effortlessly. "How's the Bureau treating you? I'm glad you're still finding time to have fun. I struggle to find balance."

Iris snorts. "So does Monroe." I give her a playful shove.

"It's going. Pretty busy with my case," I reply.

"Need any help? I'm a good sounding board," Noah offers.

"Actually, you were at Illusion Salon last month, right? There was a mishap on a day you were there."

"Oh yeah! I got my unibrow waxed." He laughs. "The accident happened after I left."

"Did you notice—"

Something hard slams into my side. My skates fly out from under me. My grip on Iris's hand vanishes. The slippery rink floor greets me as I land hard on my butt.

"Sorry! I don't know what's happening!" someone yells from above me.

"Monroe! Are you okay?" Iris is by my side a moment later, concern awash on her face.

All I manage to say is "*Owww.*"

Iris and Noah grab my arms and haul me to my feet. It's even harder to stay balanced now that I've been down. Noah goes to help someone in a St. Mary's hoodie who's also been hit. I lean heavily against Iris as she guides us out of everyone's way.

"Is this supposed to be fun?" I ask.

Iris scoffs. "You were totally enjoying yourself and getting intel before Kenny Hill nearly took you out."

Once I'm safe against the wall, I scan the room for Kenny. My eyes widen as I take in the rink. Charm dust covers the floor in gold streaks. The magic is brightest on Kenny, who's being flung around the rink by his skates.

Here we go again.

Eleven

"Help!" Kenny shrieks.

The music stops. Shouts erupt from the people around us as Kenny is flung into them.

"He's charmed," I tell Iris. "Help me over to him?"

Iris nods before looping her arm through mine and guiding us through the rapidly forming crowd of onlookers.

"Everyone, clear the rink!" the DJ announces over the speaker.

Kenny's skates seem to have a mind of their own. They fling him from one end of the rink to the other as the girl he was skating with, Nikka, watches in shock.

The crystal around my neck warms as we close in on him. "You need to take them off!" I yell.

"I—I can't," he replies as he rolls toward the DJ booth.

Iris and Noah skate after him. Iris catches up within seconds. She grips the boy's arm and tugs him to the sidelines. I inch after them at a snail's pace. Years have passed by the time I reach them, and I'm somehow out of breath.

Iris holds Kenny against the side. My crystals heat as I roll to a stop in front of them. I crouch and grab his skates—rentals by the looks of them. My hands warm, and the skates begin to glow as the magic is sucked out of the objects. It pools to the floor like sand in an hourglass.

"Is it done?" Iris asks, still holding on to Kenny.

I nod. "I need to get my bag to collect this."

"I'll help. Let me get mine too," Noah says before skating off.

"All right. Stay here, Kenny. I have some questions for you."

I don't want to bother trying to skate back to the lockers, so I make quick work of untying my skates. The rink floor is somehow more slippery in my socks. Thankfully, the skills I honed sliding around our dining room as a kid still hold up, and I make it off the rink faster than I would have wearing those deathtraps.

There's a trail of gold charm dust that leads from the rink to the skate rental, which gives me pause for two reasons: 1) Either the person who brought the charm didn't realize it was spilling everywhere, or 2) They *couldn't* have realized, because they can't see magic. It's a theory that assumes a Mundane has access to a large quantity of charm dust and is bold enough to use it on someone in public. Everyone knows the laws against the sale of unauthorized charms. The consequence for selling said contraband varies based on the severity of the case but can range from paying a fine to jail time. Who'd be bold enough to do that, and why?

I quickly grab my collector and Jordans from the lockers. As I approach the rental booth, I notice a sprinkle of charm dust along the surface. The boy who was working the booth has seemingly vanished. I glance around to see if I can spot him helping to contain the crowd of onlookers like the other employees, but he isn't in sight.

I brush the charm dust on the counter into my collector, pushing aside the tip jar to remove it all. I pause when I notice a playing card sitting in the jar that wasn't there before. Didn't Daisy have a playing card in her purse at Electric Dust?

The card is an ace of hearts. Red roses, yellow sunflowers, and cute green vines are hand-painted in the blank corners of the card. I pluck it out of the jar and flip it over to find five numbers handwritten on the back: 10308.

My curiosity spikes. Is that a birth date? A code?

I take a picture of the front and back of the card with my phone. It's odd enough to warrant documenting, even if it's unrelated to my case. I hang around for a moment, hoping the boy will return, but after a couple of minutes, I resign myself to finding him later. Right now, I need to question Kenny.

Kenny, Noah, and Iris are sitting on a bench nearby. Looks like Noah has already cleaned the charm dust from Kenny's skates. Taylor's cleaning up residue from the rink.

"What happened?" I ask Kenny.

"I—I don't know," he stammers. "One minute I was vibing with Nikka, and the next, my skates had a mind of their own! They wouldn't let me get near her!" He runs a hand through his floppy brown hair. "I was trying to ask her to prom. Fat chance she'll go with me now."

"When did you notice something was wrong?" Noah asks.

"On the rink. Everything was fine on the drive over here. As soon as I'd worked up the nerve to ask Nikka to slow skate, I was yanked to the other side of the rink."

"Did you talk to anyone?"

"Just Nikka and Liam O'Connor, who's working the rental booth," Kenny replies. "Why?" he asks. "Do you think one of them charmed me?"

"Let's not jump to conclusions yet," I reply. The only one I've come to is that Kenny and Nikka are not a match.

Taylor, who's been talking to the DJ, likely about when it'll be safe to resume skating, glides over. Her shorts and striped knee-high socks give off a real disco vibe. She stares at Kenny without much remorse.

"Can you finish explaining how the charm works to him? I need to talk to Nikka."

Taylor looks like she wants to protest, but Iris rests her hand on her shoulder, and that does it. "Fine," she grits out.

Nikka's sitting on the bench across from us, chewing her bottom lip. "I didn't have anything to do with this," she says as soon as I approach. "I don't even know Kenny that well. He asked me to go roller-skating, and it sounded better than doing homework."

I sit next to her, already feeling my muscles starting to ache. "You don't like him at all?"

She shifts on the bench. "Not in the way he likes me. He's cool, but as a friend. I didn't see anything weird go down either."

"Okay," I reply. She seems sincere and I believe her. "If I have follow-up questions, I'll come find you."

Now that all the residue has been collected from the rink, the DJ announces, "Okay, folks. Thanks for your patience. Everything appears to be under control. You can resume skating."

As skaters return to the rink, Taylor beelines for me. "What'd you learn from Nikka?" she asks.

I fold my arms. "Oh. I'm sorry, are we working together now?"

Taylor purses her lips. "Maybe I was being a bit hasty."

I snort. "You think?" I pause, then sigh. "Nikka doesn't know anything, and Kenny only started experiencing symptoms after asking her to slow skate." It's not everything I've learned, but I'm not the one who made this investigation a competition. She can learn the rest from my official report.

"All right." Taylor tilts her head, studying me. "So you and Iris? What's that about?"

I step back, a little thrown by the question. By now, the music has resumed, and the rink is full of skaters. Iris is talking to Noah near the concession stand, completely out of earshot. "What do you mean?" I ask.

"Are you really even together?" The disbelief in Taylor's voice is evident.

My lips twitch. "Of course. Why?"

Taylor shrugs. "I don't know. You don't seem like a couple. I mean, you didn't even come to the rink together."

I frown. "She had prom committee."

"And she never mentioned you before that video."

I shrug and try not to let the slow, budding panic show on my usually expressive face. "Insta love."

Taylor doesn't seem convinced. "Do you even have anything in common with her?"

"We like going to the library." I cringe when the first place I think of leaves my mouth. *The library? C'mon, Roe.*

Taylor's eyebrows jump to her hairline. "Oh, really?"

"Mhm. Yep. Reading is fun. And we—uh—also like to watch movies. She's into rom-coms." That much I know is true. "Look, it's new. We're still feeling each other out. Why are you watching us so closely?"

"Because Iris is my best friend, and I don't want her getting hurt."

"She won't get hurt," I reply honestly.

Taylor stares. "Iris is clearly still charmed. If you were a perfect match, she wouldn't be. I haven't seen you stopping any accidents when you're together either, so I know it's not one-sided. Sounds platonic to me."

I struggle to come up with an explanation that makes sense because, truthfully, there aren't any mishaps because Iris and I aren't trying to romance each other. We're acting. Our intentions don't align with the charm. "The Bureau doesn't know everything about the charm. Being a Mystic could affect how the charm behaves," I reply. "So far, all the charmed students and their romantic interests are Mundanes."

Taylor narrows her eyes. Is she buying it? Iris doesn't want our friends to know the truth, but Taylor's perceptive. That's why we're in the same class of recruits.

"Maybe," she concedes to my relief. She peeks over her shoulder at Sean, who's on his phone. "See you around, Monroe."

Iris joins me a moment later. "What was that about? Bureau stuff?" she asks.

"Not exactly. Although, I'm pretty sure she has it out for me there as well," I reply.

Iris exhales audibly. "I don't think it's personal." She glances around to make sure we're alone. "Taylor has a bit of a chip on her shoulder from her siblings failing the Bureau assessment the last two years. Her parents put a lot of pressure on her to rise through the Bureau's ranks. They think it'll bring prestige to the family name. Taylor wants to prove herself, same as you."

"Explains why she sees me as a threat," I mutter.

Iris hums. "Before I forget, I got Kenny's phone number in case you need to follow up with him. I also followed him, Chloe, and Daisy on Instagram."

"Ooh, very helpful. I hope the mishap didn't ruin your night."

She shakes her head. "I had fun watching you wobble around." I glare at her, and she laughs. "Is there anything else we need to do?"

I raise my brow. "We?"

"I mean, I'm in this now. I know you can't share everything

with me since I'm not in the Bureau, but whatever you need help with, I'm your girl. I'll help you with your case, and you help me sell our romance to Anita, remember? Speaking of which, we should commemorate our date night."

Iris holds up her phone, and this time I'm more prepared for the photo op. With a smidge of hesitation, I tug her against me. She melds seamlessly into the crook of my arm. The pose doesn't feel as stiff as the first picture we took. Iris clicks the side of her phone to capture us. She stares at the results with a strange expression on her face.

"Well? Is it up to your standards?" I ask.

She clears her throat and shows me her phone. "It's freaking cute, actually. We look like a real couple. Good work, recruit."

I shake my head at her teasing and watch as Iris types out a caption. Good Sides Only ♥

"Love it."

Iris pockets her phone. "Let's get slushies. I promise not to spill it on you."

"Ha ha. I was so late to the debrief already that I thought your mom was going to kick me out of the Bureau."

Iris loops her arm through mine and tugs me over to the concession stand. "She wouldn't. She likes you," she replies.

"Really?"

Iris hands me a menu and leans over so we can read it together. The slushies come in two flavors: cherry and blue ice.

"Yep. She's glad we're hanging out. I told her we're friends." She watches me curiously. She almost sounds nervous when she adds, "Which is kind of true, right?"

I'd be lying if I said I wasn't wondering the same thing. "Yeah. I guess it is."

Her shoulders relax, and I, too, feel the sentiment. I'm relieved to know Iris likes me as a person. Her opinion of me doesn't affect our bargain. I shouldn't care that she likes me, and yet . . .

We both end up ordering blue ice. Iris reaches for her purse, and I still her hand with mine. "My treat. You got the movie." I use my phone to pay, ignoring Iris's weak protests.

The first sip of my drink coats my mouth in sugar. "How do people drink this stuff?"

"Like this." Iris slurps down her drink, grinning. "It's better than the aspartame you like to drink."

"It's pronounced Diet Coke. And I'm pretty sure that stuff is in Sprite too."

Iris shoves my shoulder. I chug as much of the slushie as I can stand before tossing the rest into the trash. Iris giggles. "What?"

"You've got a little slushie on your mouth." She grabs a napkin and holds it out to me.

I lean closer on instinct, and her deep brown eyes widen. I remember myself with a start and take the napkin from her, forcing a laugh.

"Did you have fun?" she asks.

"I wouldn't exactly count falling on my ass and cleaning up a mishap as fun." Iris tilts her head questioningly, and I tell her the truth. "Yes. I had a good time."

She laughs. "Thought so."

I'm not quite ready for this night to end, but one glance at the rental booth reminds me I have a job to do.

"Do you know Liam O'Connor?" I ask.

"We have a few classes together. Why?" She glances around and then lowers her voice. "You think he's involved?"

"I'm not sure. There was charm dust on the skate rental counter," I reply.

Iris furrows her brow adorably. "Could he be behind this?"

"That's the thing. None of the people who are charmed are connected. I don't think one person is giving the charm to everyone. More likely, someone is *supplying* the love charm to multiple people."

It feels like the pieces are finally slotting together. With this new theory, I'm that much closer to solving the case and being offered an official role at the BMA. "Even if Liam isn't involved, he might've seen someone messing with Kenny's skates."

Iris quickly scans the rink. "I don't see him." An alarm goes off on her phone. She silences it with a groan. "My curfew is in fifteen minutes. My mom does not play about it, especially since I was charmed. I can call an Uber or ask Sean to take me home if you want to wait for Liam."

"No. That will only make Taylor more suspicious of us. I'll take you home. I can find Liam at school tomorrow."

"He might not be there. His band's playing at Hexed Hollow tomorrow night, and Liam ditches to practice whenever he has a gig."

"And you know that how?" I ask.

"He mentions ditching a lot to sound cool. I know he'll be at Hexed Hollow because I'm on prom committee. Just so you know, Promraiser is another pre-prom event that will be packed with potential charm outbreaks."

"Then we'll have to make an appearance. Babe."

Iris sticks out her tongue at my use of the pet name. Cold air snaps at our faces as we leave the rink. Iris shuffles closer to me for warmth, and I can't say I mind.

"You truly like this stuff, huh?" Iris asks as I drive us toward her house. "Investigating?"

"Yep. Part of the reason I love working for the Bureau is that I get to help people. I watched my dad help a lot of neighbors over the years, and it always brought him joy. It does the same for me."

"When was the first time you removed a charm?" she asks.

"Fifth grade. I was sleeping over at Liz's house, and her comforter that was charmed to always stay dryer-warm caught fire. I grabbed the crystal Dad made me keep in my bag for emergencies, and I just . . . vacuumed the charm. It was exhilarating." I still remember how fast my heart was beating and how proud I was of myself.

Iris smirks. "I bet. You're pretty good at it."

I turn down her street and slow my speed, not wanting this conversation to end yet. "When—"

My phone rings, and a name pops up on my car screen.

Mom

My chest squeezes. I jab the red "END CALL" button. My fingers drum against the steering wheel, an anxious rhythm I feel in my bones.

Iris watches me. "Are you okay?"

I nod, not trusting my voice to stay steady.

"Well, that's a bold-faced lie."

I park the car outside her house, and Iris doesn't make a move to leave. She's giving me the space to talk. Not even Andie and Liz know why it's so hard for me to see my mom. Both of their parents are still together and happy. Mine are two jagged halves of a whole, the edges so frayed they don't fit together anymore. I've got no idea where that leaves me.

Iris rests her hand across the console, palm up like an offering. Her smile is kind. Encouraging. "You can talk to me, you know. We're friends now."

"I don't think you'd understand," I reply. She *likes* the idea of love.

"Try me."

I rub the tension from my eyes and then let my feelings spill out. "My parents are divorced. Last year, my mom blindsided me and my dad. She said she was done, like she wasn't in love with him anymore. I was so surprised by their separation that I don't trust love anymore. It can't be something you just stop feeling."

I chance a glance at Iris. She doesn't look at me with the pity I expected. "I think it can be," she says.

"Really? I thought you of all people, with your love of love, would agree with me."

She chuckles, but it lacks much humor. "Sometimes people's feelings change. If Anita's done with me, I'll leave her alone. But sometimes, I catch her looking at me and . . ." Iris shrugs. "It's hard to move on. Breakups shouldn't deter you from believing in love, though."

"How wise. I'll stick to being blissfully single, thank you very much."

Iris shakes her head. "You're missing out. You don't like the warm feeling in your chest when you think about your crush? Or the excitement of seeing their name pop up on your phone?"

"Honestly, that hasn't happened to me in years. I don't miss the stress of liking someone."

Iris groans. "Unbelievable."

She wiggles her fingers, reminding me that she's waiting, and finally, I slide my hand into hers. There's no one watching us in the quiet of the car. No pretense to uphold. She's lending me a sense of comfort, and somehow her hand in mine feels right.

"Did your parents have some epic love story to make you so smitten?" I ask.

"I don't know about epic, but they were happy. When my dad was alive, we watched rom-coms together. Dad loved them, and I think Mom loved seeing us bond over them. Now all she does is work. The house reminds her of him. Sometimes it feels like I'm living there by myself."

The hand I'm holding twitches while her other one picks at the frayed edge of her jeans. The realization strikes me that this is the most real she's been with me. Unguarded and unrefined. It's nice.

"If it helps, you can come to my house whenever you want," I say. She glances up. "I mean you have friends, obviously. And you probably have more fun with them, but the offer is there."

She nudges my shoulder with a crooked grin. "I'm growing on you."

"Like a fungus."

The porch lights flicker on and off. Iris groans. "I should go before she grabs the megaphone."

"She wouldn't."

Iris cringes. "She *has*."

The porch lights flash again, and I think of the Director's request to keep Iris safe. "She cares about you."

Iris squeezes my hand gently before climbing out of the car. Before she closes the car door, she says, "The same could be said of your mom if you gave her a chance to show you."

Iris's words linger in my head for the rest of the night, and before I go to bed, I decide to finally text Mom back.

Hi. I was busy when you called. Dinner when?

BUREAU OF MYSTICAL AFFAIRS
RECORD OF INCIDENT

DATE: Friday, March 6

RESPONDING OFFICER: Junior Recruit Monroe Bennett

CASE NUMBER: 26-292085

LOCATION: Spellcast Roller

SUMMARY: The mishap occurred during couples' night. Kenny Hill was asking Nikka Parker to slow skate when his skates threw him across the rink. Like with Chloe Nguyen and Dante Morelli, Nikka has no romantic feelings for Kenny. Kenny made the first move. Charm dust was found on the rink and at the skate rental booth worked by FGH student Liam O'Connor. Bureau recruits Taylor Evans and Noah Cham were also present.

ACTIONS TAKEN: We collected residue from the rink and interviewed Kenny and Nikka. Liam was missing in action.

RECOMMENDATION: Find Liam O'Connor ASAP and see if he knows anything about the love charm.

Twelve

Hexed Hollow is a music venue with a small stage, a bar, and a standing area. Local bands play here on the weekends, and residents can rent it out for private events. I've come for quinces and retirement parties, but never for a school event. Tonight's fundraiser helps cover the expenses of prom, including the venue, decorations, the band, and even discounted tickets for students who can't afford the hundred-dollar price tag.

Iris stands next to me in a sage cotton dress with bows on the shoulders. I opted for something more casual, dark gray cargo pants and a white cropped V-neck. Iris coils her arm around mine as we approach a student sitting on a stool at the door. He collects ten dollars from both of us and stamps our hands.

There are a ton of people inside already. Several students are taking pictures. A few teachers loiter near the back of the hall, probably chaperoning the event or using it as an excuse to get out of the house. A few stand off to the side talking to each other while others take up the tables along the far wall. QR codes leading to the donation site are posted on basically every surface.

The energy in here is infectious. Music thumps through the venue, a solid beat I feel in my jaw. On the stage are two girls shredding on guitars, and a boy I recognize from precalc belting into the mic. Behind a mop of sweaty brown hair is Liam O'Connor on drums. As Iris predicted, he wasn't at school today.

"Roe!"

I whip my head toward the sound of my name and spot Andie and Liz at a table to the left of the stage. I'm here to work the case, but I'm also here to support Liz and let her and Andie get to know Iris better.

"The lovebirds are here!" Andie announces over the song rattling the speakers. He wraps us both in a hug. He's wearing his signature frayed jeans and a bold red mesh top. Beside him, Liz is just as fashionable, decked out in purple slacks, a sparkly silver crop top, and platform Dr. Martens. After hugging us, Liz drops into her seat and taps her fingers against the grainy table so fast they're practically a blur.

Andie leans in. "She's been like this since we got here."

"Don't be nervous. You'll do great," I say. "Are your art supplies up there already?"

Liz points to the stage. "Behind the curtain."

Iris leans across me to be heard over the band. The warmth of her body heat and the light touch of her hand on my knee shrink the entire room. "How many sets before yours?" she asks Liz.

"Not enough," Liz replies. "Thanks for coming."

Iris's hand is still on my leg, making it hard for me to think about anything other than the gentle press between ticklish and something else.

I clear my throat, hoping that will also clear my head. "I—I'm going to get us some drinks," I stammer, and then jump to my feet. "Your usual, babe?" I ask Iris. She twists her lips at the pet name, but nods.

"Simp," Andie teases.

"A gentlewoman," Iris replies, and smiles. I hope my own smile doesn't look as strained as it feels.

I elbow my way through the crowd and head toward the bar. Liam is still onstage, but the song seems to be winding down. By the time I get the drinks, his set should be finished, and I can ask him about the Spellcast Roller mishap. I spot Taylor and Jude talking to Kenny by the bathrooms, and Reggie, the St. Mary's recruit, flagging down Sasha Gordon and Dana Reeve. Looks like I'm not the only one working tonight.

Since Promraiser is a high school event, there's no alcohol being sold, and the bartenders are other students. The drink options are limited to pop, juice, and water. While I wait in line, I search the crowd for anyone who might be charmed. There are too many people here to get a clear view of everyone, though.

"What can I get you?" Sofia Vargas, a senior in my computer science class who's working the bar, asks.

"A Sprite and a Diet Coke," I reply.

She hands me the pop, and I pay with a twenty. As she fumbles through her server booklet for change, I spot something besides cash in the black organizer. A playing card: an ace of hearts with hand-painted flowers. It's the same card from Spellcast Roller.

What's that doing here?

My pulse speeds up. One time is a coincidence. Two times is a pattern. Three times is basically divine intervention.

"Hey—" I start, but Sofia hands me my change and promptly turns to the next customer. I watch as she takes a few more orders, trying to figure out how to get a better look at the playing card without her noticing. I don't want to go flashing my badge and demanding she give me the card when I don't even know if it's connected. If it is, then I'm tipping off everyone involved.

She puts the booklet on the counter by the register while she rings up Principal Walters and his wife.

I tuck the pop cans under my arms and walk around the edge of the bar, pretending to look at the list of drinks tacked to the wall. I inch forward and reach out my hand. If I can just get the booklet . . .

Someone touches my arm.

I flinch hard.

"What are you doing?" Iris asks. She's close enough that her breath tickles my ear.

I snatch the booklet as Sofia looks up and I force a smile. "I forgot to leave a tip," I explain.

I slide in a dollar and slip the playing card into my palm. I inch it up my sleeve, hopefully without Sofia noticing.

Sofia smiles. "Oh. Thanks."

I tug Iris away before I'm found out and steer us toward our table. We make it only a few steps before we're cornered, but not by Sofia.

"Iris?"

Anita Patel stands in front of us with her arms folded over her chest, one leg jutting out and her eyebrows raised.

Iris tenses next to me. "Hi, Anita."

Anita looks between the two of us, her face as still as stone. "Are you two really dating?"

All thoughts of the charm and the playing cards are shoved to the back burner with that one question. This moment was bound to happen sooner or later, though obviously I was hoping for later. Anita and I have never talked outside of class before, mainly because I stick with the two people at school I know like me.

Anita focuses her attention on Iris, who's unblinking at my side. "Well, are you? Just last week you were trying to get back together with me."

"We're dating," Iris replies, leaning closer to me to better sell our relationship.

Sensing Anita's skepticism, I add, "It's new. We're having fun."

Anita shakes her head like she wasn't expecting that reply or doesn't believe its truthfulness. "Seriously?"

"Yes," Iris says. "But thanks for your concern."

Iris flees to the safety of our table. I try to follow her when Anita blocks my path. "It's none of my business anymore, and I probably shouldn't say anything, but are you sure dating Iris is a good idea? No one likes to be a rebound. Plus, she can be a bit . . ." Anita gestures randomly with her hands.

I square my shoulders. "A bit what?"

"Fake."

I bristle at her words. Iris isn't fake. She's funny and generous. Then again, we *are* fake dating, so I've got no way of knowing whether she's being sincere when she teaches me how to roller-skate, helps me with mishaps, or tells me both sides of my face are good. All I can go on is the feeling I get when we're together.

"Well, she's not," I reply with a heat to my words that surprises me. "Not with me."

The tightness in my chest ebbs at the soft press of a hand in mine. Iris came back. Rubbing my thumb across her knuckles to ease the tension is reflexive. The gentle back and forth seems to loosen her up, if only slightly.

Our relationship may not be real, but when I slip my arm around Iris's waist and pull her to me, the stuttered breath she releases and the flash of surprise mixed with delight seem genuine.

Iris is close enough that I can count her dark lashes and study the tiny imperfections on her face that make her unique. I turn my head to whisper in her ear.

"Is this okay?" I parrot her words from the first day we started fake dating, when she kissed my cheek outside of class. Iris melts into my side and nods.

Anita clears her throat. She's watching us with a comically deep frown and a furrowed brow. Her gaze bounces from our faces to my arm around her waist.

"What were you saying?" I ask her.

"Nothing. I was . . . leaving." Anita spins on her heel and flees.

Iris deflates even farther against me but doesn't move away. I feel almost dizzy being this close to her.

"Did I say the right thing? Should I have kept it more cryptic to leave an opening for the two of you?" I ask. The plan was always for Iris to get back together with Anita, so why does my stomach drop at my own suggestion?

"You did good." Iris nods her head once, and then twice more as if she's trying to convince herself. "We'll say we're keeping things casual."

"Casual. Sure." I clear my throat. "It's a good thing Anita cornered me, right? She seems invested in us."

"Totally," Iris replies, but her responding grin has cracks in it, little fractures in the facade that lessen its strength.

Maybe she could use a change in subject. I show Iris the card I took from Sofia's organizer. "I saw this same card in Liam's tip jar yesterday. I don't think it's a coincidence."

"A clue?"

"Hopefully," I reply.

Using Andie's blue hair as a guide, we navigate back to our table. Liz has replaced Liam's band on the stage. She's wearing a smock covered in paint. An easel is tucked under one arm and a box, likely full of paint supplies, is under the other. She grabs the mic.

"For my piece, I'll be painting the audience. Everyone, try to stay in your seats for this, but please continue to talk." Liz gives us a forced smile. "The final artwork will be auctioned off at the end of the show, and proceeds will go to having the most kick-ass prom." She waves her hand in a flourish, and music clicks to life. The song has a vibrant beat that warbles through the speakers.

While Liz paints, a dancer emerges, slinking through the velvet black curtain on the stage and twirling around on beat to the song. The audience watches with rapt attention. And, at some point during all of this, Iris tucks herself against my side.

I must imagine the soft look she gives me. It's the music and the dim lighting making me delusional. Anita is probably watching us and plotting a way to get back with Iris right now. And Iris is very much caught up in Anita. Why wouldn't she be? Anita's the trifecta: smart, pretty, and popular. I'm smart and pretty, if you squint, but popularity has never been something I've cared about. And whether she admits it or not, Iris *is* popular. And a serious romantic—a trait we'll never share. So it shouldn't matter if Iris is looking at me like I'm her new favorite rom-com. It doesn't.

When the song ends, the dancer bows. Liz spins her painting around. Collectively, the audience leans in.

From this vantage point, the painting looks fairly realistic. But I know from Liz's other work that, up close, I'll see only careful brush marks to give the impression of an object. She's painted the interior of Hexed Hollow, its bright lights in the background and dark masses of people in the foreground. She's captured little details like the drinks on the tables as careful gray dashes and the streamers strung along the ceiling as pink swirls, and formed the tables lined up in the back of the room as slashes of brown.

It's so different from the floral pattern on the playing card in my pocket, even though similar colors are used.

The crowd erupts in cheers, none louder than those from my table. Liz grins for real this time and then bows.

I glance over at Iris, who's smiling as much as me, like Liz is her friend, too, and she's proud. And if Iris considers my friends as her own, then where does that leave us once this charade ends?

Liz joins us a moment later, grinning widely. All her nervous energy from before the performance is gone.

"You were incredible," I tell her.

Andie and Iris nod, and we all gush over the artwork. Liz bows again, just for us, and then points between me and Iris. "I saw you two cuddled up in the audience."

"They're cute," Andie says.

Iris rests her head on my shoulder, playing into the compliment. "We are, huh?" she says.

Liz rolls her eyes, and Andie grins. We watch more performances, and I try to remember when hanging out with Iris became second nature. The more time we spend together, the more tangled the knot in my stomach gets because I'm keeping a secret from her—the deal I made with her mom lingering. Just thinking of the Director breaks the comfortable spell I'm under.

I shift away from Iris and stand. "I need to talk to Liam before he vanishes again."

"I'll come with you," Iris suggests, getting up.

"I won't be long. Enjoy the show."

Iris shakes her head. "Someone's got to stop you from getting caught snooping."

We move through the crowd, checking every table and booth for Liam. He's not in line at the bar, or backstage mingling. He's not by the bathrooms or the photo booth or outside on the patio.

"He's gone." I kick a rock, and it skitters across the patio floor. I spent too long hanging out and not enough time doing my job.

"I'll monitor his Instagram. Maybe he'll post a story about his weekend plans. Otherwise, I'm sure he'll be in class on Monday," Iris says.

"I guess this gives me time to figure out what the playing card means. Maybe I can use it to lure out the next user," I reply.

"I can help if you want to come over. My mom works most Sundays, so she'll be gone. And I still need to get you to watch the movies I sent you because I know you didn't."

I smile sheepishly. "I've been busy, but I could probably use the pointers. You're better at fake dating than me. I feel like I need to catch up," I reply with a slight chuckle. "But come to mine? I'm on call for the Bureau this weekend. The zone I'm assigned to is around my house." If there are any mishaps, I'll be there to handle it.

Iris brightens. Her brown eyes seem to gleam in the glow of the patio light. "Perfect. But, for the record, you're pretty good at this."

Thirteen

I need to do a better job of keeping my room clean. I throw all my dirty clothes into my closet, shove the not-too-dirty ones back into the dresser, make my bed, and stuff my ever-growing collection of hair products into their bin. Then I spray a cleaning solution over every surface I can. The everlasting liquid in the bottle is charmed to absorb dust and debris instantaneously and leaves behind a lemony scent. I'm contemplating my life choices when the doorbell rings.

I glance down at my outfit—a faded Bureau T-shirt and joggers. No time to change now. I race downstairs and make it to the door in time to hear the bell announce in its monotone voice, "State your name."

"Iris James: baddie and extraordinary girlfriend to Monroe Bennett!" Iris yells jokingly from the porch.

My face warms. "Don't record that!" I yell at the doorbell.

I open the door, and Iris greets me with a grin. Dad meets us in the hallway, holding a pitcher of freshly made lemonade. This morning, when I told him Iris was coming over, he smirked. Even though our parents have known each other our entire lives, Iris has never come over to hang out. Dad didn't say anything, but his curiosity is very likely piqued.

"Hi, Iris. It's good to see you," Dad says.

"Hi, Mr. Bennett."

"Roe actually cleaned up. You'd think the mayor was coming over."

"Dad!"

He chuckles. "What's on the agenda this Sunday?"

"Watching movies," Iris replies sweetly.

"Well, I made lemonade, and I think we have some popcorn in the cabinet. Want me to set up the projector in the living room before I leave?"

"Popcorn, yes. Projector, no. I figure we can hang out in my room," I reply.

Dad nods slowly, a knowing look flashing across his face. "I don't need to tell you to keep the door open, do I?"

My skin grows hot. "W-what? Dad, we're *friends*. You won't even be here!" I'm convinced parents do this kind of stuff on purpose. There's probably a group chat for them to relay the most creative ways to embarrass their kids.

"I'm teasing, Roe. I'll be gone for a few hours. Be good," Dad says, slipping on his shoes.

"See ya!"

I grab Iris's hand and tug her toward the stairs before Dad can embarrass me more. Iris is quietly laughing the entire way. I wait awkwardly near my bed while she surveys my now pristine room.

"Is this actually your room or the guest room?" she teases.

"Ha ha." To be fair, *I* haven't even seen it this clean in a while.

Iris walks over to the whiteboard hanging on the back of my closet door, the only thing I forgot to put away. "Operation: Ace of Hearts?"

"It's a working title. On the board is everything I know so far, plus this." I take out the playing card and hand it to Iris.

She purses her lips in thought. “What do the numbers mean?”

“No clue. Want to brainstorm some ideas?”

“Okay.” Iris picks up the red dry-erase marker and draws hearts in the corners of my whiteboard and then writes “10308”. “Could it be a student number?”

I grab my student ID from my wallet and show her the number printed in the corner beneath my name. “Andie, Liz, and I swap cards to pay for food in the caf. All ID numbers start with twelve.”

“Maybe it’s a birth date?”

“Do you know anyone born on January third or October third?” I ask.

“If it’s written the European way, my dad was born on March tenth but not in 2008.” Iris plops onto my bed and opens her laptop. “I’m googling the dates to see if anything useful comes up.” Her fingers fly across the keys. “Not much, only a few random events that have nothing to do with Fair Glen High, the Bureau, or magic.”

“Okay, so maybe it’s not a date. It could be a code or a phone number like those verification messages for when you forget your password. Those are five digits.”

I grab my phone and try texting the number.

Iris chuckles. “Real smooth, Roe.”

I purse my lips, but maybe Iris has a point. No response comes. Not even a bounce-back message. *Ugh.*

“If we had access to school files, we could find out if it’s a student’s birth date,” Iris suggests.

“Good call. I’ll ask the front office on Monday.”

"Mrs. Davis will want something in return, Bureau business or not. Lucky for you, I know how to get on her good side," Iris says, and smirks.

"Then it's a date."

Iris's eyes seem to sparkle with amusement. "Do you ever take a break?"

I join her on my bed, leaving enough space between us to fit an entire person. "I am right now. So . . . did you and Anita have movie nights?"

Iris shakes her head. "She's not a huge fan of romance either. She's more into docuseries. Don't get me wrong, she never made fun of me for loving romance, but she didn't have rom-com marathons with me. We only watched them together at Electric Dust." Iris stretches out on my bed, her long legs dangling over the edge. "What do you like to watch?"

"Mostly spy movies and action comedies."

"Of course you do." Iris giggles as she clicks through her laptop. "I have a bunch of movies downloaded, but I'm afraid to say they're all rom-coms."

"I expected nothing less. Let's finish *Pretty Woman*."

"Excellent choice."

As we watch the movie, picking up from where we left off at Electric Dust, Iris leans farther into my pillow. She seems at ease, like she's done this a hundred times before. She's slotted so comfortably into my life it's hard to believe that only a week ago we were practically strangers.

The movie ends almost before I realize it. Now I understand her fire-escape-and-roses reference. Iris cues up the next movie, *Drive Me Crazy*, and I search for a summary on my phone and grin.

"Another fake dating rom-com? Trying to tell me something?" I ask.

"It's called staying on theme. You said you wanted pointers. Speaking of, our last picture together is doing numbers." Iris shows me her Instagram. This time, I'm surprised to recognize a few of the names commenting on the picture of us, like Daisy and Kenny.

"Can you go to Daisy's profile?" I ask. "I still need to follow up with her."

Iris clicks on Daisy's username: daisyguzman. I sit straighter when I see her profile picture. Daisy has her arm slung around Chloe and Sofia Vargas.

"They're all friends?" A light bulb clicks on in my brain. "Is there a way to see if they're also friends with Liam O'Connor?"

"You're asking the right person," Iris says, perking up as well. "Give me a second. In the meantime, maybe you should make your own account. I don't mind sleuthing, but it'd be easier for you to check on suspects yourself."

She's got a point. I'm a grandma when it comes to social media. The unlimited posts and reels are overwhelming. And yet, as Iris's thumbs fly across the phone, I download Instagram and create an account. I need one for the case, but I can't lie. I'm also interested in following Iris and learning more about her.

"I don't think they're friends. They don't follow each other. They haven't even liked each other's posts."

"Hm. Worth a shot. You're pretty fast at snooping. Are you sure you don't have Bureau training?" I ask.

Iris shrugs. "I'm used to vetting a first date."

"You didn't vet me."

"I already know you're too straitlaced to be a serial killer." She squints her eyes at me. "But for good measure, maybe I should go through your phone." She lunges for my phone, which is sitting on the bed. My knee-jerk reaction is to snatch it out of reach.

I don't want her to see the phone call from her mom, which I could lie about, but I'm not convinced I'm the best liar. What if Iris can tell I'm keeping something from her?

Iris is taller than me and has longer arms. She throws her body on top of mine and stretches, her fingers brushing against the bottom of my phone just as mine find the space between her ribs. I tickle her and she squeals.

"What are you hiding, Roe?" Her question is swallowed by shrieks of laughter.

She leans back to get away from me but must forget her arms are still linked with mine. We both go toppling onto the mattress. I jut my hand out to stop myself from falling onto the floor and end up hovering over Iris.

Her giggles die out. She gazes up at me, her eyes round dark pools I might fall into if I'm not careful, and yet I can't look away. I count the freckles on her nose and trace the curve of her cheeks to the arch of her parted lips. She's staring too. Each shifting glance carves a feathery trail across my face. My stomach drops when her attention moves to my lips.

A shrill ring throws me back into my body, and I flip myself off her and bury my face in my pillow, desperate for a second to assess what the hell happened between us.

My phone doesn't care that I'm processing. It continues to blare like a sensitive car alarm on the Fourth of July.

The bed shifts. "Are you going to get that?" Iris asks.

I roll over and silence the Bureau alert. Looks like there are spools of thread knotting themselves around customers at Needle and Thread instead of stitching garments.

Drive Me Crazy is still playing on Iris's laptop. The main characters, Chase and Nicole, just had a moment after they kissed to make Chase's ex-girlfriend jealous. How ironic that it feels like Iris and I had a moment too. But as I look around the room, none of my stuff is coming to life to drag Iris away from me as we play pretend. You'd think that me putting my arm around Iris at the Promraiser would have trigged some magical reaction since it was a one-sided flirtation. I don't know what to make of it.

"Do you need help?" Iris asks.

"No. I got this." A little breathing room would do me good.

Iris shoots me a small, unreadable smile and waits for me to walk her out. As she leaves, I can't help but think it's probably for the best I got a Bureau alert when I did. I need to stay focused. I can't let Iris tempt me into having real feelings for her.

Fourteen

After spending the rest of Sunday night pulling thread out of my hair and trying to catch up on homework, getting back to Operation Ace of Hearts on Monday morning feels refreshing. I text Iris while I wait for her outside the administrative hallway.

Here!

Iris: k im getting the goods now! and i totally forgot about the prom-committee meeting i have during lunch today. they act like we're organizing a presidential campaign! we might have to recap after lunch

No worries.

Also . . . sry about cutting our hang short last night. We good?

Type bubbles pop up on the screen and then disappear. My heart squeezes. I hadn't planned on running away from what happened on my bed, even though it's for the best that I did. Still, I don't want Iris to be angry with me.

Iris rounds the corner a moment later, breathing heavily. In one hand, she carries a bag of Skittles and in the other, a can of Coke. A toothy grin breaks across her face when she spots me.

All I can see is the image of her gazing up at me from the bed, the flecks of gold beneath her skin as luminous and breathtaking as shooting stars. I shove the memory into the furthest recess of my mind. "Hi."

"Hi." She bumps my arm with hers, looks me in the eyes, and says, "We're good, Roe."

Something loosens in my chest. "Great. Ready?"

She nods and we step into the front office. The choking scent of cucumber-melon lotion greets us before the school admin does. Mrs. Davis is a curvy, middle-aged woman with a love for Bath & Body Works and, apparently, a sweet tooth. She peers at us over the rim of her sleek thin-wired glasses.

"Hi, Mrs. Davis," I say.

"Ms. Bennett. You're rarely in this office. And you've brought Ms. James with you. Don't tell me there's been another accident on school grounds. If one more parent chews me out about how unsafe FGH has gotten, I'll quit," she announces with a straight face.

"No mishaps today . . . yet."

"Then what do you need? If you've come here asking about receiving credit for prom committee again, Ms. James, you know I can't do that."

"Not this time, Mrs. Davis," Iris replies. "We're wondering if you could look up a birth date in the student records for us?"

Mrs. Davis narrows her eyes. "Do you have a formal request

from the Bureau for this? The school considers all information in student records private."

I slide the Skittles and the can of Coke across her desk. Mrs. Davis looks around and grabs the snacks. Without a word, she starts typing on her computer. I look at Iris and then the door, silently asking if we should leave. Iris holds up her hand and shakes her head. Leave it to Iris to ask about extra credit enough to learn what floats Mrs. Davis's boat.

"What's the birth date?" Mrs. Davis asks.

"October third, 2008," I reply.

Her keyboard clatters. "Nothing."

"Try January third, 2008, and March tenth, 2008," I say.

Mrs. Davis looks up. "Now, what is this actually about, girls?"

"It could help us solve the love charm case," I tell her. "You don't want parents to keep complaining, right?"

Mrs. Davis huffs and then returns to typing on her computer. "Stacey Roberts was born on March tenth, 2008, but it looks like she's been absent since January. Mono. Anything else? Great." Mrs. Davis digs into her snacks, effectively dismissing us.

"Dead end," Iris says as we head to class.

Prom court signs have doubled overnight. Banners are hung on the walls. Colorful flyers are tacked to the bulletin boards that are charmed to grab the attention of passersby by yelling things like, "Check me out!" or "Over here!" Those are pricey charms, but for some students, a shot at prom court is worth shelling out fifty bucks. For those who haven't used their allowances or money earned from part-time jobs, there are good old-fashioned poster boards and markers.

"I'll keep mulling it over," I say as we stop outside Iris's homeroom.

Today, Anita doesn't even hide her staring when Iris slips her hand in mine and pulls me into a hug.

She's warm and soft and smells alluringly sweet. My head is fuzzy when she moves away. "See you later."

I wander away from the classroom, still lightheaded from Iris's closeness. My phone vibrates, and I smile at the texts she sends.

Iris: looking forward to our next movie date

my house next time?

"Damn, Monroe. Iris is already coming over? I thought U-Hauling was just a stereotype." Andie loops his arm through mine while he peeks at my phone with a cheeky grin. Liz trails behind him, smirking.

Thankfully, there are no references to our fake relationship in the thread, only a couple of memes and a funny video from Iris.

I pocket my phone with a scowl. "Don't read my texts."

Liz laughs. "You're so far gone, dude."

I nearly stumble over a pile of books. "I—I'm not. I—"

"You're useless. It's adorable." Andie stops to scan the QR code on a poster of a student running for prom sovereign—a title recently added for nonbinary and gender nonconforming students. "We're happy someone caught your attention. Now Neo and I can double-date. Or triple-date if Liz finally convinces Jess to visit."

Liz ducks as a boy throws a football to another person at the end of the hall. "Summer break, people. Mark your calendars."

Liz has been talking to another a-spec high schooler from Indiana named Jess. They met in an online coding class. Andie and I have been dying to meet them, but by summer break, my relationship—*fake* relationship—with Iris will be long over. For some reason, my stomach knots at the thought.

By the time lunch rolls around, I'm itching to work on Operation Ace of Hearts, if only to get my mind off Iris. I still haven't talked to Liam or Sofia. It will be awkward as hell confronting either of them at lunch, but it's necessary if I'm going to learn any new information.

"I'll be back in a bit," I tell Liz and Andie.

"Missing your girlfriend already?" Andie calls after me. His amusement knows no end.

I flip him off genially and walk around the cafeteria. I spot Sofia first, sitting at a table near the hot bar, but draw up short when I notice Chloe and Daisy. Chloe's drawing hearts on a stack of postcard-size flyers that say, "Vote Chloe for Prom Queen." Daisy has her arm around the back of Chloe's chair, and there's a subtle way Chloe seems to lean into the touch. That's not what stopped me in my tracks. It's the total lack of gold charm dust beneath Chloe's skin. She found a match! Chloe's no longer charmed.

"When did y'all get together?" I ask.

Chloe stares at Daisy, who reaches for her hand. Daisy's attentiveness at the movies and Chloe's hesitance to explain why she didn't flirt back with Dante now make sense.

"Recently. It . . . sort of just happened," Chloe replies, a blush working its way up her cheeks.

Daisy is uncharacteristically quiet. Is she involved somehow? "How serendipitous you're also no longer charmed," I reply. I rest my hands on the back of an open chair, my thoughts whirling. "Has there been another mishap since the drive-in?"

"None," Chloe confirms.

Sofia, who's sitting directly behind Chloe at the neighboring table, faces me. Her dark hair falls in waves around her face, obscuring the full strength of her stare, but I feel it all the same. "So it's possible for the charm to go away?" she asks. "Possible not to have any mishaps?"

I shift my attention to her, ignoring her questions in favor of asking my own. "Why do you want to know?"

I don't want to show my hand too soon, so I keep my knowledge about the playing card I plucked from her server book hidden. For now.

She drops her gaze to the table and drums her fingers against the wood. "No reason."

"Bullshit."

Sofia's eyes snap to mine. "It's not."

I hold her gaze. "Everyone's heard something. People are getting hurt."

She shrugs. "I'm not involved, if that's what you're trying to imply."

It's a weird response, considering I didn't ask if she was. Daisy shifts in her seat and rubs her hands together.

"What about you?" I ask Daisy. "What have you heard?"

"Nothing, same as Sofia," she says.

She's not exactly getting my vote of confidence. In fact, it's clear they both know more than they're letting on.

"Did you charm Chloe?" I ask Daisy outright.

Her face reddens, and she stammers, "N-no."

Chloe's eyebrows dip together. "Seriously, Daisy? Tell me you didn't."

Sofia chooses that exact moment to leap to her feet, knocking her chair into Daisy's. Daisy's bag falls to the floor and the contents spill out.

Sofia drops to the ground. "Sorry. Here," she says, eagerly reaching for Daisy's belongings.

I walk around the table, hoping to get lucky and see a playing card or even a container of gold charm dust on the floor, but that's asking for too much. Daisy finishes scooping her things back into her bag just as I reach them. And then the end of lunch bell rings.

Sofia's on her feet and packing up her food in a blink. She rushes from the table like she's late for a job interview, rather than early for fifth period.

"Daisy—" I start.

She steps closer to me. Her voice is as sharp as a blade. "You have no proof I did anything to Chloe. I *like* her. I always have. And the fact that the dust is gone means she feels the same. So don't ruin this for us."

Daisy walks away, disappearing into the throng of students filing out of the cafeteria.

As I head back to my lunch table, I mull over our conversation. Daisy knows something. I could dig dirt up on her to get her to talk, but how long will that take? The Bureau needs proof. Liam might be more forthcoming about where the charm came from, but I might run into the same issue I have with Daisy. No proof, no punishment.

Iris is waiting for me outside the cafeteria, her hand extended. Andie coos, and Liz smirks. I ignore them. My heart starts racing as soon as I take Iris's hand. *Get it together, Roe.*

"How was lunch?" Iris asks as we head toward her next class.

"Chloe's not charmed anymore," I blurt out.

Iris stops. "Oh my God. How?"

"Chloe's with Daisy. They're *together.* I saw them holding hands, laughing, and everything. No mishaps or a single speck of dust in sight. Chloe said they clicked after the movie night."

Iris starts walking again, her steps energized and her hand tugging me along. "So as soon as Anita starts liking me back, the charm will be broken. Anita already seems jealous. That must mean she still has feelings for me."

Hot flames burn inside me at her words—a feeling too close to envy for my liking. I shove away the pesky emotion. Iris is love-obsessed, and I'm too jaded about love for us ever to be a match. Iris wants someone who's perfect for her. Someone who'll float on a door with her in the ocean, climb fire escapes with roses in their mouth, and do all the rom-com stuff she deserves. I don't know the first thing about romance.

Iris tilts her head. "You good? What's with you right now?"

"Whoops." My thoughts are so scattered I've unintentionally walked us past her classroom. Warmth sears my face as I shuffle us in reverse. "Sorry. Thinking about the investigation."

Iris studies me with narrowed eyes, like she's trying to catch me in a lie.

"Students, take your seats!" the teacher calls from inside the classroom.

"That's my cue." Iris lowers her chin and kisses my cheek.

I'm pretty sure I'm holding my breath, and my back is stiffer than my hair after an at-home press and curl. When I look at Iris and the curious curve of her mouth, a sensation creeps up on me. It's the same one I get when I hold charm dust in the palm of my hands—a desire for more.

Iris waves goodbye, and I spin on my heel and bolt toward my homeroom as my heart thumps wildly. Liking Iris is the last thing I need right now. The second we hold hands or cuddle up to make Anita jealous, a mishap is going to rip us apart. Unless I'm right about the charm impacting only Mundanes. Or Iris is also catching feelings for me. Ridiculous thought. I saw her two minutes ago, and she's still charmed. Dust lingers on her skin. If she liked me back, it'd be gone. Besides, Iris is obviously still focused on winning back

Anita. I can't like her or want anything real with her, which is for the best. Relationships don't last. The people in them always hurt each other, and ultimately, everything ends in disaster. Best to stay far away from the romance trap.

So I shove my feelings about Iris *deep*, deep down and will them to vanish. I'm a recruit, meaning it's my job to stay indifferent. Iris may have managed to wedge herself under my skin like charm dust, but my crush ends now. Prom is not even a month away, which means I have less than three weeks left of fake dating Iris. I just need to figure out who's dealing the illegal dust before then so I can impress Director James and keep Iris from any more mishaps. Easy.

Fifteen

The library is quiet when I enter to volunteer during my open period. I take the final bite of my turkey sandwich, toss the wrapper, and stride over to Mx. Michaelson's desk.

"I'm giving a tour of the school to a few prospective parents this afternoon. Can you hold down the fort for an hour?" Mx. Michaelson asks as they vacate their seat.

"Sure thing," I reply. I point to a stack of books on the desk. "Do these need to be shelved?"

"Yes. They have new call numbers. See you in a bit," Mx. Michaelson calls over their shoulder.

The sparkly purple book on top of the pile reminds me of Iris's eyeshadow. When I crack it open, the book begins reading the words on the page aloud with a posh British accent. The customizable charm is commonly used and is especially helpful for people with disabilities.

I trace the spine, wondering whether the numbers on the playing card could be a call number rather than a birth date or student number. The format doesn't match, but maybe that's the point. The charm could be hiding in a hollowed book among the shelves.

I head upstairs, processing what I know. So far, everyone experiencing mishaps seems to be dusted shortly before the accidents occur and always in a public setting around students from FGH. None of the victims seem to know each other, bringing me to my second theory—either one person is charming everyone, or multiple people have access to the dust. The playing cards could be some kind of currency, a signal, or a referral system for students.

As I scan call numbers, hushed voices coming from the charmed literature section draw my attention. And then someone screams.

I bolt down the aisle, my breath coming in short bursts. Books fly off the shelves, pages flapping wildly and yapping in voices from Tom Holland's to Daffy Duck's. I dodge left as a book narrowly misses my head.

I skid to a halt when I spot two people lying in a crumpled heap at the base of a bookshelf. Books and papers cover their tangled frames. There's a hand covered in gold charm dust peeking out from under the pile. I drop to my knees and hurriedly toss aside books.

I uncover a boy I've seen around but never talked to named Hollis Williams. He's sporting a dark welt on his forehead, and his skin shimmers gold. Sitting next to him is Sofia Vargas. A red mark blooms on her arm, but otherwise she seems unharmed. In her hand is a vial of rippling gold dust.

"Whoa. Is that the charm?" I ask.

Sofia glances at the vial in her hand. Her head then swivels toward the stairs. Her brows are furrowed and calculating when she jumps to her feet.

"Don't even think about running," I tell her.

She grabs her bag and bolts, taking the stairs two at a time. Groaning, I sprint after her. I jump onto the railing and slide down to catch her, but she's surprisingly fast. She's already halfway across the library by the time I stick the landing.

"I only want to talk!" I yell.

I don't want to lose track of her in the school. She's the first person I've seen with the charm. If she disposes of it improperly, more students could get hurt.

My mind shuffles through the list of charmed gadgets I own. The only thing that might help in this situation is my self-securing hair tie. I tug my hair loose from the elastic band and chuck it at the door handle like a lasso. The band is charmed to wrap around anything it touches. My aim is solid enough, and the hair tie knots around the handles of the library's double doors.

Sofia tugs on one handle and tries to remove the band, but I catch up to her before she can.

"Don't. Just talk to me. Why did you charm Hollis?" I ask, slightly out of breath.

Sofia faces me. We stare at each other for a beat, and then Sofia releases a defeated sigh. "I was trying to ask him to prom. I didn't think the charm would hurt him. I was told it would make him like me."

"Who told you that?" I ask. "Daisy?"

Sofia drags her foot across the carpet and tightens her lips.

"Listen, no one wants to be a snitch, but stalling won't help you. I'll find out either way, and then you and whoever told you about the charm will be in serious trouble. If I tell Principal Walters and the Bureau Director that you cooperated, it might help your situation."

The authority figure vibe I'm giving off is very much not me. I'd rather she answer me honestly or, I don't know, *not* charm her crush? But this is the only way to get ahead on my first Bureau assignment.

Sofia grimaces. "*Fine.* I got an Instagram message from a burner account, okay?"

"Elaborate, please."

"I don't know who contacted me, but I added a heart on my prom registration form like they said to."

"Like *who* said to?"

Sofia rubs the back of her neck. "Daisy. I overheard her talking to people in homeroom about how she bought a charm to get her crush to be her prom date. The buyer adds a red heart emoji in the additional information box when registering for prom. I wanted to take Hollis, so I tried it, and a burner account DM'd me on Instagram and told me there would be a playing card in my server book at Promraiser . . . only it wasn't there."

So I was right; Daisy's involved. That's why she had a playing card in her bag at Electric Dust.

"What's the card for?" I ask, not sharing that I am the card thief.

"I'm not sure. I didn't get that far in the process. I tried asking for another card, but no one messaged me back. When I overheard you talking to Daisy and Chloe at lunch today, I figured here was my chance to still use the charm. I took what I hoped was the charm from her bag."

"You knocked over her bag on purpose," I say. Sofia drops her gaze, all but confirming she did. "The person selling the charm lied to you, or they don't know what it actually does. It was never going to make Hollis like you. Its purpose is to prevent mismatched love."

She gasps. "I didn't know that. Swear on my life. I thought there wouldn't be any issues, like with Chloe and Daisy." Sofia runs a hand down her face. "I've been waiting for Hollis to notice me for just as long."

"I thought we were friends," Hollis says, appearing at the top of the stairs.

"We *are*. But . . . I also really like you, and I didn't want you to ask anyone to prom before I could muster up the courage to tell you how I felt," Sofia replies.

Hollis squints. "You get how messed up that sounds, right?"

"I'm truly sorry," Sofia says. "I didn't think you'd get hurt."

Hollis cradles his head. "Well, I did."

"I'll call the nurse in a sec," I tell Hollis. "Sofia, show me the Instagram messages."

She grabs her phone and pulls up a thread of messages from an account called @Charmedlife33. How original. There are no pictures or posts when Sofia navigates to the person's profile.

"I've tried contacting them several times, but it's been days since I was supposed to get the card. They never responded."

"Maybe they suspect you've been compromised, so to speak," I suggest.

The same playing card in Liam's tip jar at Spellcast Roller was given to Sofia. Now that I have that card, whoever is selling the charms will need to put a new card in rotation. With any luck, I can intercept them. As for how students are getting the card, I'll need to check the prom registration files. Good thing my fake girlfriend is on prom committee.

Hollis moans again, so I quickly call for the nurse.

"I'm cooked, right?" Sofia asks once I'm off the phone.

"Probably."

Admittedly, I feel a bit sorry for her. It's against local regulations to distribute unauthorized charms, and against FGH rules for students to use such dust on others on school grounds. She could be suspended, and all for love? Doesn't seem worth it.

"I didn't want him to get hurt," Sofia whispers.

"I know. But when love is involved, someone always does."

Sixteen

Incoming Call: Director James

The devil works hard, but Bureau agents work harder. It's been only twenty minutes since the mishap, and already the Director has gotten wind of the accident.

I answer the phone immediately. "Hi, Director."

"Monroe. I received word about another mishap at your school. Is it true you caught someone using the charm?"

"It's true."

"Good work. A senior agent will be there to gather more information shortly. I expect a write-up. In the meantime, tell me what you've learned so far."

Before the Director called, I was making two piles of books to separate, those with gold dust on them and those without. I add a book to the pile to be cleansed. "Over the last week, four Fair Glen High students were charmed, including Iris."

"Who are the others?" the Director asks. "I've checked in with Taylor about the mishap at Spellcast Roller and read your report, but I'd like to hear it from you to confirm."

"Chloe Nguyen, Kenny Hill, and just now, Hollis Williams. I can send you the list."

"Good. I'll compare it with what I've gotten from the other recruits. Have you conducted interviews?"

"Yes. I've also interviewed a few potential suspects."

"Names?" I hear typing on the other end of the phone, like the Director is taking notes. I pause long enough for her to notice. "I understand that some of these people might be your friends, but this helps everyone."

"I know. Besides Sofia Vargas, a boy named Liam O'Connor and a girl named Daisy Guzman might have used the charm. According to Sofia, Daisy was originally in possession of it, which tracks since I saw a card in Daisy's purse at Electric Dust. I'm not sure who's distributing the charm yet. Liam is a good initial guess since I think he's been intentionally avoiding me."

"Let me know once you've spoken to him. Anything else?"

I check to make sure I'm truly alone in the library before I put the Director on speaker so I can debrief and clean simultaneously. Gently, I scoop the dust into my hand and dump it into my collector, where its magic will be neutralized.

"Based on how many people have been affected in such a short amount of time, I'd say there is a large quantity of dust stashed somewhere. I think students are finding out about the charm by word of mouth. They're contacted by a fake Instagram account after registering for prom. There's also a playing card involved, but I'm not sure of its purpose. If I can find another one or the next person being contacted, I can probably find out where the charm is being kept."

"Excellent work, Monroe. This is exactly the kind of thinking that will help you as an agent."

My heart fills with pride. Once my collector is full and not a speck of dust remains, I trek down to the first floor.

"How did Sofia Vargas learn about the charm?" the Director asks.

"Daisy Guzman. I'll question her again."

"Good. I also want you to try to find out who might use the charm next."

"Got it. What will happen to the students caught with the contraband?" I ask.

"The Bureau takes this seriously. Charming someone is against local laws. If it turns out they are involved, they'll be suspended at the least, but more likely, arrested."

"I understand."

"You're doing great work, Monroe. I'm sure your parents are proud. How's your other case coming? How is Iris? Has she had more mishaps?" the Director asks.

I pause before leaving the library. It's between classes right now so the hallways are empty. The chance of Iris hearing me talking to her mom about her is slim to none. I'm paranoid, though, and decide to take the back stairs down to the floor my locker is on.

"None," I confirm.

"Good. Collections has matched the residue you've deposited to the love charm we have on file, right? It's unlikely we're dealing with multiple charms that look the same and present similar mishaps, but it's protocol. Plus, R&D needs dust to test dissolvers."

"I haven't gotten a notification about a match. Should I have?" I ask.

The typing on the other end of the phone slows. "By now, yes. Have you asked them about the holdup?"

"Um . . . no."

"All right. Let's visit R&D together. I want to make sure that you're leaving samples in the right place. I have back-to-back meetings today and tomorrow. How does Wednesday around three-thirty work for you?" the Director asks.

"Perfectly. Just so you know, the collection bin is always overflowing," I reply.

The Director sighs. "I know. Unfortunately, the system isn't perfect, but charms should still be getting processed. We'll find out more on Wednesday. In the meantime, keep your focus on Iris."

Little does she know that Iris is the only person I seem to be able to focus on. Keeping Iris safe would be easy if I didn't have feelings for her. All the more reason to snuff them out. *Iris wants Anita*, I remind myself. Getting Anita to fall back in love with her is how to clear the charm dust.

"I will, Director," I reply, my throat suddenly tight.

"Stay on this path, and you'll be promoted to junior agent in the fall. Do you need anything else from me? I need to check on another team."

"No, ma'am."

"Okay, then. I'll see you on Wednesday," she replies and then hangs up.

The Director mentioning Collections makes me wonder whether Noah could have some insights into where this kind of contraband would be hiding and why the samples I've deposited haven't been logged yet. It's been almost a week since I left the Electric Dust sample. I've read the Bureau handbook cover to cover half a dozen times. I'm definitely depositing samples correctly, so what's the issue?

I text Noah, thankful he gave me his number.

Hey it's Monroe (garden gnome girl). Are you free for coffee sometime this week?

Not as a date. I want to pick your brain about something.

Noah: Bureau bugging you already? How's coffee on Wednesday? Not a date lol

Sounds perfect 4 p.m.?

Noah: 👍 See you then!

I pocket my phone and head to physics. It's hard to concentrate on my science teacher explaining how force is an interaction of one object with another when one of my classmates could be breaking hearts. I text a snapshot of the handle @Charmedlife33 to Iris.

Recognize this person?

Iris: nope. the handle is a little on the nose, no?

Not the most creative by far. Meet me after class? Time to change tactics . . .

Iris is waiting for me outside of physics. I hold my hand out for her, and she leads us toward the closest study hall room.

"Do you have a list of the students who've registered for prom? I need to search it for heart emojis," I say as we find seats. Only a few other students are here, and none of them pay us any attention.

"Yep. I'll pull up the names on my laptop. We've been using Jotform, so looking for a heart should be easy." Iris opens her computer and navigates to the site. "Okay, I've sorted by date of registration." She glances around and drops her voice. "Sofia Vargas randomly added a heart in the additional information section. Oh, so did Liam O'Connor, and a few others."

"Hm. Either they used the charm and had a love match, never used it, or never got it for whatever reason. I'll need that list of names."

"Already emailing you."

"Can you check for the last person who added a heart?"

Iris scrolls to the bottom of the list and then points to a name. "Devin Miller bought tickets last night. And see, there's the red heart emoji."

"Do you know him?"

"The name sounds familiar." Iris scrunches her nose in thought, and I can't help noticing how cute she looks. She grabs her phone and navigates to her Instagram. Iris is truly friends with everyone because a second later she says, "Oh! *Devin*. He hangs out with Anita sometimes. They're in photography club together."

"When does the club meet?" I ask.

"Tomorrow." Iris leans her elbows on the desk. Her arm brushes against mine, and my skin flames. I do my best to ignore it. "You want to crash photography club? I'm down if you are."

"I'm down, but promise not to laugh at my pictures."

"Oh, you know I will," Iris replies with a wink.

BUREAU OF MYSTICAL AFFAIRS
RECORD OF INCIDENT

DATE: Monday, March 9

RESPONDING OFFICER: Junior Recruit Monroe Bennett

CASE NUMBER: 26-292085

LOCATION: Fair Glen High School—library

SUMMARY: Sofia Vargas admittedly charmed Hollis Williams in the FGH library, after which several books flew off the shelves and landed on top of them both. Hollis was injured and taken to the hospital. Sofia confessed to stealing the remainder of Daisy Guzman's charm—which I suspect was used on Chloe Nguyen—from her bag at lunch. She heard the charm would ensure her crush (Hollis Williams) liked her back. This doesn't appear to be the charm's MO.

ACTIONS TAKEN: I retrieved the stolen charm from Sofia, cleaned up the residue, and called the nurse for Hollis.

RECOMMENDATION: Recon to find the next student who will receive the charm and intercept the exchange.

Seventeen

On Tuesday, Iris and I venture into the basement of FGH, where the visual arts classes are held. The temperature dips, and cold air rushes up to meet us as we follow the trail of voices to an activity room. The door is open, revealing tables and chairs facing an old whiteboard. Iris and I find two open seats near the front of the room.

Anita sits at the table across from us, prim and proper in her ivy polo sweater and black jeans. She shoots us a questioning glare. Next to her is a boy who I'm guessing is Devin Miller, looking the opposite with messy hair and piercings. Best-case scenario, Devin already has a playing card but hasn't used it to get a charm yet. Worst case, he already has a charm, and I can try to stop him before he uses it.

The club advisor, Mr. Michaelson, is a middle-aged man with graying locs who teaches freshman English and is married to Mx. Michaelson. He grins when he notices me and Iris.

"I see we have some new faces here today. Love it! We're just about to learn how to control the camera's shutter speed and take some pictures outside. Cars, people, anything you can find in motion," Mr. Michaelson tells us with an excited grin that creases his kind eyes. "Once you're done, feel free to return here."

We spend twenty minutes learning the ins and outs of the school's donated cameras, although most club members have their own. Once we've learned enough to get by, Mr. Michaelson leads us outdoors.

By now, FGH is practically deserted. Spring is in hiding today, so I bundle up in my jacket and tug my beanie down over my ears. Iris is wholly underdressed in her miniskirt and lightweight jacket. The wind fiercely blows her braids into her face.

I pull off my beanie and nudge it toward her. "Take it." She looks at me like I've grown another head. "Unless you want to freeze to death? I mean, if that's your goal, fine, but I'd have to find another person to fake date and it's on *such* short notice so—"

"All right!" Iris laughs and snatches my hat from me. She tugs it over her ears and grins. "How do I look?"

"Very cute." I clear my throat and hope she can't tell I'm breathing too fast.

I drop my gaze to the bushes in front of me. There's a spider stringing a thin silvery web along the branches. I pretend it's the most fascinating thing I've ever seen.

Mr. Michaelson lets us wander FGH grounds as we please, so long as we take photos of five different things in motion. I snap a picture of the spider weaving a web, while Iris meanders a few yards away, chasing down a squirrel. I hate that I find everything she does charming. Crushes are such an inconvenient hazard.

To take my mind off Iris, I hunt down Devin and find him taking pictures of cars racing down the block, despite the school-zone speed limit.

"Hey, Devin!" I yell.

He turns, dark hair falling into his face. "Yeah?" he replies, his shoulders nervously climbing toward his ears.

"You added a heart to your prom registration. Have you gotten a playing card yet?" Devin blanches, and his muscles lock. I hold up my hands. "I only want to talk."

"I—I don't know anything."

"That's not true. Listen, I'm not the bad guy here. I'm trying to prevent more students from getting hurt. Did you know someone had to be taken to the hospital yesterday? This charm is dangerous. It can't be controlled or predicted. Just tell me what you know. Please."

Devin toys with an expensive-looking camera dangling from his neck. I lift my own camera and take a picture of the movement. Counts, right?

"I heard Sofia Vargas is being suspended," he says.

"Is that who told you how to get a charm?" He looks away. "How do you know her?"

Devin moves toward an oak tree across from us where a bird is plucking at a nest. He watches for a moment before taking a picture. "Chem lab. She said she knew a way to ensure my crush likes me back in time for prom."

"Sofia is spreading misinformation," I huff.

Devin turns away and snaps a picture. I follow the direction of his camera to the park across the street. The merry-go-round spins and spins. I catch a blurry glimpse of Iris's broad grin. Of course she's with Anita. Iris, ever the flirt, could trigger a mishap any second now, if Anita's not into her.

With my attention elsewhere, Devin takes the opportunity to run. He sprints back toward the school, mumbling something to Mr. Michaelson as he goes. Damn. I had more questions.

For a split second, I waver between chasing after Devin or going to Iris. But it's hardly a decision at all. I sprint toward the playground. Once I'm within earshot, I catch a snippet of their conversation.

“So you’ll come to my party?” Anita asks, sounding, dare I say, hopeful. She plucks at a loose seam on her shirt. “You can bring Monroe.”

“I’ll ask her,” Iris replies as she slows to a stop. She pats the metal wheel she’s sitting on, a gesture meant for Anita. Only, before her hands even leave the merry-go-round, gold magic spreads from her fingers to the bumpy metal surface. The ride starts to spin.

Anita has yet to notice. She’s still rambling about her party, but Iris’s eyes double in size. I reach for my necklace, heat already pulsing against my skin as the crystal readies to deactivate the charm.

“Iris, jump!” I yell.

Anita whips her gaze toward me, but her focus is rapidly yanked back to the merry-go-round when Iris leaps off it with a screech. She lands on the wood chips beneath her, knees bending until she’s plopped forward on her hands. I grab the spinning bars, tugging against the momentum to slow down the wheel. Residue flies away, inert now. I sigh in relief. Iris could’ve been hurt on my watch.

“What was that?” Anita asks.

“Um . . .” I’m not sure what I’m supposed to say. Iris clearly has feelings for Anita, who still doesn’t trust her. “A game we made up.” I extend my hand to Iris and haul her to her feet. “I tell her to jump once the merry-go-round is spinning fast to see if she’ll do it or chicken out.”

Anita glances at Iris, a skeptical dip between her contoured brows. “Really? What movie is that from?” she asks.

Iris frowns. “None.”

Anita purses her lips. “Okay. Well, I should take more pictures since I’m actually *in* this club, and not trying to be a detective,” Anita says to me. Then, to Iris, “See you around?”

Iris nods, and once Anita has scampered off, I help Iris dust the wood chips off her clothes. Pro tip from a Bureau recruit: Always keep your collector on you. I get to work gathering as much of the residue as I can.

"You were flirting with her," I say. I hate how my voice sounds all tight and high, like I'm making an accusation rather than an observation.

Iris scoffs. "I wasn't. I mean, I don't think I was."

"You triggered a mishap."

"Old habits or whatever. I'm sorry," Iris replies. I back down, letting my arms hang limply at my sides. Iris nudges my shoulder. "You know, before the mishap, Anita was inviting us to her house party next weekend."

I screw the cap onto my very full collector and shove it back into my bag. I'll empty it tomorrow at the Bureau office when I meet the Director. "Are you sure that's a good idea? We got lucky today. We might not be at a party," I reply.

Iris leans against the blue pole of the swing set, watching me curiously. "Is that the only reason you don't want to go?"

I shrug, jostling the camera around my neck. "I never said I didn't want to go. I'm saying it seems like a lot of work for me to try to keep mishaps at bay during a party. But we can go." My stomach suddenly feels very weird, like I ate expired yogurt.

Iris kicks off the pole with a sigh. We cross the lawn and head toward the school to warm up. Mr. Michaelson seems to be enjoying the cold air while advising the photography kids. He must be part polar bear to be out here wearing only a T-shirt. I'm chillier than the slushies from Spellcast Roller.

"Can I share my thoughts with you?" Iris asks.

"Always."

Iris chews her bottom lip. "Anita wouldn't have invited me to the party if her feelings weren't starting to change. She's probably not sure how she's feeling just yet, but she's getting there."

"That's great," I reply dully.

Iris stops outside the school entrance. "Is it?"

"Yes, I want you to be happy."

She shakes her head. Continues. "Right. Okay, thanks."

Iris is being very weird for someone who is starting to get exactly what she wants . . .

The inside of FGH isn't exactly a sauna, but there's no wind, which instantly makes me warmer. Iris leads the way back to the activity room. "The party's theme is the roaring twenties. I figure this is our last big hurrah before the breakup. If we split after the party, we'll have another two weeks before prom. That gives me plenty of time to ask Anita and you to ask whoever you want."

"I'm not going to prom."

"You're—"

"Anti-romance," I remind her and myself. I put the borrowed camera next to the others on the desk. Iris does the same. She has that strange expression on her face again, the one I can't seem to crack.

"Still?" she asks. "I thought for sure I'd change your mind." My mouth parts in surprise. "On account of our movie date," she clarifies. I swear there's a hint of mischief in her gaze.

I rub the back of my neck with a chuckle. "There's time to persuade me. Anyway, I still need to finish my conversation with Devin. Know where I can find him?"

"No, but I can find out. We could do recon tomorrow," Iris suggests.

"I have two meetings tomorrow. Want to come with me to get coffee with Noah?" I could go alone, but I've gotten used to hanging out with Iris, and something about this all ending soon has me in my feels. I want to spend more time with her, even if it's as a fake girlfriend.

"Picking his brain about your case?" she asks knowingly.

"Yes, but also, I might just want to get coffee with you." I lean against Mr. Michaelson's desk. "Maybe I'm asking you on a date. A real one." Would it be so far-fetched? I can't cross that line with her, and yet my curiosity is insatiable. When Iris's eyebrows jump to her hairline, I backtrack as fast as possible. "I'm kidding." *Why did I open my mouth?*

Iris tilts her head, her face unreadable. She steps closer and rests her hands on the desk behind me, her arms brushing against my hips. On her mouth is a smirk that would steal my breath if it weren't already gone.

"That's too bad. I might've said yes."

Eighteen

On Wednesday, I head directly to the Bureau after school. The building is bustling with agents. They speed walk through the lobby carrying collectors and discuss their cases while waiting for the elevators. Someone brushes past me wearing a safety vest commonly worn by agents in Distribution and pushing a bin labeled "Approved." It's full of mops, brooms, and dusters wiggling around like they're itching to get to work.

The elevator arrives, and I squeeze in with the full-time Bureau agents. On the fifth floor, the Director is waiting for me, her eyes glued to her tablet.

She looks up when I approach. "Monroe, you made it."

She gestures down the hallway, and we walk in sync, passing researchers projecting microscopic charm dust on monitors in the labs, likely trying to match the genetic patterns to charms already in the system.

We walk to the Collections drop-off bin, where today a tall woman around my parents' age with thick, green-rimmed glasses and finger tats types away on the computer. The bin beneath her is empty.

"Is this where you've been depositing your collections?" the Director asks.

"Yes. The bin has always been full, though," I reply.

"Things get backed up during the holiday break, so we have a backlog for the first few months of the new year. We're caught up now," the technician explains. "How can I help you, Director?"

"I've been overseeing a case, and my junior recruit said there have been no updates in the database," the Director says, her voice level—devoid of any accusations.

"Case number?"

"26-292085," I reply. The Director spares me an impressed glance.

"Okay, let's see." The technician's fingers fly across her keyboard. "A match is pending."

The Director folds her arms. "Why is it still pending? Ms. Bennett has been depositing samples for a week. Don't matches usually take forty-eight hours?"

More typing. "It looks like the samples have been scanned but haven't been processed and matched yet."

"Why not?" the Director asks. "We need to understand the charm's makeup to find and test existing dissolvers. I'd hate for this substance to hit the entire town."

The technician types so fast that her fingers practically disappear. I swear a bead of sweat drips from her brow. I'm glad I'm not the only one who finds the Director to be an imposing badass. "I understand, ma'am. I can take you to the location where collected samples of the love charm should be stored. There might be a glitch on our end."

The technician jumps up and rushes over to the door separating the Collections booth—a small narrow room just big enough for a chair and a computer desk—and the storage locker. She swipes her key card, and the door unlocks. She spins around, as if remembering the Director and I are still in the hall and says, "This way, please."

Cold, stale light illuminates the large storage locker, containing shelves full of glowing charm dust in clear containers. Dozens of rows are laid out before us. Signs hang from the ceiling, labeling the passageways. The room is basically a fancy grocery store, except instead of food, the shelves are stocked with charms.

We enter an aisle categorized as "Sentiments" and stop at a metal shelving unit labeled "Love." The tech points to vials of dust on the shelf, checking her tablet to confirm the classification number. "Here it is."

"Let's test that to be sure," the Director says. "Shelving mistakes happen."

The technician grabs a pen-size vacuum from her tool belt and collects a sample. She reverses the suction and releases particles of dust onto the reader attached to her tablet. The Bureau-designed app will compare the sample with a list of charms in the Bureau's database. After five seconds, the reader beeps and a classification populates: fearless charm.

The silence that follows is unsettling, so I state the obvious. "Where's the love charm?"

"Let me check the log sheet," the technician replies hurriedly. More rapid-fire typing on the tablet, like she's trying to win the Guinness World Record for most words per minute. "The love charm was initially found several years back by a Mystic cleaning out the house of her late grandmother, who was a self-proclaimed matchmaker. The granddaughter knew the gold dust was contraband and called the Bureau. We confiscated the charm and that was that. A month ago, junior recruit Noah Cham matched a collection of the residue from Illusion Salon & Spa to this original charm, but that's where the record stops. I'm sorry, Director. No one noticed that the charm on the shelf wasn't the love charm in question."

The Director pinches the bridge of her nose. "Are there any other logs of the residue?"

"Nothing, ma'am," the tech replies, frowning at her tablet.

"I swear I dropped off those collections! Taylor must've dropped off collections, too, after the rink incident," I reply. I reach for the collection I gathered on the playground yesterday. "What should I do with this sample and all future ones?"

"I'll handle it directly," the tech replies. She swiftly takes my collector and empties the dust into a crystal-lined jar. "I'll log the deposit as soon as we're done here."

The Director rubs her fingers across the shelf where the vials of dust *I* collected should be. "How did this happen? Could the collections still be with R&D?"

The technician swallows hard and then shakes her head. "All transfers to other departments would be recorded, and I don't see a record of any new vials in the system."

"Send me a list of every agent and recruit who takes care of collections so I can look into them," the Director says to the tech. She turns to me. "Who was working at the desk when you stopped by?"

"Noah Cham."

"You're sure?" she presses. "Because if that's the case, we've got a real problem. Noah could be tied to this. If not him, someone with connections to the Bureau doesn't want us to find out the truth. The question is: Why?"

Ten minutes later, I arrive at the coffee shop across the street from the Bureau, my mind reeling. Could Noah really be taking my collections and what—dumping them? No wonder the Bureau hasn't located a dissolver. The Bureau isn't in possession of the charm! Neither the new nor the old dust is there.

Noah seems so nice. Why would he agree to meet me if he has something to hide?

I tell myself to act cool, which might be difficult considering he's just been added to my suspect list, along with Daisy and Liam. Should I have roped the Director into this meeting? Probably, but I want to prove I have what it takes to be an agent. I don't want the Director to think I can't handle this on my own. Things will only get tougher as an agent. I'll be assigned multiple cases at once, and suspects won't be limited to my peers but will include the entire community. Dad had a case once that took him almost a year to solve because he had over thirty suspects.

Charmed Coffee Co. is a redbrick, two-story coffee shop popular among sleep-deprived agents and students. It makes sense why Noah—a recruit and student at St. Mary's—would pick this place. Iris is waiting for me on a bench outside. Her magenta dress and signature denim jacket are paired with well-loved combat boots. She always looks nice, but of course, my brain can't help noticing *how* nice today. The sun even seems to shine a little brighter when she smiles at me.

"Hey, you. Coming from the Bureau?" she asks.

I nod, debating whether to tell her about the latest update before or after we talk to Noah. I settle on after. "You're early."

"I'm punctual. You like it."

"We're supposed to be doing things we hate, remember?" I ask while I hold the door open for her.

She brushes past me, the sweet scent of her perfume clouding my thoughts. "Doing one thing you like won't make you fall for me."

If only it was just one thing. It's so hard to stay neutral around her.

Charmed Coffee Co. is packed for a late Wednesday afternoon. The line to order trails along the counter, wraps around the bins of coffee bags, and stops short of the door. Half the people in line are wearing suits with ties undone and blazers draped over their arms. The rest are dressed in sweats and carry bloated bookbags, the dark circles under their eyes likely permanent fixtures at this point.

I search the sea of faces for Noah, spotting him only after Iris tugs us toward the back of the shop. Noah's wearing a purple Northwestern University hoodie and has one arm slung around the person next to him. I'd know that mop of blue hair anywhere.

"Andie?"

They both look up at the sound of my voice. Andie's mouth drops open. "Monroe? *You're* the junior recruit he's meeting today?"

"Yes . . . How do you two know each other?" I ask.

"This is Neo. Well, that's his nickname. He goes by Noah at the Bureau. Though, I promise I didn't know he worked there when I first mentioned him," Andie replies.

Neo. Andie's boyfriend. Of course. But also, shit. My best friend's boyfriend could be betraying the Bureau. Andie has kept his relationship close to the chest, which is unusual. He must seriously like this boy.

I plop into the seat across from them, slightly numb. Noah seems completely at ease, no nervous movements or sideways glances to suggest he's keeping a secret. Or maybe he's just that good.

An awkward silence ensues. Andie rolls his eyes and stands. "Okay, let's get coffee while these two talk." He holds out his hand to Iris. She takes it with a bemused shrug, and Andie tugs her to the line to order.

"Are you going to Northwestern next year?" I ask.

Noah nods, his eyes crinkling at the corners. "They have an art theory and practice major. College is expensive, but I'll figure something out." He glances over to the café counter, then back to me. "So what'd you want to talk about? The line for coffee may seem long, but it moves fast," Noah says.

"You know the case the field recruits have been handling?"

Noah nods.

"Yesterday, the Director was wondering why we don't have more information by now considering we've been dropping off samples for the past week. And I was curious why my samples still say 'Pending' in the database. The samples were never logged or sent to the research team to be analyzed. All the recent samples and the original love charm are missing from Collections."

Noah stills. "What do you mean?"

"I mean the love charm is literally not on the shelf anymore. You know anything about that? I left two samples with you last week, and Taylor dropped off at least one." I think about all the case files I've reviewed. "Reggie and Senior Agent Rudd too."

Noah sits up straighter, finally catching on. "I logged them in the database; I swear. And I shelved the dust in the Sentiments aisle."

"Could you have shelved it wrong, or left your post for a little too long? Stuff happens." Although, that doesn't explain where the charm from years ago went.

Noah wipes his brow and drums his hands against the table. I can't tell if he's sincerely surprised or nervous because he's cornered. "Are you saying someone stole the charm from the Bureau?"

I nod. "The collection bin isn't exactly secure."

"The bin and all charms are in a secure building on a secure floor full of agents. I don't see how someone could have stolen the samples."

"Anyone with a Bureau key card could have access to it, and the first time we officially met, you weren't exactly guarding the bin with your life," I say, remembering how it was unattended when I dropped off the residue from the garden gnomes. "All I'm saying is, managing the bin is a big job for one person. Is it possible someone working at the Bureau could've taken contraband without you noticing?"

Noah flushes. He chews on his bottom lip and takes a long time to answer. "It's possible," he concedes. "*Unlikely*, but possible."

I lean forward. "Where would someone hide enough contraband to charm multiple people? Best guess."

"The vials of dust themselves wouldn't take up much space. For example, if the dust was divided into a dozen two-ounce jars for easy distribution, it would only take up about a square foot. I'd personally keep a few crystals on hand to dispel any dust should some of the charm leak or a vial break."

I narrow my eyes. "That's a pretty detailed theory but doesn't exactly answer my question." The charm could be hidden anywhere.

Noah parts his lips at the same time Iris and Andie return carrying two drinks each. I fix my face and force some cheer into my voice. "Let me guess, something sweet?" I ask Iris.

She grins. "Duh."

Noah seems to remember himself when Andie sets a cup down in front of him. "How much was it?" he asks. "I'll pay for both of ours."

Andie pats his cheek. "I got it. It's fine."

Noah grabs his bag from around his chair anyway and fishes out his wallet. My gaze snags on the familiar art on the front flap of his bag. No way it's the same, is it?

At this point, I've stared at the playing card long enough to know those outlined flowers anywhere. Roses, sunflowers, and vines twist around the front pocket of Noah's JanSport and along the zipper of his cloth wallet.

"That design . . ." I start.

Andie grabs the wallet and holds it out for us to see, beaming proudly. He *really* likes Noah. They're cute together, and that makes Noah's potential involvement in the case suck so much more.

"Cool, isn't it? Neo paints them himself," Andie says.

"You painted this?" The question comes out barely above a whisper.

"Yeah." He rubs his thumb across the paint, a faint smile dusting his lips.

Iris leans forward in her seat. "What else do you paint?"

"Uh, mostly just plants," Noah replies.

"Do you paint other mediums too?" she presses.

"Canvas kind of bores me. I like cloth"—he gestures to his bag—"fabric, glass, metal—"

"Paper? Like say, note cards or playing cards?" Iris offers.

"Um. Yeah. Sometimes," Noah replies.

Iris and I share a look. It's not as discreet as it should be. Even though Noah doesn't notice, Andie does, and he narrows his gaze at me.

"Roe—"

"Well, thanks for agreeing to chat. We, um, have to go to a . . . thing," I say quickly, gathering my coffee and my bag. "Right?" I nudge Iris.

"Yep!" Iris snatches her smoothie off the table. "It was so great seeing you both."

"Monroe, wait," Andie starts. "Why did you really need to talk to Neo?"

"My case. I'll explain later, okay?"

Andie crosses his arms, unconvinced. "You better."

Iris and I shuffle out of the coffee shop and onto the sidewalk. I lean against the building, my heart racing. I inhale shakily.

"Smooth," Iris says.

"I panicked! You saw his bag."

She nods. "Same as the playing cards. You think Noah's selling contraband around FGH? He so quiet and sweet."

"More like inconspicuous. He also had a pretty good idea for how the charm could be stored. His motive would need to be worth risking his job at the Bureau. He said he's attending Northwestern next year. I'd have to sell my kidneys to afford that tuition."

"Money could be a motive. I don't think he'd make enough selling charms to pay for college, but it might be enough to cover food and books," Iris says. "But why target FGH students rather than ones from his own high school?"

"You get a bigger pool at our school, fewer eyes on you. Those two St. Mary's students at the baseball game just got caught in the crosshairs. And remember, Diego goes to SM and was the first to be charmed."

I push off the wall. Iris links her arm around mine, and we head toward my car. I try my hardest not to lean into her touch.

I'm not sure, so I won't tell the Director about my suspicions until I'm certain. Noah could lose his job or, worse, get arrested. Andie would never forgive me if I'm wrong.

We stop in front of my car, and I fiddle with my keys. I should go but linger like a simp.

"Friday is senior night at Jinxed Adventures. Fair Glen versus St. Mary's. Based on their recent posts, Devin and Liam are likely to be there," Iris says.

"Let's go," I reply a little too quickly. Senior night sounds like the perfect opportunity to investigate. I also wouldn't mind having actual fun with Iris. "Are you doing anything right now? We could game-plan for Friday," I suggest.

There's no real reason to hang out more, and yet I can't seem to help myself. Anita isn't around to make jealous, and telling myself I need to bounce ideas off Iris for my case is true but unwise. I should be working to get rid of this crush, not fueling the fire.

"I'm going shopping with Taylor for Anita's party next weekend," she replies. "You could come."

"Thanks, but hard pass. I'm still traumatized from my last trip to the mall—dress shopping for eighth-grade formal."

Iris laughs. "Not a dress girl?"

"I could be if the dress resembled a skirt and was sewed down the middle, so both of my legs were covered with fabric."

Iris snorts, her eyes creasing at the corners. "You literally just described pants, but noted." She drags her gaze down my frame. "You'd look great in a suit."

"Tsk-tsk. No flirting," I remind her amusedly.

"I'm not flirting; I'm making an astute observation. I saw you in your Bureau one for a few seconds before I spilled my drink all over it. Very dapper." Iris bumps her shoulder against mine and waves. "Later, Roe."

"Later."

I can't stop smiling the entire drive home.

Nineteen

Jinxed Adventures is an outdoor obstacle course on the outskirts of town. I arrive early on Friday, geeked to spend time with Iris after a long week of school. A couple of people I recognize are dressed in protective vests and helmets while playing a very active game of Dodge the Charm—Fair Glen's version of paintball. The course is rigged with obstacles like rubber structures charmed to change shape to make it extra hard to win. You have to dodge all the unpredictable charms to get to the flag. The Bureau conducts regular assessments of the course to ensure its safety.

Iris arrives on time wearing loose jeans and a lacey top I haven't seen her wear before. It hugs her frame perfectly.

"New top?" I ask, when I mean to say hi.

Iris glances at her shirt, beaming. "Yep. Found it at the mall along with the *perfect* outfit for Anita's party. I may have picked up something for you too."

"Please tell me you didn't get us matching dresses."

"I wouldn't do you like that." Iris's lips stretch in amusement. "Although, we should've added matching outfits to our list of do's to prevent falling in love."

“Hey, I draw the line at torture.”

We enter the building, and Mr. Ngata greets me with a large grin. “Monroe! You finally came to one of our events!”

“I couldn’t pass this one up,” I reply honestly.

“Don’t show off too much!” He winks.

The full ticket price is thirty dollars, but Mr. Ngata charges me and Iris thirty bucks total because I’m a regular here and one of their highest-scoring players. Once we’ve paid, he gives us green helmets and vests and wishes us good luck. Across the room, a few boys still wearing their St. Mary’s uniforms are putting on blue vests and helmets.

I search for Liam or Devin. If I can show them I’m on their side, maybe they’ll help me. What better way to do that than to beat St. Mary’s?

Iris watches me with a curious expression while I help her get her vest on and check that her helmet is tight.

“What?” I ask. “You don’t want a concussion on your bingo card today.”

Iris rolls her eyes playfully, and I tug her outside. Several FGH students are chatting near the start of the field.

“There’s Devin,” I say when I spot him a few yards from us, tightening the straps of his vest.

We move closer until we’re in earshot.

“I’m *definitely* going to score more points than you,” Devin says to Kenny Hill, the victim from Spellcast Roller.

Kenny laughs. “You’re not. I come here all the time. Better stick to what you know. Photography won’t help you on the field.”

“Wanna bet?” Devin asks, a gleam in his eyes.

I step forward. “I do.”

Devin tenses. “I wasn’t talking to you.”

"Aw, c'mon. That's no fun. If you score more points than me, I'll leave you alone for good. But if I score more than you, you have to answer my questions," I say.

In Dodge the Charm, players score two points for their team per opposing player they eliminate. Twenty points are awarded for capturing the opposing flag.

Kenny grins. "I'd take that bet, Devin. If Monroe plays like she skates, winning will be a piece of cake."

Too bad Kenny and Devin don't know that I basically had to play this game as part of the Bureau recruitment test. I'm going to mop the floor with him.

Devin folds his arms. "Promise I won't get expelled."

"I can't promise that if I don't know what you did," I reply.

Devin digs his shoes into the dirt. "Fine," he agrees.

I grin. Iris is bouncing on the balls of her feet by the time we make it onto the field. "You're going to win, right?"

"Obviously."

The referee blows his whistle. Members of the Fair Glen High team immediately try to find the best spots to hide from the onslaught of blue paint from St. Mary's. A spray of bright blue lands at our feet. I grab Iris's hand and pull her behind a huge hay bale covered in bright pink dust. It's charmed to unravel, but if memory serves, we should be safely hidden for a few moments. Iris's gaze finds mine. Her eyes are as bright as fireflies on a hot summer night.

"A little different than skating or watching a movie," I murmur.

Iris nods. "But equally fun with you."

My heart stutters in my chest. Before I can respond, the hay bale unravels, revealing our position to the St. Mary's team. Crap. I got distracted.

I catch a glimpse of movement and a flash of blue. I raise the paintball gun and eliminate the opponent just as he aims for us.

After that, I rack up four more points by taking out two more players running through a charmed rubber tunnel that peeled open like a banana before they were halfway through. Being a Mystic gives me a leg up in that I can see which obstacles are charmed, but I've also memorized what the charm does by playing the course a dozen times.

Across the field, Devin seems to be having an easy time picking off the blue team and inching toward their flag. If he captures it, twenty points are his, and I'll be forced to find another way to get through to him.

A twig snaps behind me. I spin to find a girl aiming at me. A ball of green paint lands on her shoulder before she can get off a shot. Next to me, Kenny gives a thumbs-up and continues across the field.

I tug Iris closer to my side, her lavender scent washing out the smell of grass and mud. Together, we weave through a maze of inflated cones that are charmed to pop in and out like a game of Whac-A-Mole.

Next to us, blue paint explodes across a boy's chest. He yanks his helmet off with a groan and turns toward the edge of the field, but not before I glimpse his face.

"Was that Sean, Taylor's boyfriend?" I ask Iris.

She stares after him with a frown. "I think so. He probably came with his friends." She points to a stack of car tires a few feet away. "Come on. Those give us a better vantage point."

We keep playing, Sean all but forgotten. Twenty minutes in, and I'm starting to sweat, and my thighs are screaming from crouching. Iris seems to be enjoying herself. She manages to take out two people in the span of a second, popping out from behind a giant red ball and nailing one in the leg and the other in the arm.

Iris doesn't have time to get back to safety before paint flies toward her. She throws herself onto the ground at the last second and grins up at me in what I assume is supposed to be triumph, but her entire back is splattered with blue paint.

I shake my head in amusement. "Nice try, but you're hit."

The other team tries to fire off another shot. I duck and roll. My gaze snags on a red flag hanging on a wooden stake. Across from me, hiding from a round of fire, is Devin.

"I'll come back for you!" I yell to Iris.

She waves her hand. "Go!"

I race toward the flag. I'm running low on paint but manage to take down two more St. Mary's players. I'm up to ten points. If I get the flag, I'll be at thirty, which is more than enough to beat Devin.

Unfortunately, he has the same idea.

We share a glance before he takes off, racing me for the flag. Devin reaches it first, his hand outstretched and his fingers nearly touching the fabric. But his foot collides with the rubber mat around the base of the pole. Like a booby trap, it's charmed to buck off anyone who steps on it. He yells as he's tossed back. Meanwhile, I'm already diving for the flag. My hand closes around it, and I tug the flag against my body, then throw it up high.

The referee blows the whistle. That's the game. We won! *I* won!

Iris runs up to me, full of smiles. She doesn't say anything. She doesn't have to. She pushes my glasses further up my nose. I reach for a smear of blue dye on her face. Flecks of charm dust shine like glitter beneath my thumb when I swipe at her cheek.

Devin clears his throat. I drop my hands and take a step back, chalking up my temporary lapse in judgment to my excitement at winning the game. "Ready to tell me what you know?" I ask.

Devin seems both annoyed and impressed. "I should've known the bet was a trap. At least we beat St. Mary's." He sighs. "I'll tell you what I can."

We exit the field and find a quiet spot near the entrance to the building. Devin fishes his phone out of his pocket. "So like I said before, Sofia told me how to get a charm, but I haven't picked it up yet. After I added a heart to my prom registration form, I got a DM." He shows me the messages from the @Charmedlife33 account on his phone. "Someone put a playing card in my locker today. I'm supposed to send the numbers on the back of the card, and then I'll get instructions on how to pick up the charm. I haven't done it, though. I didn't want to get suspended, and I didn't want to hurt anyone, especially not Anita."

Ah. So that's who he was taking a picture of during photography club. "I need to see the card." If I DM the account as Devin, I can get instructions on how to pick up a charm and maybe catch the person putting it there.

He nods toward the building. "It's in my bag."

The three of us head inside, and Devin goes to the cubbies to grab the card. Iris and I return our gear while we wait. Ahead of us, Sean stands with his arm around a girl our age who laughs into his chest. Said girl is *not* Taylor. She's wearing a St. Mary's polo with a plaid skirt rolled at the waist to shorten the length.

The muscles in Iris's jaw flex. "Sean, who the hell is this?" she asks.

Sean whirls around. He's not covered in any charm dust that I can see, and neither is the girl he's with. A small blessing, I guess.

"Iris." Sean jumps away from the girl and holds up his hands. "It's not what it looks like."

"It's *so* what it looks like," Iris snaps.

"Yeah, you're caught, dude," I add.

"You said no one would notice us here!" the girl complains. "I'm not doing this with them." She whips her silky black hair over her shoulder and storms out.

Iris glares after her but ultimately turns her focus back to Sean. "You're literally dating Taylor."

Sean pinches the bridge of his nose. "I care about her, but Taylor's been different lately." He scratches his forehead.

Iris scoffs. "What are you talking about? Taylor hasn't seemed different to me."

Sean tilts his head and releases a dramatic sigh. "Well, you haven't exactly been hanging out with her, have you? Too busy with your new girlfriend to pay attention to your friends, same as usual."

The weight of his judgment knocks Iris back a step. I glare at Sean. He's not necessarily wrong, though. Iris has been spending a lot of time with me lately, like sitting with me and my friends during lunch and hanging out most days after school.

"What do you mean, Taylor's been different?" I ask.

Sean glances around as if Taylor's going to pop out any minute. "When I try to talk to her, all I get is one-word answers. It feels like we're putting on a performance. I'm not saying this as an excuse for coming here with another girl. I'm saying she won't care much that I did. We've been on and off for a long time. The last fight we had was kind of my last straw. Taylor knows that."

He sounds sincere and a little hurt. I don't know their relationship well, but when I do see them together, they aren't talking or laughing or paying each other much attention. Sean is always on his phone, and Taylor is busy talking to her friends. They're together, but mentally separate.

"I need to check on Giselle. I'm sorry; I gotta go," Sean says before he stalks off.

Iris groans. "Unbelievable. He honestly wants us to feel sorry for him when he's cheating on my best friend."

"It sounds like he and Taylor broke up," I offer.

"They do that often. Taylor never mentioned they were on the outs again." Iris grabs her phone. "I need to call her."

"Yeah. Of course. I'll find Devin."

Devin's by the cubbies, still taking off his gear. He sighs when he sees me and holds out a card. King of hearts. The same vines and flowers are drawn on the card, and the same numbers are written on the back in black Sharpie. Sticking with hearts was clever. So is making the user text a confirmation code and keeping everything anonymous. Let's hope I can outsmart them.

"Can I send a message from your phone?" I ask.

Devin hesitantly hands over his cell, and I message @Charmedlife33.

DMill111: I got the card. What's next?

We wait a few minutes for a response. And just when I think this won't work, dots appear at the bottom of the screen and a message comes through.

Charmedlife33: What numbers are on the back?

DMill111: 10308

Text bubbles appear and then vanish. Devin raises his brow as the seconds drag on. My palms begin to sweat.

Charmedlife33: FGH basement. The card will guide you to the right locker. On Monday, put the card inside along with $50. I'll message you the combination for the locker. The charm will be there at 3 p.m. Don't be late.

A locker? Noah did say a dozen vials of contraband would fit into a small space. But how could he have a locker at Fair Glen when he goes to St. Mary's?

"Thanks, Devin. Text me when you get the combination. Not that it's up to me, but since you don't plan on using the charm on anyone, I see no need for you to be suspended or anything," I say.

Devin nods and walks off. I find Iris outside still on the phone with Taylor. I can't shake what Sean said about his relationship with Taylor feeling performative. Iris and my relationship felt the same in the beginning, but recently, it's been easy. If a real relationship can feel fake, and a fake one can feel real, then nothing makes sense, and grass might as well be blue.

At least there's one thing that seems to ring true: Relationships bring nothing but trouble.

Twenty

On Monday, I head straight to the school basement with the playing card in my hand and a battery cam in my pocket. The Bureau can't detain the culprit without evidence, so a video of the person coming back for the cash and playing card should work. I just have to find the locker.

I study the playing card. Could the painted flowers be a clue? Perhaps the locker is in the art room. Most of the student lockers were replaced with smart lockers three years ago. Our current locker numbers are four digits, not five. But I think a few metal lockers remain in the basement. I never memorized my old locker number, only its prime location next to the vending machine. I drank way too much Diet Coke freshman year.

I turn the corner and nearly knock into Jude Featherstone coming out of the art room with her head down and her steps quick. Her eyes widen when they land on me.

"Jude?"

She ignores me and takes off. I race after her but stop before I reach the stairs. Finding the locker is more important. We have a Bureau meeting tomorrow anyway, so I can follow up with her then. Is she a step ahead of me in solving this case?

I double back, and when I enter the room, the scent of linseed oil hits my nose. It looks like Jackson Pollock went hard on every surface. Paint is splattered on the walls, the old wooden desks, and the concrete floor. It's also unreasonably cold in here. You'd think it was a meat locker.

Liz is standing in front of an easel signing her name on an impressionistic painting of the school. "Hey, Monroe! What are you doing down here?"

"I'm looking for a locker. Maybe you can help," I reply. "Was that Jude Featherstone making a break for it like she stole a bunch of paint?"

Liz nods amusedly.

Could Jude be involved? She doesn't have access to R&D like Noah, but all recruits can get to the collection bin. And she could have swiped his key card. But again, *why*? Is she for or against love?

Liz wipes her hands off and unties her smock. She gathers her supplies and walks over to a locker. My eyes widen when I notice the numbers. Five digits.

I brush past Liz and beeline toward the lockers lining the walls. My fingers trail along the metal tags drilled into the locker doors. When I find the right one, tucked away in the corner with the dust bunnies and the cobwebs, I can hardly believe my eyes.

Locker number 10308 has a lock on it. I try the handle for no reason other than to fail. I shove my face against the slits and try to make out what's inside. Darkness greets me.

"What's in the locker, Roe?" Liz asks.

"If I'm lucky? The charm taking out our student body." I use the flashlight on my phone and point it toward the narrow openings. It's an awkward slant, and the flashlight isn't much help. I change the angle a few times. The beam of light catches on something that could be glimmering and gold. I inhale sharply.

I spin to face Liz. "Does this locker belong to someone? The others aren't locked."

"No idea. Sorry," Liz replies.

"That's okay. I think I know how to find out."

Mrs. Davis shakes her head when she sees me coming. "Ms. Bennett, the bell rings in six minutes. What could you possibly need before school begins?"

"This will only take a second. I might've made a break in the case. I don't have any snacks, but I promise to bring some later today."

Mrs. Davis sighs. "This has already taken longer than a second."

"I could stop the love charm mishaps with your help. That means no more parents calling to complain, remember?"

Mrs. Davis leans her elbows on her desk. "I'm listening."

"Does locker 10308 belong to anyone? It's in the art room."

"If it's in the art room, then it belongs to no one in particular. It's probably used as storage by the studio art students."

"All of them have access?" I ask.

"Yes, and students in pottery club who meet in the art room. No one should be using those lockers for anything personal, though."

That doesn't exactly narrow down my search. I glance at the clock behind Mrs. Davis's desk. Five minutes before the bell rings and I still need to set up the battery cam and drop the money and the playing card in the locker.

"I can see who it belonged to before it was used by studio art and pottery club. Would that help?" Mrs. Davis asks.

"Yes!"

"Okay." Slow typing and clicking ensue. I tap my foot on the old carpet to expel some of my energy. "It looks like the last person the locker belonged to was Noah Cham. He transferred after his freshman year."

Noah went to our school? I mainly kept my head down freshman year and never noticed him. Odds are slim that Noah's not involved when his old locker is tied to the charm *and* he was the last person to see the charm dust I collected.

"Are you sure?" I ask shakily.

Mrs. Davis narrows her gaze and taps her fingers against the computer monitor. "The system may be outdated, but it doesn't lie. Better hurry. The bell is about to ring."

I thank her and then race to class. There's no time to set up the battery cam and drop off the money with the playing card. I'll just have to do it during lunch. Fingers crossed no one is using the room.

I duck into homeroom, cringing as the charmed door announces, "Monroe Bennett: one minute late."

I plop into my seat with a groan and decide to salvage the morning by diving into Noah's socials. I check his TikTok and public Snapchat stories only to find a lot of reposts, film quotes, and photos of his art. On TikTok, he's posted a lot of videos of himself painting and reviewing different art materials. Nothing helpful in establishing a motive. Though I do watch a video of presumably his parents recording his reaction to getting into #Northwestern #Wildcats #EarlyDecision. They're cheesing bigger than he is.

Could money for college really be a good enough reason to risk his Bureau job? And why befriend me? To make sure I don't crack the case? Maybe he's trying to throw me off his scent by dating Andie. But you'd think he'd want to distance himself from me or use me to find out exactly what the Bureau knows about the charm. So far, he's done neither.

Better luck during lunch, I hope.

I do not, in fact, have better luck at lunch. There's a class in the art room, which leaves only the open period an hour before school ends. Hopefully the seller doesn't return to the locker before then. If Noah is responsible, I doubt he's visiting FGH during school hours.

"Do all art students get keys to this space?" I ask Liz, as she, Iris, and I head to the basement to install the battery cam.

"Most don't," Liz replies. "I begged Ms. Anderson to lend me a key because my parents won't let me paint at home. You know how the fumes mess with Mom's allergies and give my dad headaches." Liz pushes open the door and flicks on the lights.

"You think Ms. Anderson has lent out the key before? Maybe to a student in the past like Noah?" Iris asks.

"She's extremely nice, so yeah, probably," Liz replies.

"If Noah copied the key, he could come and go as he pleases," Iris says.

"Without someone noticing?" I ask.

"Well, not for long," Iris replies.

Our free period is forty-five minutes, which is plenty of time to set up the camera, assuming no one enters. Iris grabs a stool from the nearest table.

I pick a locker directly across from number 10308 so we can have a clear view. I step onto the stool and place the camera on a pile of dust, making sure it's not visible. I have it aimed on the locker only. Nothing else is getting recorded, and there's no audio.

"Is it noticeable?" I ask.

"Nope. And no one comes in here besides the art and pottery students and apparently the desperate and lovesick."

"I *desperately* hope this works." I drop the playing card and fifty dollars (from cleaning with Dad) through the slit.

"I'm putting it into the universe that we catch whoever's behind this, whether that's Noah or someone else," Iris announces.

"I'm honestly wishing for anyone else because Andie really likes him," I reply.

But if Noah isn't involved, someone is doing a good job making it look like he is. I could straight-up ask, but I don't for the same reason I don't just open the lock using a charm. I don't want to tip him off or lose a lead by moving too quickly. If this recon doesn't work, I'll open the locker myself.

Liz clears her throat loudly. That's the signal. Someone's coming. Iris and I shuffle out the door as Liz grabs the handle and closes it.

Ms. Anderson rounds the corner. She's a tall red-haired woman with a floral tattoo sleeve. "Hiya!"

"Hi, Ms. Anderson. I was showing my friends my art," Liz announces before looping her arms around me and Iris and steering us down the hall. "Bye!"

I glance over my shoulder to see Ms. Anderson shaking her head, grin still plastered on her face. We race upstairs before she can ask questions.

"You seriously think Andie's boyfriend is involved?" Liz asks as we navigate around a group of girls showing each other pictures on their phones.

"It's possible," I reply.

"Have you told Andie?" Liz asks.

"Not yet."

"Tell him sooner rather than later, but *only* if you're sure his boyfriend's a criminal," Liz says.

"I'll do a deeper dive into Noah's social media to shore up a motive right now," I reply. "Liz, you coming?"

She shakes her head. "I have an assignment due at three. See you later, lovebirds."

Iris and I wave goodbye and find an open classroom to do some research into Noah. First, I quickly check the camera footage. So far, Ms. Anderson is putting away supplies while a girl works on her painting. No sign of anyone going to the locker.

I open my Instagram and navigate to Noah's posts, passing pictures of him and Andie at Bewitched Buns and drawings done in a similar style to the art on the playing card. He's tagged in photos from St. Mary's events like art night and a talent show, but there are no pictures at FGH. That'd be too obvious anyway.

Is he working with someone? He carpools with Taylor, Jude, and Daisy. Any one of them could be working with Noah. He's also dating Andie, but Andie wants nothing to do with the Bureau. Sure, he watches *Love Island*, which one could argue makes him invested in other people's relationships, but selling contraband is not his vibe.

I check the camera stream again. Adrenaline shoots through my veins, and I jerk upright. "Iris, look!"

Iris leans against my shoulder, her sweet floral scent making my head fuzzy. "Is that—"

"Jude."

Jude slips on a glove and then twists out the lock's combination. She looks over her shoulder. Iris and I tense when her gaze locks with the camera. She must not notice it, because a second later, she tugs off the lock and opens the door. She moves around what appear to be papers and books then grabs the cash and the playing card. She doesn't put anything inside before slamming the door shut and briskly walking off.

I jump to my feet. "Come on."

Iris and I rush out of the classroom and toward the basement.

"You're friends with Jude. Does she have any reason to sell the charm?" I ask as we race down the hallway.

"No way," Iris mumbles. "I mean, she's the only one of us who's never had a partner. Like, she's had crushes, but nothing's ever turned into a relationship. Even though she's beautiful and smart."

"Selling charms illegally certainly got the attention of the Bureau," I reply. Could she be helping other people get out of love ruts in her own misguided way?

We enter the hallway leading toward the stairs. The final bell rings, signaling the end of school. Students flood out of the classrooms, slowing us down. We weave between them and race to the basement.

Jude's nowhere in sight.

"I don't have any charms on me that will open the lock without completely breaking it. I need to find Devin. @Charmedlife33 should've messaged by now," I say.

Iris loops her arm around mine, and we head for the stairs. "Okay, update me when you get in. If I don't leave soon, my mom will start panic texting. She's been surprisingly chill about the whole being charmed thing. I thought for sure she'd try again to send an agent to bodyguard me," Iris says.

"Yeah, that would suck." My stomach churns, but I force a laugh. "So have you talked to Taylor?" I ask partly because I'm curious, but mostly to distract myself from the fact that I'm lying to Iris about one of the reasons I agreed to fake date her. I don't know if I can keep doing this.

"Yep. I called her yesterday, and she seemed really happy to talk to me and not at all that sad about Sean. I guess he was right. I've been neglecting my friends. I mean, clearly. I had no idea Jude was involved in your case."

"That's not on you, and she might not be. Maybe her investigation led her to the locker, same as us. It's not like recruits are sharing all their notes—we're too competitive. Maybe you should sit with them tomorrow during lunch. I think we've sold our relationship to the entire school by now."

"Just say you don't want to eat lunch with me," Iris teases. "You won't even miss me."

Against my better judgment, I reply honestly. "False. I'll really miss you." Iris watches me closely, her gaze warming my face. I clear my throat and step back. "Anyway, I won't keep you."

Iris smiles. "Later, Roe."

"Later," I mumble, watching her go.

Once I come to my senses, I shuffle farther down the hallway to Devin's locker, where he's packing his bag.

I lower my voice and ask, "Did @Charmedlife33 message you?"

"Nope," Devin replies.

"But it's three p.m."

He shrugs. "Maybe they're running late or someone spooked them. I gotta go, but I'll text you a screenshot if they send another message."

Devin closes his locker, then disappears into the throng of students, leaving me wondering whether Jude knew it was a setup or somehow tipped off the real culprit. I grab my camera from the art room, hoping there's useful footage I missed in the recording, then head home.

When I get there, the last person I expect to see is waiting for me.

"Monroe!" Mom jumps to her feet.

We look alike. Same short build, pouty lips, and dark eyes. But that's where our similarities end. In personality, I'm more like

Dad. We're both committed and steadfast in our love for the Bureau, despise shopping, and love planning. Mom is spontaneous and couldn't care less about magic. She's not a Mystic. She's a preschool teacher.

I drop my school bag onto the couch and cross my arms. "What are you doing here, Mom?" I don't like how gravelly my voice sounds. It gives away how I really feel. Hurt.

Mom rubs her hands together, an act that makes her appear nervous. "You haven't been returning my calls. You text, but it's so brief and we never nailed down a time for dinner."

"I've been busy." I glance over her shoulder and into the kitchen. "Is Dad here?"

"He's working. He knows I'm here. I was hoping we could catch up." She waves me over.

I stay put. "Catch up on what?"

Mom sighs as though I've disappointed her. "Monroe, you can't ignore me forever." She nods toward the table. "I brought your favorite, Mystic Pizza."

"I can't be won over with pizza," I complain, although I inch closer to the table, the cheesy goodness calling to me.

Mom holds up her hands. "Fine. Can you humor me at least? How's school? How's the Bureau?" Mom leans her elbow against the table so casually and comfortably, it hurts.

"Everything's fine," I mumble.

"Fine? Monroe, I'm your mother. I want to know about your life."

Seeing her reminds me of how everything has changed. She yanked the rug out from under me, and I haven't quite yet caught my footing.

"Sometimes parents get divorced. You do know I didn't leave because I didn't love you anymore, right? I simply couldn't make it work with your dad. I wanted you to come live with me. Still do, but I'm not going to force you."

I plop down into the closest chair and hug my arms around my knees. "Why didn't it work? Because you stopped going on dates? Was he, like, not romantic enough or something?" I don't think I remember a time when they did any of the things Iris and I have done in the past two weeks. Maybe that was the problem?

Mom shakes her head. "Love is more than dates, chocolate hearts on Valentine's Day, and 'I love you's. Those things are nice, and romance is definitely a part of relationship building, but alone, romantic gestures can't make a love last that isn't meant to be."

"How can romantic love not last?" I ask.

"Sometimes people grow apart. It isn't necessarily anyone's fault. People evolve and find they like different things than they once did."

"I never noticed you and Dad growing apart. You rarely fought."

"We didn't when you were home. We did our best to shelter you from the shifts in our relationship. Have you talked to Dad about this?"

I shrug. Dad's been putting on a brave face. I don't want to bring up anything that would hurt him, but it sounds like I don't have the full picture like I should.

"Love seems like a waste of time," I grumble.

Mom places a hand on my arm. "Not always. Your dad and I made great memories together, and best of all, we got you." She smiles.

"You have to say that because you're my mom."

"Doesn't mean it isn't true," she replies with a nudge.

I wouldn't know. The only thing I have to compare love with is a fake romance and my own budding relationship with the Bureau. I'm not even sure I have what it takes to be an agent.

"Please, don't be mad. I know the divorce has been hard on you," Mom says.

I exhale audibly. "I'm not *mad*. I don't get how love is worth the effort if it could all end anyway."

"That's a risk we all take, baby," she replies, patting my shoulder.

I shake my head. "Not me."

Mom sighs and turns the pizza box toward me. "Here. Have a slice."

She doesn't play fair. I can't resist how amazing it smells any longer. Reaching for a slice feels like a concession.

Mom nods encouragingly. "So is school good? Are you going to prom? Dad tells me you've been spending time with Iris James."

I tense at the mention of Iris. "We're . . . friends."

It's true. We *are* friends. Magic can't lie. No mishaps mean there's nothing between us. On the off chance that what I'm feeling for her is more than friendship, being a Mystic must keep mishaps at bay. Even if she feels the same, it can never happen. Iris wants romance, movie nights, and picture-perfect dates—all the things we did to fake a relationship. What if a real one doesn't match up to her expectations? What if I put myself out there for real and end up regretting it? I'm not one to set myself up to fail.

Twenty-one

On Tuesday morning, I arrive at the Bureau early for a check-in with Director James and the rest of the junior recruits. I'm wearing my crisply pressed Bureau suit rather than a borrowed, dank sweatshirt like last time. Luckily, junior recruits are only required to come to the office for briefings twice a month.

The Director is already in the conference room when I enter, furiously typing on her laptop. A sleep mask and a bonnet peek out of her open briefcase. *Does she sleep here?*

Taylor and Jude are here too. Taylor appears the same as usual, not at all like someone going through a breakup. When my parents got divorced, Dad had permanent shadows under his eyes and Mom's shoulders drooped like a weight hung around her neck. Even Andie stopped gelling his hair and lining his eyes for a month after his first boyfriend dumped him last summer. Maybe Taylor is fine because she finally admitted to herself that Sean wasn't her person.

"Something on my face?" Taylor asks in a clipped tone.

"Nothing," I reply.

Jude starts to laugh but quiets when I narrow my gaze. I'm itching to ask her about yesterday, but the Director never gives me the chance.

"All right. Let's get started. Monroe, why don't you kick us off? I'm assuming everyone has read your report, but why don't you tell the team what you've learned so far?" the Director asks.

All eyes turn to me. My hands are suddenly sweatier than a glass of ice in the summer. I clear my throat. Here's my chance to redeem myself from the debacle during our initial debrief two weeks ago.

"Okay. Well. I'm pretty sure everyone who's been charmed is connected, either by a friend or a friend of a friend. They're instructed to add a heart on their prom registration form and then are contacted on Instagram by a burner account called @Charmedlife33. Thanks to Devin Miller, we know FGH students receive a playing card with a number on the back for a locker that's located in Fair Glen High and are asked to pay fifty dollars in cash," I tell them.

"Do you think the culprit is a student at FGH?" the Director asks.

"Most likely. Since charms are being delivered during the school day, someone at St. Mary's would need to skip class or have an open period."

Taylor drums her pink nails against the table. "It could be a teacher or anyone in the community with access to a charm."

"The original charm was stolen from the Bureau, so only people with access to R&D could've gotten to it," I reply.

"And the same recruit was working on days residue was deposited. Noah Cham has been placed on probation," the Director says, all but confirming Noah might be compromised.

The table is silent while they process. Taylor shifts in her seat and says, "Anyone could've stolen a key card from Noah."

"Agreed. I also haven't seen a playing card circulating through St. Mary's. I think whoever has the charm is storing it at Fair Glen

High, but selling it to kids at both high schools," Reggie, the St. Mary's recruit, says.

It's true. And our town is so small, I'm sure there're multiple friend groups that overlap between our schools. Noah is proof of that. He's friends with multiple FGH students.

"Besides Diego, the others were charmed during a baseball game against FGH," Reggie continues.

Before the debrief, I reread Reggie's report of the baseball game mishap. I recognized Zeke's name since he's Sean's rival, but I wasn't familiar with Yesenia. I did a quick search of her name on Instagram and found a picture of her holding up a foam finger at a game. Sasha Gordon, the FGH softball player, was also charmed during practice.

The person giving out the charm might like sports or have a reason to attend games. They also attend a lot of school events. Sofia got her card at Promraiser, and Liam received his at Spellcast Roller. Noah was at the rink and at Illusion, but he wasn't at Promraiser. Jude wasn't at Spellcast Roller, but she was at the other events. What if they're working together for different reasons?

"Reggie, does Diego usually go to St. Mary's events?"

"Nah. He keeps his head down, only hangs out with his mathlete friends."

"Diego could be an outlier, then. Everyone else has way more school spirit. And since he's the first victim, Illusion could've been a trial run to see how the charm worked," I suggest.

Reggie runs a hand down his crisp fade. "It's possible."

"Okay, keep working at this, recruits. Fair Glen High's PTA wants to postpone prom, and I'm inclined to agree with them, though it's not up to me," the Director says.

Murmurs fill the room. Iris is going to be so disappointed if they end up not just postponing but canceling prom because of this. She's been working hard on the committee since before we started fake dating.

"Make sure you're working together," the Director continues. "Share ideas, compare notes—that's part of what it means to be a recruit. We'll check in again in two weeks. Good job, everyone."

I glance up from my notes once chairs stop screeching on the floors. It's only me and Jude left in the room. She seems to be reviewing notes too. I seize the opportunity to talk to her while we're alone. I want to hear her side of things before I show the Director the footage.

"Jude, can we talk?" I stand and close the conference room door for privacy. "I saw you at the locker. Are you selling the charm?"

Her jaw drops open. "No! I found out the locker is the pickup point for the charm."

"How?"

"You're not the only recruit working the case. I read your report on Chloe's mishap at Electric Dust. Chloe's in my homeroom, and when I saw she was no longer charmed, I asked her about it and whether anything new happened since Electric Dust. She told me about her and Daisy. I wrote an essay for Daisy last semester, so she owed me. I said we'd call it even if she told me what she knew. That's how I found the locker. Then I used this to open the lock."

Jude lifts a black shimmering glove out of her bag.

"Is that sanctioned?" A charmed object that can open any door must've been flagged as potential contraband because it's dangerous.

"Sure is," Jude replies, but I don't really believe her. She puts the glove away and slings her bag over her shoulder. "The locker had scratch paper, a playing card, and fifty dollars inside. No charms, though. Daisy must've been mistaken."

"I don't think so. Devin Miller led me to the locker too. Did you ask Daisy anything else, like how she heard about the charm?"

"I asked her if she knew who was dealing it, and she said no. Any specific questions you have, you'll need to ask her yourself."

I roll my eyes. "Fine. Let's check the locker once more. You must've missed something. Oh, and I want my fifty dollars back."

When we arrive at school, Jude and I immediately go to the art room. She slips the charmed glove over her hand and twists the combination lock on the locker. It pops open. Papers, books, and art supplies greet us.

"Told you. Nothing magical is in here," Jude says.

I can't believe this is a dead end. "Why have a lock and change the combination after each sale if the only thing in the locker is a bunch of books and pens? We must be missing something."

I toss aside the textbooks and supplies, running my hands along the shelf and the sides. The cold metal seems normal. I drop to my knees and peer underneath the locker. Nothing's there but dust. I start to stand, using the bottom shelf to push myself up, when I notice the shelf seems higher than my locker's. These aren't the same models, so maybe I'm tripping, but on the off chance I'm right, I check the locker next to this one to compare their structure. Sure enough, the bottom shelf is about two or three inches lower despite being the same make and model.

I feel along the top of the shelf and press. A flap folds down, revealing a shallow compartment. I think back to what Noah said: *It would only take up about a square foot.*

"Holy crap!" Jude exclaims, and at the same time I yell, "Yes!"

The chamber is full of vials of gold charm dust!

Along with the charms are four rounded selenite crystals. Stars are etched into the smoky white surface, and holes have been drilled through the centers so they can be strung together. The stars are imperfect, which makes me think someone made them themselves. Artsy Noah Cham, perhaps? Or Liam, who's been dodging me since Spellcast Roller, which obviously means he's guilty of something? Or even Jude, who's currently shifting on her feet? I snap a few pictures of the locker.

"Who are your suspects so far?" I ask. When Jude's lips pinch into a narrow line, I add, "Listen, the Director said we should work together at the debrief. Don't shut me out just because Taylor does. I won't report you and your glove if you talk to me."

I'm gambling about the glove being contraband. You can find similar charms not on the Bureau's radar at estate sales or in junkyards. I wouldn't be surprised if Jude is using contraband to get ahead if she's desperate enough, though. That's why she and Taylor make good friends.

Jude grumbles but says, "Fine. Liam O'Connor is at the top of my list. He works at Spellcast Roller and has been avoiding me. His parents are active agents, which gives him knowledge of charms and access to high-clearance ones. I'm still parsing out his motive."

Liam's parents are agents? He could've used their key cards to enter R&D and steal the charm, but Noah's card was used. Could it have been cloned? This locker previously belonging to Noah might be a coincidence.

"Should we tell the Director?" Jude asks.

"I'm texting her now." I send the Director the pictures I took of the locker. She replies almost immediately.

Director James: Excellent work! Bring them to R&D as soon as you can.

Grinning, I stuff everything that was inside the locker into my bag. Finally, a win.

I wait outside the cafeteria, mostly for Iris so I can walk her to class, but also for Daisy to ask her my lingering set of questions. I sift through the faces and see Daisy with her arm linked through Chloe's. It seems like Chloe has forgiven her or Daisy managed to convince Chloe that she didn't charm her. Either way, Daisy attempts to change directions when she spots me.

I catch her arm. "I know you charmed Chloe, and I know you told Jude about the locker in the art room." It's risky coming on so strong, but I need to catch her attention.

Daisy's widened eyes snap to mine. Chloe balks. "Daisy, you said you didn't!"

Well, there's the answer to that question.

Daisy winces. "I need to talk to Monroe. I'll catch up with you later."

"Daisy—"

"Later. I promise."

Chloe swears under her breath but walks away, disappearing into the crowd. I nod toward a quieter corner of the hallway so Daisy and I can talk.

She follows me and pinches the bridge of her nose. "You couldn't have waited? You might've sabotaged my chance to go to prom with her."

"You did that on your own, when you charmed her," I reply. "Now can you tell me how you got the dust?"

Daisy groans. "Whatever. It's not like I started this." She inhales slowly and says, "I was complaining to a few friends during pottery club about wanting to take Chloe to prom but not knowing if she'd go with me. The next week, a playing card was in my locker. I got an Instagram message with instructions shortly after that."

"From @Charmedlife33," I guess.

"Yep."

The culprit is smart. They've managed to stay anonymous and avoid any personal exchanges.

"Who's in pottery club with you?" I ask.

"It's new this year, so attendance varies. Ms. Anderson's our advisor. We meet in the art room."

A light bulb turns on in my brain. Maybe the locker isn't Noah's, but someone's in pottery club. I need to figure out who's gone to meetings.

I thank Daisy for the info before heading toward the cafeteria doors, where Iris holds a Diet Coke in one hand and half a sandwich in the other. My stomach growls.

"You didn't eat lunch, did you?" she asks, shoving the sandwich and pop into my hand. "There's more to life than the Bureau, you know."

I could kiss her. I shovel food into my mouth instead. "Like fake dating?"

Iris loops her arm through mine. "More than that too."

I glance at her. "What does that mean?"

She clears her throat and straightens her back. "Nothing."

"I'm not buying it, but I'll let it go for now because I have news. I found vials of the charm," I tell her, keeping my voice down.

Iris's mouth drops open. "Roe, that's awesome!"

I grin, a bubbly feeling running through me. "It really is. I still need to figure out who's the seller. Luckily, I got a lead from Daisy just now. Do you know anyone in pottery club?" I ask as we head toward her locker.

"Jude and Taylor suggested we go, but I don't know if they actually did. I didn't," Iris replies.

"I'll ask them. How was lunch?"

"Good. Taylor was happy to see me."

We stop in front of her locker. "No mishaps?"

"My Sprite sprayed everywhere like someone shook it right before I opened it. Does that count?" she asks, grabbing her books for next period.

"What happened before that?"

"Taylor suggested me, her, and Jude all go to prom together since they're both single now."

I finish off the sandwich she brought me and toss the wrapper into a nearby trash can. "Probably a coincidence."

"Figures. You wanna get ready together for Anita's party this Friday? You could come over after school." Iris says this casually, and yet she's fiddling with her braids and chewing on her bottom lip in a way I've come to associate with nerves.

"Sounds fun. Your mom won't mind?" I ask, thinking this might account for her worry.

"Nah. She'll be at the Bureau late, as usual," Iris replies.

"I did notice a bonnet in her briefcase this morning."

"She slept there last night. It happens sometimes, so she keeps a spare bonnet with her." Iris laughs, but it's as harsh as Fair Glen's winters.

"You know, if you wanted to spend time with her, I think she'd be down," I say. "She cares."

I wish I could tell Iris that her mom asked me to keep her safe. It's way too late to come clean now. Iris would feel like our entire relationship was just another assignment.

Iris crosses her arms. "You work one case with her and now you know her?"

"Not like you," I reply gently. "But I do think you could give her the chance to be more present."

"Is that what you're doing with your mom?" she asks.

"Actually, my mom came over yesterday. It honestly wasn't bad. I miss hanging out with her. I think I could cut her some slack. My parents' divorce isn't about me."

Iris sighs. "I guess I should probably do the same for mine."

Iris gifts me with a wave and a warm smile before walking into class. My stomach swoops traitorously.

Get it together, Roe.

The game's almost over. One wrong step, and we could both end up hurt by this love charm.

Twenty-two

The porch lights are on at the Jameses' house when I arrive at seven on Friday night. Anita's party is the last official event with Iris as a fake couple. I feel like I swallowed a bunch of rocks. I really don't want to stop hanging out with her. Maybe we could still be friends after all of this? If Anita isn't the jealous type.

Twilight settles around me in streaks of navy blue. The wind blowing through my open car window rustles my afro and promises a chilly night. I rummage in my bag for my phone, brushing aside the battery camera with a sigh. I watched the recording, and nothing, or rather no one, turned up besides Jude. The good news is, I dropped the vials of charm dust off at the Bureau after school on Tuesday. We're still missing some residue collections, but hopefully there is enough charm to start working on finding a dissolver.

I text Iris.

Here!

She replies with a voice note that says, "The door's unlocked. I'm upstairs."

I get out of the car and take her steps two at a time, a strange nervous jitter running through my legs. The welcome mat outside shudders when I step on it, and when I open the door, it nudges my feet and dumps me into the hallway as if to say *Get on with it.*

The first floor is open concept, so I can see the living room, dining room, and kitchen from the front door. The charmed objects don't stop at the rug. Her house is teeming with magical items. The record player in the living room plays the ultimate welcoming kickoff song, "My House" by Flo Rida. A flock of kitschy napkins circles me, inviting me into the kitchen before returning to a woven basket. There are snacks and water bottles on the island.

Upstairs, notes from a Billie Eilish song guide me to the last door on the left. Iris's room is bright and lived in. Purple polka-dot pillows are fluffing themselves on her bed. Posters from her favorite movies—*Pretty Woman* and *Clueless*—hang on the wall.

Iris sits on a furry white chair in front of a vanity, braiding her hair. She catches my eye in the mirror, and a bright smile lifts her face. "Hi."

"Hi."

We stare at each other for a beat before she seems to remember herself. "Sorry I didn't come get you. I was mid-braid when you texted."

Her hair, like the rest of her, is divine. She's glammed up her usual makeup, adding sparkling eyeshadow and bright red lipstick. The white sequined fringe dress that cinches at the waist hugs her frame perfectly. Combined with the small pearls strung along her collarbones and the shiny bracelets adorning her wrists, she fits the party's 1920s vibe perfectly.

Iris gestures at her outfit. "What do you think?"

"I—I like it," I stammer, and then immediately wish I'd fall through a hole in the floor. Could I be more ineloquent?

Iris doesn't seem to mind, though. "I thought you'd say that. I got you something to match." I shake my head and open my mouth to protest, but then she says, "Not a dress." She pulls something red from the plastic bag near her feet and holds it up. "I took a cue from *She's All That*."

"Another rom-com?" The sleek red vest she thrifted for me matches her lipstick perfectly. I slip my arms through and am not surprised to find it fits. It goes well with my black jeans, suspenders, and white shirt.

Iris beckons me closer. "Photo? Last one. For the fans." Even though she smiles when she says this, it doesn't reach her eyes.

"We'll still be friends," I tell her with a nudge, hoping it's true and not my own wishful thinking.

She rests her head on my shoulder, and I resist the urge to tug her even closer to me, trying to keep it friendly. I *do* inhale the sweet floral scent of her perfume. Her phone camera flashes. The picture looks more authentic than all the others combined.

"I have an update, as promised," I start, plopping down onto her bed. "Jude and I found a false bottom in the locker. She seemed shocked but not in the gotcha kind of way."

"Oh, clever. Can you get fingerprints from the locker?" Iris asks.

"Fingerprinting is a task for the police. The Director hasn't roped them in yet, but she might if more students get hurt."

The Bureau is the first call for magical mishaps, but occasionally, other government agencies are looped in for more large-scale, serious issues. Last spring, a water fountain in a park downtown started spurting coffee instead of water. What started out as free caffeine quickly turned into flooded streets and dying plants. The Department of Public Works had to be called to drain and repair the roads.

"You think they'll cancel prom?" Iris asks, laying down her edges.

"For my own sanity, I hope not. You and Andie will never let me hear the end of it," I reply with a small laugh.

While Iris finishes her hair, I scroll through Liam's Instagram. There are mostly photos of him with other FGH students like Anita, Taylor, and Devin. I stop when I reach a picture of him and Luna, the girl who charmed Diego at Illusion Salon. They both go to St. Mary's. Liam seems to have a large friend group.

"You figure something out?" Iris asks.

I raise my head. Iris has finished getting ready and is as bright and stunning as a roaring twenties movie star. Suddenly, I just want to enjoy her company. "Not really. Anyway, Operation Ace of Hearts can wait."

The corner of her mouth quirks. Her bed squeaks as she plops besides me. Her sweet scent and warmth lull me into a sense of peace.

"You know how I saw my mom this week? Well, I thought my parents fell out of love because they stopped doing romantic stuff together, but she said it was more than that. They grew apart. Apparently, there's more to love than romantic gestures."

A dimple appears between Iris's eyebrows. "Well, duh. Perfectly swoony moments can only carry a couple so far."

I exaggerate my gasp. "What have you done with the real Iris?"

She shakes her head. "I'm serious, Roe. All the dates we went on should have been perfect but ended in disaster, and yet, they were still . . . fun." Her eyes flick across my face.

"They were, but having fun and falling in love are two different things," I say, more to convince myself than her. "You and Anita did a lot of cute stuff together, but you genuinely fell for her. Your relationship was real."

Iris spins to face me fully, our knees pressing together. "What if perfect dates are the reason I thought Anita was perfect? What if she's right, and I was only in love with the idea of being with her? Maybe I *was* building it—her—up in my head."

"You weren't. We wouldn't be doing all of this if you didn't love her." Iris must be getting cold feet because we're so close to the finish line. She wants her ex back. She said so a few days ago.

"I guess," she mumbles.

We're sitting so close together, I can feel her body heat in my bones. She shifts to face me fully, and our hands brush together, spiking my heart rate. All I can think about is how utterly beautiful she is, so smart and resourceful and optimistic about love. I should look away. Better yet, I should get up and put some distance between us, but it suddenly feels like I'm glued to the bed.

I want nothing more than to kiss her right now. And the thought alone jolts me like a thousand volts. I can't give in to my desire for several reasons. *You don't like her*, I tell myself.

The distance between us seems to shrink. We're so close I can count her eyelashes as they flutter closed.

You don't want her.

Her breath ghosts against my mouth, sending a tingling warmth down my spine.

You're frien—

The blanket on her bed tangles around Iris's arms and yanks her back. I startle to my feet. Momentarily stunned, it takes another second for me to remember I'm a Mystic. I grab my necklace with one hand and the blanket with the other, quickly diffusing the charm.

Iris kicks off the blanket, huffing. "Was that . . ."

"A mishap," I confirm, my heart racing. So much for my theory that Mystics are immune to the love charm. Why haven't we had a mishap before now? I've been crushing on Iris for a while. "Are you okay?" I ask.

Iris nods. Her face is flushed, and her dark eyes blink rapidly.

I feel so visible under her gaze, like she can see the fluttery panic rising inside me. She asks, "Were you going to kiss me?"

Jesus, I could die. I force a laugh. "No. *No.* I might've been about to hold your hand or something equally dumb," I lie, rubbing my face to dispel the heat. I could've sworn I had everything under control. "It was a momentary lapse in judgment. It won't happen again."

"Oh," Iris replies, her brows dipping together. "But I—"

"Maybe we shouldn't fake date anymore," I blurt out.

Now Iris looks panicked, likely because she hasn't gotten with Anita yet. She fidgets with her braids. "That was a tiny mishap. We can get through a party, at least."

I want to push back but get lost in the depths of Iris's gentle brown gaze like a simp. "All right," I concede, despite feeling like this last hurrah will be easier said than done.

Twenty-three

Anita lives in a big brick house on the edge of town with a perfectly sheared lawn, trimmed foliage, and a flagstone walkway. The thumping bass of a hip-hop song plays loud enough to hear inside Iris's parked car. Girls in sparkly dresses stand outside taking selfies while a group of boys in bow ties and top hats point as their rhythmless friend tries to dance on beat. The music seems to laugh with the friends—a trumpet blares notes that sound like *ha, ha, ha*.

I nod toward where Daisy and Chloe are arguing in the driveway.

"Is it weird that the charm supposedly finds love matches, but Daisy wasn't even honest with Chloe?" I ask.

"Maybe their relationship started off as a lie, but they truly are meant for each other," Iris suggests.

"Maybe." I unbuckle my seat belt and desperately try not to apply her theory to us. "Ready?"

Iris nods, and we climb out of the car. When she reaches out, I slip my hand into my pocket before our fingers touch. Her responding frown sends a wave of guilt crashing over me, but I'd rather be safe than sorry.

The cobblestone walkway flashes bright pink and purple as we approach the house.

"Priority number one is finding Liam," I say.

"Always working, even at a party," Iris says.

I fiddle with the buttons of my vest. "I'm going to get answers. I can feel it. I don't want to lose momentum."

Iris gently stills my hand with her own. "I was joking. I like that you're focused, Roe." That traitorous warmth in my chest blooms at her kindness. I snuff it out by thinking of the deal I made with her mom. Iris wouldn't think so highly of me if she knew I've been lying by omission. I should remind myself of that whenever I feel like we're getting too close.

We squeeze past a couple making out by the door to get into the party. As we wade through the mass of sweaty teens, I can't tell what smells worse, the cheap cologne or the BO. Most people have dressed for the theme, although a few are in regular clothes, too, clearly not reading the memo or not caring. Black and silver streamers hang from the ceiling, a strobe light flashes around the living room, and balloons are taped to the walls, charmed to change shapes. One second they're ovals and the next they're hearts.

Iris leads us deeper inside the house. She's totally in her element, waving at a few girls on prom committee. Surprisingly, I recognize people here too. Sofia Vargas is sulking in the corner with a group of teens in all black. Taylor's laughing with Jude near a twinkling record player, which might explain how the music seems to react to the vibe of the party. People nod when they spot me and Iris like we're a popular couple.

In the kitchen, there's a line for punch. A boy ladles some into his Solo cup and those of his five friends. The amount of punch in the bowl constantly refills. The glass shimmers faintly with pink dust. Endless bowl charm. A fan favorite for parties.

"Anita's family owns Conjurer's Corner, right? Are you sure there aren't unapproved charms floating around? It's more common than you'd think," I say, thinking of the defective sponge Dad's client bought and Jude's gloves.

Should Anita be a suspect? She does have access to charms and crystals. *But* not the Bureau—unlike Liam and Jude—so it'd be difficult for her to steal the collections from our archives. Besides, why would Anita charm Iris, who's made it clear she wants Anita back? Unless Anita had her eye on someone else, even though that's insane because Iris is . . . Iris. Who wouldn't want her?

"I know the Patels. They aren't selling contraband," Iris says, handing me a cup of punch.

I take a sip and gag. There's so much sugar in the juice I can feel cavities forming. The slightly bitter aftertaste confirms it's spiked. I set my cup on the counter. I can't do my job if I'm tipsy.

Iris guides us back through the living room, where a ton of people are now dancing to Kendrick Lamar. Hugging the wall is a girl who looks a lot like Yesenia Rodriguez, the St. Mary's junior who was charmed along with Zeke Hart at the baseball game.

While Iris greets a few students on prom committee with her, I take the chance presented to me.

"I'll be right back," I tell her.

Yesenia pouts when I approach and show my badge. She says, "I already talked to Reggie. Besides, we're at a *party*."

"I can multitask. Can you think of anything you didn't tell Reggie? Like a description of anyone suspicious."

Yesenia sips her drink. "Someone wearing an FGH baseball hat and sunglasses knocked into me at the game, but I didn't see their face."

"Were they tall? Short?" I ask.

"They were shorter than me and had a slim build. After they

bumped into me, I grabbed my boyfriend's hand and the bench I was standing on collapsed. People thought it was a freak accident until Zeke lost control over his bat a few minutes later. A couple Mystic parents saw all the dust on me."

That description rules out Jude, who's taller than most of the boys in our grade, but Yesenia is equally tall, so it's not saying much. "Are you sure?" I ask.

"Positive."

But before I walk away, I ask, "Are you and your boyfriend still together?"

She snorts. "I found out he was cheating on me a couple of days later, so no."

"I'm sorry."

Yesenia shrugs and resumes drinking her punch. "Love sucks."

See?

I thank her and search the crowd. Despite Iris's initial theory that the love charm could be defective, the stuff hasn't been wrong yet.

Iris is right where I left her, chatting with her prom committee friends. A bushy-haired boy who seems to be around five foot seven leaves the kitchen carrying a Solo cup.

"Liam!" I yell over the music.

The boy turns, and relief fills me when I realize he is indeed Liam. I rush over to him. "You're harder to find than Carmen Sandiego."

"I don't know who that is," Liam deadpans.

"Context clues, dude. You've been avoiding me like I'm personally doling out suspensions."

Liam inclines his head. "Sofia got one, and she didn't deserve that. She only had a crush on someone who wouldn't give her the time of day."

"Is that what happened with you and Kenny?" Liam bristles, and his eyes get all wide and shiny. I soften my stance, familiar with this flavor of gay panic. "Liking anyone is hard, especially when you're queer and your crush isn't. What I don't understand is why you'd charm Kenny at Spellcast Roller and then flee the scene."

Liam's eyes clear as some of the fear leaves him. "Kenny and I are friends. He doesn't know I'm bi. Not many people do. That's why I've been hiding from you. Buying a charm wasn't about prom for me. I only wanted a fair chance with him. I had no idea his roller skates would freak out."

"Who told you about the charm? Daisy? She used the charm right before you." Sofia never got a card but did steal some dust from Daisy.

Liam sucks on his teeth. "No one. I overheard Daisy talking about it in homeroom. And I DM'd the account myself."

"Who do you think is behind it?"

Liam shrugs. "Someone willing to exploit people trying to find love. I was told there'd be no consequences. I can prove it."

He grabs his phone and shows me a message from @Charmedlife33: I tested the charm myself this semester. It's safe. Are you in?

Wait. This is huge! My pulse races as I think through the possibilities. What if earlier tests all led to real love matches but the first reported mishap was at Illusion? I bet the seller was there to see if the charm worked. They were also at the baseball game against St. Mary's wearing an FGH hat. That leaves Luna Le, the salon owner's daughter; Noah; Taylor; Anita; or Iris. Luna's been abroad. Anita doesn't have direct access to the Bureau and has no real motive. That narrows it down to Noah, Taylor, or Iris (please no).

Noah needs the money for Northwestern. We've yet to confirm whether the use of his old locker is a coincidence. I wouldn't put it past Taylor to stir up trouble at our school, only to "solve it" and get promoted to junior agent. Plus, she *does* carpool with him. Are they working together? As for Iris, I highly doubt she'd charm herself, especially since she seemed genuinely surprised the day I told her she had gold dust all over her. Unless she charmed herself by accident . . .

I'm practically shaking by the time I find Iris talking to Taylor outside on the patio. Even though it's barely spring, the built-in pool is uncovered, revealing shimmery blue water charmed to dance in crisscrossing designs like a fountain. Anita's leaning against the railing twirling a lock of shiny black hair around her finger while she glances at Iris, who waves me over. It's hard to disregard the fiery heat of jealousy raging through my veins.

I want to question all of them immediately—mostly Taylor, who seems annoyed to see me—but just when I open my mouth, my phone rings. My heart drops at the name on the screen.

Incoming Call: Director James

Iris stares. "Why is my mom calling you?"

"Um. There's probably an update on the case." I'm lying again, and it makes me sick. *She could also be lying to you*, my mind supplies traitorously.

"She hasn't called Taylor," Iris notes.

I attempt to keep my voice light. "Maybe she will after this?"

The call goes to voicemail, which does nothing to help my nerves. I'll find a quiet spot to call the Director back later.

Incoming Call: Director James

"She's calling again?" Iris asks, her face twisting with confusion.

"I—I should answer this." I jump down from the patio and onto the spongy grass, shooting Iris an apologetic look over my shoulder. Desperately, I search for a place to take this call that won't have Megan Thee Stallion rapping in the background.

I settle on a spot beneath a tree in the corner of the yard facing the neighboring house and answer on what is likely the last ring. "Hello?"

"Monroe! Finally. Is Iris with you? She's not at home or answering my texts." The Director sounds frantic on the other end of the phone, worry clipping her vowels.

"She's with me. We're at Anita's house," I reply.

"Anita? Her ex-girlfriend? I must be missing something."

"I think they're friendly again." The words ring true but leave a bitter taste in my mouth that I swallow down. "She must've forgotten to mention it."

"Must have," the Director says carefully, like she's trying to make sense of the words.

"I'll have her home by eleven. She's safe. I'm watching out for her, like you asked."

"Good. Thanks, Monroe."

The Director hangs up, and I slump against the tree with a sigh.

"You're watching out for me, huh?"

I spin around to find Iris standing next to me, her arms crossed and a dark expression on her face.

"Why'd you tell my mom that, Roe? Why is she even calling you on a Friday night?" The suspicion in Iris's voice, coupled with the deepest frown, stills me. My first instinct is to lie, but I've done enough of that. "Tell me the truth," she demands.

I inhale deeply and steel myself for her response. "Your mom asked me to keep you safe. She was worried about there being more mishaps."

"So this"—she gestures between us—"was about the Bureau the entire time. What'd she promise you? A guaranteed spot in the agency next year?"

When I look away, she gasps. "Are you for real right now?"

Taylor chooses this exact moment to walk over, her lips pinched to the side, and Anita joins her, a little less sure in her steps but still seemingly curious.

I swallow hard. "Can we talk about this somewhere else? I'll explain everything—"

"No." Iris's hands tremble at her sides. "We can talk right here."

I work my jaw as I try to salvage this and lower my voice. "Fine. Yes. I was offered a spot on a task force this fall for junior agents if I protected you."

A bitter laugh escapes Iris's lips. I hate the sound. "So *that's* why you really agreed to date me," she says slowly. "It wasn't to save a bunch of people with crushes. It was to help your own career."

"No. *No.* It was partly for the case, but I also thought dating you was the best way to stay close without you becoming suspicious of me or your mom."

"So I was a mark. You *used* me."

I scoff. "*You* used *me* too. I know I lied about protecting you, but Iris, our *whole* relationship was a lie so you could win back Anita. Maybe she was right, and you've been watching and reading too many romances. You've been playing with people's emotions. I only wanted to keep everyone safe."

Iris steps back, her eyes watery with unshed tears. *Shit.* I reach for her, but she turns and runs toward the house. She disappears through the French doors a second later. Anita glances between me and Taylor before following Iris in a huff. Taylor shoots me the dirtiest look, and then she's hot on their heels.

I shake off my stupor and run after them.

Twenty-four

My heart is beating so hard it feels like it might leap out of my chest. Iris is nowhere in sight as I push through the swarm of dancing, drinking, and laughing bodies. The air is stale and hot inside; the rooms are both too large and not large enough.

I catch a glimpse of boho braids and smooth brown skin turning the corner, the silky strands of Anita's hair right behind her. I sidestep a boy footworking, and then an arm juts out and stops me in my tracks.

Taylor. She shakes her head, lips pinched like she swallowed a lemon. "Let Iris cool off first."

"I need to apologize." I knock Taylor's arm out of the way. She moves, blocking me in with a wall on my left and a horde of partygoers on my right.

"She can be hotheaded. A little overdramatic," she says.

"I don't think Iris is being overdramatic. I messed up, and I need to explain myself."

"Trust me. Give her a few minutes," Taylor presses.

I cross my arms. "And why should I trust you? You've only seen me as competition."

Taylor rolls her eyes. "That was about work. This is about my best friend. She's not going to be happy that you lied to her."

"I didn't outright lie, I just . . . didn't tell her everything." I should've told Iris the truth the moment we started getting close. I was scared she wouldn't want to stay friends, that she'd question whether our conversations would stay between us. Which they have.

"The Director isn't calling the rest of us on the weekends. I can't believe you pulled something behind Iris's back for a leg up. Do you even like her, or have you been playing her this entire time?"

"I do like her, not that it's any of your business," I snap.

I'm not listening to her for another second. Again, I attempt to go around Taylor, but every step I take she's right there like an annoying little cousin. Finally, I manage to brush past her.

"You weren't a good fit for her, anyway!" Taylor calls after me.

I ignore her and continue moving through the party. I check the front lawn, where there's a group of people making reels, the kitchen, and the line for the bathroom. My last resort is checking the bedrooms.

It's quiet upstairs, the music and chatter muffled and distorted. Voices filter through an open door at the end of the hallway followed by Iris's watery laugh.

I don't mean to tiptoe or eavesdrop. I mean to run to Iris and make an impassioned speech about how I was wrong to keep a secret from her and will never do it again, and yet the dread of what Iris could be doing in a bedroom with Anita makes me clammy and slow.

Through the crack in the door, I see Iris sitting on the bed. Anita stands in front of her, one hand resting against the bed frame, photographs of her and her friends on the wall behind them. Anita's other hand is cupping Iris's chin. She leans in and—

I spin on my heel and run. I can think of nothing else except getting away. The hallway is blurry as I head toward the stairs, and it's only when something wet hits my cheek that I realize, in horror, I'm crying.

I swipe at my eyes. I'm not actually dating Iris, so it's not like she's betraying me. In fact, she's getting exactly what she wanted. Our scheme worked. I held up my end of the bargain. Success shouldn't feel this shitty, though.

A tumultuous rattle that isn't part of the music seems to bleed into the floorboards, vibrating against the soles of my feet. I draw up short. Someone screams. No, not someone. Iris.

My blood freezes into icy slush. I race back upstairs to Anita's room, my heart lodged in my throat. I reach the open door in time to see Iris being tossed into the air like a ragdoll. The bed stops shaking—the source of the rumbling—and a second later Iris hits the ground with a sharp cry of pain.

Anita scrambles against the far wall. She stares with her mouth open at the scene in front of her.

"Anita, get help!" I yell.

She snaps out of her frightened daze and runs for the door. I drop to my knees and crawl over to Iris, who's curled on her side.

"Iris, are you okay? I'm *so* sorry."

She rolls onto her back with a groan. Her brows are pinched together, her breath labored, and her arm is cradled against her chest.

"Say something," I plead.

The floorboards creak as someone runs into the room.

"What happened?" Taylor asks, jogging over to us. She nudges me aside. "You good, Iris?"

Iris shakes her head with a grimace. "My arm."

My breath catches in my throat. I can't bring myself to move from my spot on the ground as Taylor does what I wish Iris would let *me* do: loop her arms under her and help her stand.

"I've got you," Taylor whispers.

"Iris . . ." I trail off as they pass me.

Iris leans heavily against Taylor's shoulder. They stop briefly. Iris's mouth twists in a grimace. Her gaze is cloudy with pain. I start to apologize or offer to take her to the hospital or tell her about the strange tightness in my chest and ask her what that means, but she shakes her head, sharp and quick. Her disappointment is as visible as the charm dust shimmering on her face.

And then she's out the door.

I clean up the residue as fast as I can and then head to the hospital. We aren't a couple, but I've sat through enough of Iris's favorite rom-coms to know you chase after the girl. Since Iris drove us to the party, I'm without a car, but I do have a bus pass. I catch the line heading through town and Google Maps the correct stop for the Fair Glen Medical Center. The entire ride, there's a scratchy feeling in the back of my throat, and my leg won't stop bouncing.

When the bus reaches my stop, I fling myself from the seat and sprint across the street. The hospital's sliding doors open, revealing dozens of faces waiting for help. None of them are Iris.

I jog toward the check-in station, where a nurse in scrubs peers up, her eyes droopy with fatigue. "I'm looking for Iris James. There was an accident at a party, and she hurt her arm. She was brought in maybe twenty or thirty minutes ago?"

The nurse sighs and clicks her mouse. "Second floor. You'll need a visitor's badge—"

I'm gone before she can finish her sentence, opting for the stairs rather than waiting for the elevator. The hallway smells like a mix of ammonia and bleach. Everything is so white it's blinding.

I turn the corner and stop in my tracks when I see Director James in casual clothes. A heavy weight seems to press down on her, bowing her shoulders and neck.

"Director!"

"Monroe?"

"Is Iris okay?" I ask as I approach her, feeling my anxiety spike.

The sigh, coupled with the unyielding crease in her forehead, tells me everything I need to know. "She has a fractured radius and is in quite a bit of pain. She'll need a cast," the Director replies, her voice shaky in a way I've not heard before. "Taylor explained what happened when I got here, but I'd like to hear your side of the story."

Through the exam room window, I spot Iris sitting on the stiff hospital bed while a doctor wraps her arm. I'm the reason Iris got hurt. I got distracted by all the pesky feelings in my chest and lost sight of my job to keep her safe. This is further proof that romance is a trap.

"I'm sorry, Director. I only took my eye off her for a moment," I say.

The Director shakes her head. "This was an accident. You couldn't have watched out for her every second. That's too big of an ask, especially for a junior recruit."

"Well, it shouldn't have been too big, considering they're dating. Or were."

My stomach drops to my knees. Taylor's standing right behind us, holding two cups of steaming coffee and sporting her typical smirk.

The Director narrows her gaze in my direction. "What do you mean, dating?"

"I—I . . . well, not *dating*—"

"You've been telling everyone you're a couple for weeks," Taylor says hotly.

The Director stiffens. "Monroe, is that true?"

A bead of sweat slides down my spine despite the frigid hospital air. My rapid heartbeat pounds in my ears, nearly drowning out the hum of the fluorescent lights, the creak of opening doors, and nurses paging doctors over the intercom system.

"It was fake," I blurt out. "It wasn't real. We were pretending to make Anita jealous. Iris asked for my help, and I figured I could keep a better eye on her if I said yes. But I promise, Director, I would never—"

"So you *don't* like Iris?" Taylor interrupts.

"I . . . No. We're friends."

Someone clears their throat. We all turn to find the doctor who was checking out Iris standing in the doorway holding a clipboard. The door to Iris's room is open, and to my absolute horror, fresh tears stream down Iris's face. She heard me. Can the floor crack open and swallow me already?

"Mrs. James?" There are deep bags under the doctor's eyes, and her graying curls are a sign of how hard she works. "I've finished wrapping your daughter's arm. I'm going to grab an info packet, and then I'd like to go over what to expect in the coming weeks."

"Okay, thank you," the Director replies. Once the doctor has gone, she turns a disappointed stare on me. "I asked you to watch Iris's back, not date her. Or pretend to. You've blurred the lines between professional and personal."

I drop my gaze to the linoleum flooring, not finding it in me to come up with an excuse. "Am I off the case?"

"You're too close to this, recruit," the Director replies. "I think it'd be best if you took a step back."

Hearing those words stings as much as the tears welling behind my eyes. I look up and lower my voice. "And the recommendation for junior agent?" I ask.

"We'll see. I need to know you're still focused."

"I am," I reply.

The doctor returns and gestures for the Director to follow her inside Iris's room.

"We'll talk more later," the Director says before entering the room. She closes the door behind her.

"Go home, Monroe," Taylor says.

I almost forgot she was here. I ignore her. My body is heavy with guilt while I watch the doctor instruct Iris on how to care for her arm. Iris doesn't look at me.

Once the doctor is done, she exits the exam room, followed by the Director, who makes her way to the nurses' station, likely to handle discharge paperwork. Iris emerges from the room a moment later, her arm in a sling and her face wet.

My stubborn feelings for her swell until I feel I might burst. I can't pretend she doesn't mean anything to me anymore. I don't *want* to. The last time I ran away from my feelings, Iris got hurt. "Iris—"

"Don't." The word lances through my side like a dagger, and all the hope I had of fixing this bleeds out. "Just leave me alone, Monroe. We're done."

Twenty-five

I catch the bus to the Bureau to drop off the residue. I wait until the technician processes it, and then promptly head home in a daze. The words "we're done" replay in my mind. I feel off-balance, and I can't keep my thoughts from veering to Iris. I'm so unfocused I miss my stop and have to walk four blocks back home, cold air nipping at my face. I feel like I'm in a nineties R & B music video. All that's missing is some rain.

I get home right before curfew and find Dad in the living room watching TV.

"Hi, honey!" he calls to me. "How was the party?"

"Fine," I mumble, breezing past him and practically running for the stairs.

His frown is unmistakable. The worried expression on Dad's face promises a long conversation, but for now luck is on my side, and he doesn't stop me.

Once I'm in my room, I gracelessly drop onto my bed, my body feeling heavier than a semitruck full of bricks. My gaze snags on the investigative board, and for the hundredth time, I try to make sense of the clues. But trying to work on Operation Ace of Hearts has the opposite effect of clearing my head. All I can see are the cute little hearts Iris drew in the corners of my whiteboard that night we watched rom-coms. She's found a way to ingrain herself into every aspect of my life, and I can't picture her anywhere else. I want her and now she's gone.

I throw the covers over my face so I won't be tempted to look at those hearts anymore. I resurface only when my phone buzzes. I check the notification. Someone tagged me in a comment on Instagram. I open the app and find myself staring at a photo of Iris with her arm in a pink cast, the caption reading: partied too hard tonight.

My stomach twists as I read the comments.

Where's your knight in shining armor **@JustRoe17**?

Prolly trouble in paradise

Noooo

I start to reply but decide it's better to text Iris directly.

Hi. I am so sorry about today . . . for not telling you everything and for the mishap. I should've been there. Can you forgive me?

When twenty minutes pass and there's no answer, I send her another text.

Please respond.

At some point, I fall asleep watching *Love Don't Cost a Thing*, a movie Iris recommended, while waiting for a reply that never comes.

When I wake on Saturday morning, the drama of last night comes flooding back the moment my gaze lands on my phone. Hope blazes through my veins as I check my messages. It fizzles out a second later when I see Iris still hasn't replied, but I do have ten unread texts.

Mom: Hi honey! Do you have plans this weekend? Perhaps we can get together?

No plans tomorrow . . .

Getting kicked off a case and losing a friend in one fell swoop warrants at least one day of wallowing.

Mom: I'll stop by then 🙂

I like her message and then check the rest of my unread texts.

Andie: how was the party?

Liz: Yes tell us all about life as a popular kid!

Andie: she's probably asleep on Anita's front lawn

Liz: Or with Iris 👀

Andie: Roe, are you alive?

Andie: HELLO

Liz: Answer your phone or we're sending out a search party!

Andie: ok that's it. we're coming over

The doorbell rings ten minutes later, and the automated voice announces that Liz and Andie have arrived. I check my appearance in the mirror. It looks like I got into a fight with a pack of hungry raccoons. I throw on a semi-clean T-shirt, slip on a beanie to hide my bed head, and greet my friends.

"She lives!" Andie says, holding up a half-eaten bag of tortilla chips.

Liz sits on the floor by my bed with a bowl of avocado dip between her ankles. "Wild night?"

I fall back onto my bed with a sigh. "I'd rather talk about anything else."

"Okay. When were you going to tell me that Noah is your prime suspect?" Andie asks. "I was tempted to withhold the chips and avo dip, but Liz made a good argument on the way over that I should hear you out first. You seriously think I have such poor taste in guys that I'd date a criminal mastermind?"

Okay, maybe not anything else.

"No. I'm sorry." I pick at the edge of my comforter. "But Noah has the means and opportunity. He works in Research and Development, and his old locker at FGH is being used to store the charm. Did you know he went to our school?"

Andie raises his eyebrow. "When?"

"Freshman year, before you moved here," I reply.

"Okay . . . I didn't know that, but maybe because it never came up. Look, Noah didn't do this, Roe, and my reason is gonna sound flimsy, but believe me . . . he's really not the type to go rogue. He's lawfully good and would never risk his job at the Bureau. He loves working there and keeping Fair Glen safe from magic misfortunes as much as you do."

"That's not enough. I need evidence or an alibi or—"

"When do you think he's been selling the charm?" Andie asks.

I level my gaze. "You can't claim an alibi for him because you think it will get him off my suspect list."

He shrugs. "I can try. Tell me."

"During school."

"Oh, then he's for sure innocent! Neo wouldn't skip class. He's a total rule-follower," Andie replies. "He starts sweating whenever I jaywalk."

It's not enough to let Noah off the hook. Our schools are only ten minutes apart in drive time. He was also working every time charm residue was deposited but not logged at the Bureau. The Director confirmed that herself during the last check-in. Still, I let Andie have the win. The last thing I want to do is argue. "That's . . . helpful."

"Mm-hm. See, if you'd come to me earlier, I could've proved his innocence sooner."

I load a chip with dip. "You're right. My bad."

Andie waves me off. "It's fine. Love makes us all a little insane sometimes."

I choke on the chip, avocado spewing on the carpet. "Love? Iris and I aren't . . ." I inhale deeply. "Our relationship wasn't real."

Telling my friends the truth should feel like a weight lifted off my shoulders. I hated lying to them. Instead, I'm strangely sad.

"What are you talking about?" Liz asks with a frown.

I explain the arrangement Iris and I came up with, relaying

our parameters and what we both got out of it. All the while, my friends quietly munch on chips and dip and occasionally react to the bombshell I'm dropping with a raised eyebrow or a quiet hum.

"Fake dating? Like the romance trope?" Liz asks.

"It may have started off fake, but y'all are for real into each other. The pull between you two is plain as day," Andie replies.

"Iris doesn't like me back. There was a mishap yesterday when we were alone. And I basically saw her kissing Anita."

"Basically?" Andie asks.

"They were leaning in and a second away from making out when I ran," I tell them, a sour taste forming in my mouth. "They're probably already back together."

Andie and Liz share a look, and then Andie grabs his phone. "You need to see something," he says.

He navigates to Anita's Instagram. The newest post is a picture of her and Devin Miller, who's holding up a floral-themed sign asking her to prom. I stare at the two of them, trying to make sense of what I'm seeing.

"I don't know what you saw, but Iris and Anita aren't a thing," Andie says matter-of-factly. "Anita is going with Devin to prom. As friends, but still."

"What? All Iris wanted to do was get back with Anita. That's why we fake dated."

"Maybe something changed her mind," Andie replies.

"Or some*one*." Liz shoots a pointed glance in my direction.

Could Iris really like me back? No. How else do I explain the mishap? Besides, I can't be that oblivious. I would've noticed. I'm a Bureau recruit. Paying attention to detail is part of my job.

"You should talk to her," Liz says. "Tell her how you feel."

"So she can reject me? That's why I don't *do* love. It's not worth the heartache."

"It might not end in heartache. You can't predict the future," Andie says.

"Take things one step at a time. Apologize and see how she feels," Liz suggests.

"I guess I can do that," I mumble. "Although, I doubt Iris wants anything to do with me now." I lied to her. She has every right to shut me out.

"It'll work out," Andie tells me.

This isn't one of Iris's rom-coms, so it might not. But I'm starting to wonder if that's the whole point. Even if a relationship fails, at least I tried to get a happy ending.

Twenty-six

After Andie, Liz, and I finish off the chips, we have a gay revival pretending to walk the runway while *Pose* plays on my laptop. By the time they leave, my mood has significantly improved, enough to venture into the living room. I find Dad sitting on the couch, a bowl of salt water in front of him already purifying a few of his more well-loved crystals, like his quartz ring and tourmaline necklace. After, he'll recharge them in his cleanser. When I was younger and he was still working at the Bureau, I'd help him. I was so eager to soak up any knowledge I could. Now I have my own crystals to recharge and my own case to solve. It's funny how things change so fast.

"Are you going to tell me what's wrong, or do I have to pry it out of you?" Dad asks, patting the space next to him.

My family never was the type to ignore our issues, always speaking up and working through the problem, which is why me avoiding Mom has been so unusual.

"I messed up," I tell him. "The Director gave me an assignment, and I failed. Iris got hurt because of me."

Dad taps his fingers against his thigh in thought. "Did I ever tell you about my first case at the Bureau? Contraband was being sold at a resale shop, and I lost some of the dust we collected. I thought for sure I was getting fired, but I found another way to get the evidence we needed. Laura—the Director—was my partner on that case. She'll understand. She knows this line of work is hard. Is Iris going to be okay?"

"She has a broken arm."

"Ouch. I know it seems bad, but you're only a recruit. Mistakes happen. It's part of the job and life."

I drop my head against the back of the couch. "I know, but I like her, Dad."

He snorts. "That much was obvious, kid."

I roll my eyes. "I haven't been honest with her or myself about how I feel."

"If there's one thing I've learned over the years of being with your mom, it's that it's always best to be honest, even if you're scared of how the person will respond," he says.

I mull over his advice while I dip my quartz necklace into his cleanser. My situation sounds a lot like Operation Ace of Hearts. Students were promised a magic charm to make their crush like them back, but the charm only prevented the wrong people from falling in love. Even if a person turned out not to be a match for their crush, at least they tried to find love. It's not okay to risk hurting someone for your own gain, but taking no risk at all only hurts yourself.

I've spent the past few weeks pretending my feelings for Iris aren't real because I was terrified of something good ending horribly, yet my actions only pushed her further away.

"Why did you and Mom separate?" I ask, my voice barely above a whisper. "It was so sudden."

Dad sighs. "We'd been having problems for a while, honey. I'm glad we were able to keep much of the fallout from you. Your mom wanted me to retire from the Bureau years ago. She thought I worked too much. I think the separation was the first time I really understood where she was coming from. Being an agent required a lot of me. I was ready to leave when I did, but by then, the damage to our relationship had already been done."

I sit with that, thinking of how many nights growing up were just me and Mom. And then a picture of Iris doing the same thing with her dad when he was still alive comes to mind. I don't want work to be the only thing I live for. And I like that Iris has taken up real estate in my head.

"Say I get the courage to tell Iris how I feel. What if she doesn't want to be with me? Or what if she does and it all goes sideways like—"

"Like me and your mom?" Dad guesses. His sigh is heavy. "You know parents aren't perfect, and neither is their love. No relationship is, really, but that's part of the beauty of it. Love is rediscovering and coming together stronger. Sometimes it works out. Sometimes it doesn't. It might not last forever, but love is worth experiencing."

I pull my legs up and rest my head on my knees. "I don't know . . ."

"Look at it this way. The Bureau wasn't a sure shot, but you still went for it, right? You love magic and helping people enough to give it a real chance. There's no guarantee you'll be a junior agent in the fall, but that didn't stop you from becoming a junior recruit, did it?"

"No. I guess not."

"Exactly," Dad says. "The chance at something great is worth the risk of failure, love included."

"Isn't that different? You were heartbroken after the divorce."

"Yes, but I don't regret being with your mom. And I want to give love a chance again one day with someone new."

"You do?"

Dad nods. "Love is worth the potential heartache. If you could go back in time and never be friends with Iris, would you? Was nothing you did this month memorable?"

"All of it was," I reply. And suddenly, the conversation I had with Mom begins to make a lot of sense.

Dad nods like this is the answer he'd been expecting. "Then I say go for it. Tell her how you feel. It can't get worse. You might even be surprised by her response."

"In a good way, right?"

Dad grunts. "Here's hoping. I hate seeing you mope."

" 'Mope' is a strong word."

"I almost called your mom."

I laugh. "We're actually hanging out tomorrow."

"Oh?" Dad plucks our crystals from the cleanser and lays them out to dry on a paper towel.

"We're . . . trying." Since her impromptu visit, I've been replying to her texts. I've missed her more than I realized. The divorce is still a tender bruise on my spirit, but pushing Mom away won't make it heal faster.

Dad smiles. "Glad to hear it. Now go win back your girl."

But first . . . to the salon.

"Where to?" Mom asks as she drives us toward town on Sunday.

"Illusion Salon & Spa." Luna Le should be back from her exchange program, and she's the last person I need to speak to.

Mom glances at me briefly. "Who are you, and what have you done to my daughter? Monroe hates getting her nails done."

I chuckle. "*You* don't, and I need to talk to someone who works there."

After my conversation with Dad, I decided that even if Iris doesn't want to be with me, I can still help her by uncovering who's behind the charm. I'll double down on the investigation—prove to the Director I'm still focused and would make a great agent, all while winning back Iris's trust. I hope that'll be enough.

"Oh, good. You are still my kid," Mom says.

When we arrive at Illusion, Mrs. Le greets us with a smile. "Back again, Renae? And you brought Monroe. Are you going to let us give you a manicure this time?"

I glance at my dry cuticles with a frown. Maybe they could use a little shaping. "Okay, but only if Luna does them," I reply, glancing at the girl with black glasses and a bob.

Luna gestures to an open table while Mrs. Le helps Mom. "You really should come more often," Luna says as she examines my nails.

"They can't be that bad."

Luna laughs. "They are, but also we offer a student discount. A bunch of kids take advantage of it."

"Like who?"

"From FGH? Taylor Evans, Iris James, Anita Patel, and some others," Luna says as she buffs my nails.

"Do you talk about personal stuff with them?" I ask.

"Sure. School, family drama—"

"Crushes? Like yours on Diego?" Luna freezes, and her dark eyes find mine. "Who gave you the charm?"

"Um . . ." She drops my hands and glances at her mom, who's filling the foot tub with water.

"She thinks you know better than to use contraband. I don't want to burst her bubble, but you'll need to tell me the truth."

Luna jiggles her leg nervously. "Fine. I like Diego. I have since I first saw him. Earlier in the day, before he got hurt, I received a DM and a charm in my work locker. At first I thought the vial was empty, until I shook it and realized it was kind of heavy."

Luna shows me her phone and a single Instagram message from @Charmedlife33.

Check your work locker. Use it on your crush.

I was right. The dealer was at Illusion the day Diego was charmed. The person behind this is Noah Cham or Taylor Evans or both.

At school on Monday morning, Iris dodges me like a virus. I can't exactly blame her. I lied about the job I was doing for her mom and also failed to do said job. Not my finest moment, but we learn and grow. I watch as she disappears around the corner with Taylor by her side.

After lunch, I catch myself heading toward her locker out of habit. Blessedly, I remember myself before she returns.

I spend the entire week torn between confronting Iris and wallowing. I want to tell her how I feel at the perfect moment. In the middle of school with her arm freshly in a cast and her mean best friend/a possible contraband dealer watching is not that moment. Besides, since she put me on game to rom-coms, I know my confession needs to be big and memorable.

Over the weekend, I do a cleanup job with Dad to clear my head. A ballerina's pointe shoes won't stop doing sautés and pirouettes around the ballet studio. While charmed sporting goods exist, most athletes are encouraged not to use them. The owner of the shoes looks mortified by the time Dad and I catch them and vacuum the dust. One glimpse of the girl's purple leotard and Iris is back on my mind for the rest of the night.

By Monday morning, I'm feeling more optimistic about talking to Iris. On my way to my locker, I'm handed a QR code for last-minute prom tickets. Could prom be the perfect grand gesture? I'm so focused on coming up with a plan that I bump right into the back of someone.

"Watch it! There's space over there," the girl says pointing to a small opening in a mass of people loitering around.

"Why is everyone standing—?"

I cut my sentence short, my entire body tensing when I spot the reason for the crowd.

Taylor's in the middle of the hallway holding up a glittery cardboard sign, the words "Iris, will you go to prom with me?" made using letters cut out from magazines. It's so nineties chic that I'm surprised I haven't seen it in one of the cult classics Iris made me watch. Taylor's playing "I Say a Little Prayer" on her phone and swaying to the beat. The crowd swoons, particularly the freshmen and sophomores who are enamored with the idea of prom, too young to have experienced the stress of finding a date, an outfit, and the money to cover the ticket.

Iris appears genuinely surprised to watch Taylor shimmying up and down the hallway. She covers her open mouth with her hand. Taylor doubles down, doing a spin and dropping to her knees. A few teachers have poked their heads out of their classrooms to get a better view of the commotion.

I can't look away despite how painful this is to watch. Iris is nodding slowly, each bob of her head sending a sharp pain through my chest. When I imagine Iris at prom, it's not with Taylor. It's with me. Prom was never something I was planning on going to, but for Iris, I would. I'd do the promposal, get dressed up, dance to slow songs—the whole nine yards—if it meant we'd be there together.

The locker next to Iris flies open. Taylor clutches a quartz crystal dangling from her neck and slams her hand against it in time with the beat of the song. The action almost seems like part of the routine, except for the charm dust.

I didn't even know Taylor was queer, yet the subtle mishap makes it clear this promposal isn't purely platonic for her. And if the mishap wasn't enough evidence of Taylor's interest, she's staring at Iris with pleading heart eyes. It's the same expression I've seen on Daisy's face, Sofia's, Andie's, and everyone who's ever had a crush. Taylor wants this. And Iris, seemingly somewhere between embarrassed and flattered, says yes.

Twenty-seven

That ridiculous—fine, it was a little creative—promposal replays in my head like a bad horror movie for the rest of the day. I thought Taylor, Iris, and Jude were all going to prom together, yet Taylor's asked Iris to the dance like it's a proper date.

Taylor *likes* her. Taylor, who was at Illusion and the baseball game against St. Mary's to support Sean. Taylor was at Spellcast Roller when Liam received a playing card. And Promraiser when Sofia was supposed to get hers. She even mentioned attending pottery club to Iris. And, based on that public promposal, she's got a thing for Iris, which gives her a clear motive to charm her. Maybe it's not about getting ahead at the Bureau.

The hallway expands, or maybe that's my pupils dilating from adrenaline. The evidence is circumstantial. I'll need solid proof that Taylor is the dealer before bringing this to the Director. She knows that whoever's been doling out the charm has also been tampering with collections. If I can find a connection between Taylor and R&D, I can prove she's involved.

As soon as school ends, I drive over to the Bureau. Larry, the security guard, is talking to two teachers leading a field trip for grade schoolers in matching T-shirts. He gives me a thumbs-up, and the weight of how much I want to work here permanently hits me full force. Just as I'm getting settled at the Bureau, I fumble the opportunity to stay. I can't completely drop the ball on my chance to be an agent.

When I arrive at the collections window, I'm surprised to see Noah and Andie. I thought Noah was suspended until he was cleared as a potential suspect. Behind the computer is the same technician who was working when the director and I visited. She adjusts her green glasses and gives me a nod.

"Hey, Roe! Neo and I are dropping off residue from his sister's diary. It started reading her entries aloud. You'd be surprised how often a twelve-year-old girl thinks about Jung Kook. We're hitting up the tux rental after this. Do you think it'd be too cheesy if we wore matching suits to prom?"

"Prom?" I can hardly think beyond solving the case.

"Yes, prom. The biggest event of senior year outside of graduation. Happening this weekend." Andie tilts his head. "You good? You seem a little tense. You're not going to accuse my boyfriend of being a charm dealer again, are you?"

Noah looks from Andie to me. A light pink tint colors his cheeks as he stuffs his hands into his pockets and rocks back on his heels. "I know I'm technically on probation, and we aren't supposed to bring civilians in here, but Andie does have a visitor pass and I'm only dropping off some dust I collected," he rambles.

"It's chill. I'm not here to bust you," I reply as I try to gather my thoughts. "I have a question for both of you anyway." I grab the playing card from my bag and show it to them. "Have you seen this card before?"

I keep my gaze locked on their expressions, searching for cracks in the facade. Neither one of them gives me anything. Andie appears confused, whereas Noah actually breaks into a grin, his pale eyebrows lifting in surprise.

"Where'd you get that?" Noah asks.

"You recognize this?" I ask.

"Recognize it? I painted it. I painted an entire deck. Gave it to Taylor for her birthday this year," Noah replies.

"Taylor Evans?"

"Yeah." Noah reaches for the playing card, and I let him take it. "See how the white of the flowers is a little bit muted by the green in the leaves? That's because I did these alla prima, which means wet-on-wet. The green wasn't totally dry when I added the white."

I study the playing card and see the faint smudging he's talking about. Taylor really is guilty. She was everywhere the charm was spotted and has a connection in R&D—Noah. Not to mention she owns the deck of cards used to exchange contraband.

"Why do you look like you just learned Santa isn't real?" Andie asks slowly. "What's going on?"

"Did Taylor ever visit you here?" I ask Noah. "Have you maybe let her into the storage locker?"

The slow budding recognition on Noah's face is enough to confirm my suspicion.

"She visits me sometimes," he starts, his shoulders stiffening. "I started working at the Bureau last year, and Taylor's an overachiever. She comes to me for advice. Small tips to get ahead. She's not . . . Taylor's not a criminal."

"I wouldn't be so sure about that."

"You don't think Taylor has something to do with this, do you, Roe?" Andie asks.

"I think she might have everything to do with it. And I'm still trying to figure out if Noah helped her or not," I reply.

Andie crosses his arms. "I already told you he didn't."

"What do you need to clear my name?" Noah asks. "Do you want to see my time logs? Or there's got to be security footage we can pull up to prove my innocence." He looks at the technician working the desk, clasps his hands together, and asks, "Please, can I look up my timesheet?"

The tech studies him for a beat. "Fine. Make it fast." She points toward a shelf in the back. "I'll be right over there."

She slides out of the chair and Noah takes a seat. He immediately starts typing on the computer.

"The video footage from literally every time the love charm residue was deposited has been deleted. The Director checked," I reply. "Are there any samples there now? I dropped off one on Friday."

"Let me check . . . There's one from Friday. It's labeled 'in progress,' so R&D should have a match to a dissolver soon," Noah replies.

At least there's some good news. "Where were you on Wednesday, March fourth?" I ask. That was the day I deposited the residue from Electric Dust.

Noah spins the monitor around so I can see his timesheet. He jabs his finger at an empty row. "Wednesday . . . Yes! I wasn't here! See!" He navigators to the security logs, and frowns. "It shows me swiping in. That's impossible. I was on a date with—"

"Me," Andie says, showing me a photo on his phone of them at the local history museum. This wasn't on Instagram. "The museum is free on Wednesday afternoons. See those wristbands? They have a date on them. And you can check with the man at the front desk who sold us our tickets."

"Taylor must've taken my key card the day before. We carpool a lot," Noah says.

"What about on Friday, March sixth?" I ask, looking at my notes on my phone. "That was the night of the Spellcast Roller incident."

"I gave Taylor a ride to the Bureau that night to drop off samples. I waited in the car," Noah replies.

"She must not have deposited them," I reply. The seller isn't Noah or Jude or Liam or Iris (thank God). It's Taylor. She's clearly gone rogue. "I'm sorry I thought it was you," I tell Noah.

"You were only doing your job," Noah replies. "You honestly think Taylor did all this? Why would she?"

Because she likes Iris. Taylor's probably the person who dusted her. She was lying in wait to ask Iris out. I'm sure she's overjoyed with me and Anita out of the way.

I'm technically off the case, so if I bring this theory up to the Director, I'll need to be certain. "I'm not sure, but she's the seller, and I'm going to prove it."

On the drive home, all I can think about is Iris going to prom with Taylor. More than anything, I want her to have the happy ending she deserves. I want to keep her safe, even if it's no longer my job to. I text her again.

Hi. It's Roe. I hope you're ok. This is going to sound very jealous but hear me out. You can't trust Taylor . . . She's behind the mishaps.

Iris: why should I believe you? you lied to me for WEEKS!

I know. I'm sorry. But I'm not lying now. I promise.

Bubbles appear and then vanish. I hang my head and debate sending one final message. Love is about taking risks even if there's no guarantee the gamble will work out. It's about taking a leap of faith despite the chance of a mishap. So I type out what's in my heart and hit send.

Also, I miss you.

Tuesday is a haze of last-minute promposals, announcements for limo rentals, and chatter about charmed alterations at Needle and Thread. Girls want their dresses to have weightless pockets. Boys want their ties to glow in the dark. The entire school has prom fever. I'm pretty sure even Liz has FOMO, but she can't miss her brother's wedding.

When I see Taylor outside the cafeteria, I bite my cheek to stop from confronting her lest I tip her off. I brush past her, heading to our lunch table, which has whittled down to three. The chair where Iris sat is annoyingly empty. To take my mind off her, I center my attention on the case. Proving Taylor is behind this helps me and Iris. That's my focal point.

I pick at my leftover lasagna and force myself not to look at Iris's lunch table, where I can hear her and Taylor laughing. I wish I could access the @Charmedlife33 account, but I'm no hacker. Asking the Bureau is out of the question because I'm no longer on the case.

"I need to take Taylor down," I grumble.

"It won't be easy. She's willing to let Noah take the fall for her. Hell, I bet she's hoping he will. No way she's giving up without a fight," Andie replies.

"What if you get her to confess?" Liz suggests.

"She's been smart so far. I'll need leverage to force her hand," I reply.

"Hm. Maybe let her think she's won. You have the element of surprise. She doesn't know you're onto her," Liz says.

"Unless Iris tipped her off," I mumble.

Andie shakes his head. "I doubt it. She wouldn't betray the Bureau like that, especially her mom. But speaking of Iris, any plans to win her back?"

I glance at Iris's lunch table. "I want to apologize and tell her how I feel in a big way, so she knows I'm serious."

A slow, mischievous grin spreads across Andie's face. "You could do it at prom. Your prime suspect will be there with the girl of your dreams. We can't have that, can we?"

Andie has been trying to get me to go to prom all semester, and this time, I pull up the registration form using the QR code I got yesterday.

Seems like I'm going to prom after all.

On Saturday afternoon, I invite Mom over to help me get ready for prom. I dust off the gray fitted suit I wore to Dad's retirement party. Dad irons all the wrinkles out of my blazer and then sits me in the folding chair in the garage and gives me a last-minute haircut that looks professional. The sides are tapered, and it's left long on the top. Mom helps define the curls and then pulls out her makeup case and gets to work. She brushes on sparkly eyeshadow and lines my eyes.

Dad hands us two glasses of his homemade lemonade, and it almost feels like old times again. Seeing my parents work together solely for my benefit makes me realize that all those things Mom was saying about their marriage being worth the subsequent heartache because of the good that came from it may be true.

Shoving down my feelings and avoiding a relationship because it might blow up in my face could mean missing out on something great. And right now, the great thing I'm missing is a real chance with Iris James. One I desperately want.

Twenty-nine

After tolerating my parents taking a dozen pictures of me with Mom dabbing at her eyes and Dad giving me a thumbs-up, they drop me off at the Glamoured Manor, the only hotel in Fair Glen. The ballroom isn't huge, but the prom committee has ensured there's a red carpet for us to walk down so tonight, the hotel feels extra fancy.

Bureau agents are posted around the perimeter, their utility belts full of charmed gadgets. Based on Dad's tools from his time as an agent, gadgets include anything from endless rope and adhesive gloves for scaling a building to bubble gum flexible enough to capture a person. Looks like the Bureau is taking no chances tonight, which puts me a little more at ease.

Outside the entrance is a folding table where Mr. Michaelson, the photography club advisor, is checking tickets. Anita's sitting next to him wearing a pink off-the-shoulder dress. She has a stack of wristbands in front of her, and she looks me over with a raised eyebrow.

Mr. Michaelson smiles. "Monroe. We missed you in photography club this week. Are you not interested in continuing?"

"I—uh—was only trying it out," I reply.

"You're always welcome to stop by again." He scrolls through the list. "Hm. I don't see your name. I'm sensing a theme." He chuckles to himself. Anita lifts the corner of her mouth in amusement. I guess they still remember me crashing photography club.

"You bought a ticket, right?" Mr. Michaelson asks.

"Yep," I reply.

Mr. Michaelson shakes his head. "I'm sorry, but I don't see you."

"That's impossible." Could Taylor have messed with my registration because she knows I'm onto her? Did Iris say something?

Grumbles and sighs sound from behind me as the line lengthens.

"Why don't you stand over here until we get this sorted," Mr. Michaelson says.

I grind my jaw but move out of the way. Clearly someone doesn't want me to get in. Good thing I have backup. I text Andie, who's already inside with Noah.

Slight problem. I can't get in.

Andie: leave it to me!

Ten minutes later, Andie bursts out of the entrance with Noah hot on his heels. They're wearing matching tuxes, although Andie has glammed his up with a sequined rainbow bow tie. His glittery eyeshadow is framed by the sharpest cat eye I've ever seen. Meanwhile, Noah looks like a mixed James Bond, his light brown hair gelled into a perfect swoop.

"Someone's trying to spike the punch!" Andie exclaims.

Mr. Michaelson whips around, bug-eyed. "Where are the other teachers and agents?"

"Breaking up a fight on the dance floor," Andie lies.

"Jesus. All right. Anita, can you help the rest of the students in line while I check on this punch spiker? You two"—he points at Noah and Andie—"come with me."

While Andie and Noah leave with Mr. Michaelson to find the nonexistent punch-spiker, I'm left with Anita.

"Nice little diversion. There's still me to get through, though." She folds her hands across the tablet and smirks.

I cross my arms. "Shouldn't you be inside enjoying the dance?"

"I'm covering until Mx. Michaelson comes back. Wardrobe malfunction." Anita leans back in her chair. "Are you here for Iris? She's inside with Taylor."

I swallow hard. "I'm surprised *you* aren't here with her."

"Devin asked me as a friend. I wanted to go after sitting through prom committee meetings all semester and didn't want to come alone."

"Devin was going to use the love charm," I say. On Anita, no less.

Anita scrunches her nose. "But he didn't. We all know the feeling of liking someone who doesn't like you back."

"Really? Because after that kiss with Iris, I assumed—"

"What kiss?"

I frown. "At your house party."

Anita throws her head back and laughs. I swear my blood boils. "Iris and I didn't kiss. She pulled away from me, but not fast enough to stop a mishap, I guess. She said she liked someone else. I'm assuming that person is *you*."

"Wh-what?" I stammer.

"I admit, I was a little jealous when you two first started dating. She's different with you. I thought maybe she really changed. And when she pulled away from me, I *knew* she had. I'm not who she wants anymore. You are."

“What Iris and I had . . . it wasn’t real.”

Anita’s smile is laced with pity. “It wasn’t real with *me*. I wasn’t right for her. Her broken arm proved that. She never let me see the messy bits, you know? Everything always had to be perfect. But with you, she seems comfortable and genuine. Your relationship might be the realest one she’s ever had. I think you like her, too, or you wouldn’t be trying to sneak inside to see her.” Anita eyes me with a sly grin. “Love the outfit, by the way. Now go, before Mr. Michaelson comes back. Get your girl.”

A feeling of weightlessness comes over me. I don’t have to be told twice. I mouth a thank-you and then rush through the doorway.

Prom is lively, the music thumping even in the hallway. There are three times as many people here as there were at Anita’s house party, not just the popular kids. Everyone is dressed to the nines in their suits and gowns. Between the flashing camera lights, the loud music, the laughter, and the mass of bodies dancing around, I imagine this is what a club is like. The atmosphere certainly has an energetic quality to it.

I spot Andie and Noah talking to Mr. Michaelson by the DJ booth. Andie shrugs in response to a question he’s asked while Noah seems like he’s trying very hard to keep a straight face.

I turn away from them, in case Mr. Michaelson glances in my direction, and head off in search of Iris and Taylor. They aren’t on the dance floor, or by the finger food, or in the lounge area. I start to check the second floor when I notice a purple sleeveless dress and brown shoulders glittering in the chandeliered light.

I rush toward Iris, but someone grabs my arm and yanks me to a stop.

"Not so fast. You aren't ruining this for me." Taylor spins me around. She's wearing a yellow dress that complements her tan skin. "How'd you even get in? I deleted your registration."

"You owe me a hundred bucks. Luckily, I had help."

Taylor inclines her head. "You don't quit, do you?"

"Most would say that's a good quality to have," I reply.

Her grip tightens on my arm. I glance down and freeze. She's wearing a bracelet made of smoky white selenite crystals with star etchings—the same design I found on the crystals I saw in the art room locker. I photographed the contents with Jude. Taylor wearing the bracelet now is solid proof she stored the contraband there. It's enough to bring her in. I got her.

"Nice bracelet," I mutter, desperately trying to come up with a plan. "The crystals are so unique."

She eyes her wrist. "Okay. And?"

"And they make it super easy to identify the crystals as the same ones in locker 10308."

Taylor's eyes double in size. She rips her hand away, but the damage has been done.

"Is that true, Taylor?"

We both spin to find Iris standing behind us with her arms crossed as well as possible with a cast on. The sweep of her gaze leaves a flame of heat across my skin.

Taylor's eyes flick between us. "N-no."

Her body language says otherwise. Her gaze is shifty, and the planes of her shoulders are tense.

Iris shakes her head. "I don't believe you."

Taylor scoffs. "You're gonna take Monroe's word over mine? I'm your best friend. She lied to you. I did this for us."

"Did *what*?" Iris demands.

Taylor chews her bottom lip. "I like you, okay. I have for a while."

Iris's mouth drops open. "*You* charmed me?" she asks, barely loud enough to be heard over the music.

"You weren't supposed to get hurt. The charm was supposed to be temporary, just until I could tell you how I feel. You were so obsessed with Anita, but turns out, she wasn't who I had to worry about." Taylor narrows her gaze in my direction.

Iris inhales slowly. "What about Sean?"

"I don't feel about him the way I do you. I never did."

Iris throws her hands up. "You couldn't have talked to me about this?!"

"I've tried! You're always so flirty and not only with me but everyone, and I—I needed you to notice me without everyone else getting in the way."

"Being a flirt doesn't mean I deserved to be *charmed*. I'm in a cast at prom because of you!" Iris snaps.

"I know!" Taylor rubs a hand down her face, smudging her makeup. "I'm not saying what I did was right." Taylor reaches for Iris's hand. "You're amazing. I asked you to prom, not as a friend but because I want us to be together."

Iris grinds her jaw and says through her teeth, "I don't want that."

She rips her hand from Taylor's grasp and steps back. Her butt hits the table full of finger food and little dancing salt and pepper shakers. In the blink of an eye, the charm dust spreads.

The tablecloth yanks itself off the table, sending the salt and pepper shakers flying. It wraps around Iris's arms and pulls her away from Taylor. The butterfly napkin holders, charmed to flap their wings, take flight, weaving through the crowd on the dance floor. Surprised shrieks erupt as they land on people's heads. The Bureau agents run toward the commotion, and Taylor uses the opportunity to flee, disappearing into the throng of people.

My crystal bracelet warms, and I quickly suck up the magic and unravel the tablecloth from Iris's arms. We share a glance—a moment that lingers like the charm dust on her skin.

"Go," Iris says.

I don't want to leave her. I want to tell her the truth—that she's everything I want. But she and the other victims deserve the mayhem to end. So I give chase, following Taylor as she winds between students and ducks to avoid flying napkin holders. When she reaches the tables, she tosses a chair behind her. I leap over it, but it clips my shins. Pain sears across my skin, but I don't stop.

"Give it up, Monroe!" Taylor yells over her shoulder.

I think through my options to subdue her. My hair ties won't work since she's not by a door. I don't have an endless rope, but I do have pomade that's charmed for semipermanent hold. I grab the jar from my pocket and spread some onto my hands. I just need to get close.

Taylor rushes toward the stairs, but she's wearing heels that slow her ascent. My loafers come in clutch as I jump over a stair, my hand outstretched. I latch onto her arm, and the pomade locks us together like two magnets. She trips, and we both go down hard.

"Ow!" Taylor yells.

"It's over," I tell her breathlessly.

Two Bureau agents rush over with Iris and Mx. Michaelson, who's wearing a black velvet suit.

"What is the meaning of this?" Mx. Michaelson asks.

"Taylor's been selling contraband," I say.

The Bureau agents share a look. "Start from the beginning," a female agent demands. "Right now."

Taylor hangs her head, but it seems she's finally lost some fight. "Ugh, fine! I was hanging out with my neighbor, Noah, at R&D last month when I found a love charm." Taylor turns to Iris. "This was right after Anita broke up with you. I thought if I was supportive, you'd realize she wasn't the one. *I* was. But all you could do was talk about her and flirt with everyone else to mask your hurt. I needed a way to clear the space for me to make a move."

Iris folds her arms. "So you stole the charm."

"I honestly didn't think anyone would notice. There are hundreds of charms being processed at any given moment," Taylor replies. "I wanted to see how it worked before I gave it to you. I tested it on my older sister, and nothing happened when she flirted with the hot barista at Charmed Coffee. I figured it might be because she's a Mystic. So I wanted to try it on a Mundane. I knew Luna was in love with Diego since she talks about him every time I get my nails done. I figured she would be a good person to test out the charm. There was a mishap with the fans, but I wasn't sure that it was related, so I did another test on Sasha. I sprinkled some on her softball uniform before the game. By then the Bureau was bringing us in for a debrief, and I knew I needed to act fast. I sprinkled it on you hoping to prove we'd be a love match, but then you started dating Monroe."

"How'd Daisy, Sofia, Liam, and everyone else buy from you?" I ask, ignoring Taylor's glare.

"People talk about their love problems, especially at the height of prom season," she replies. "I needed to get rid of the remainder of the charm, and I wanted to help other people who were desperate to find love. I knew if I told students what the charm really did, they'd think it was too risky and wouldn't buy from me. I didn't know it'd cause so many mishaps, though. Sometimes it didn't, like with my sister."

"Or maybe your sister and the barista actually vibed?" I sigh and then ask, "Why'd you take the residue from the Bureau?"

"To delay finding a dissolver until I could ask out Iris. I knew when residue was being deposited by reading the reports. Most times, I was able to get to the Bureau before the dust was processed, but I missed one."

The deposit I collected from the playground after Iris's mishap. I gave the dust directly to the tech and never wrote a report.

"Why did you charm students from St. Mary's?" I ask, trying to plug the holes in her story.

She hesitates to answer until a burly Bureau agent clears his throat and prompts her to continue. "Don't stop now."

Taylor sucks her teeth. "To divert attention away from FGH, from me. Sean made me go to one of his baseball games. I dumped some of the dust into a player's baseball mitt and more into a girl's purse next to me in the stands. I admit, it was reckless."

"No shit. You broke the law and our oath to uphold it as recruits," I snap. "Did you need money that bad?"

"It wasn't about the money at first," Taylor says, glancing at Iris. "But I knew people would be more suspicious if I handed out the charm for free. Plus my family could use the extra cash. Our car is always breaking down, and bills are overdue."

"I'll call this in. You can explain yourself further to the Director herself," the female Bureau agent says. "In the meantime, here."

She holds her crystal and touches where Taylor and I are joined together. The pomade lifts away in a plume of pink dust. The agent hauls Taylor to her feet.

Taylor turns to Iris. "I didn't mean for you to get hurt. I only wanted to know if I had a real shot with you."

Iris doesn't respond. She doesn't even look up. The agents give Taylor a nudge to continue walking, and Mx. Michaelson follows, leaving me and Iris alone on the steps. The moment feels charged, like the air before a storm.

The DJ yells into the mic, "Fair Glen High, thank you for your patience while the agents cleared things up. How about we get back to having fun? Want to hear this year's prom court?" He drops a chest-thumping beat laced with sirens to pump up the crowd.

"That's my cue," Iris says. "I'm supposed to hand out crowns."

She doesn't give me the chance to reply before taking off down the stairs. I feel my window of opportunity closing.

Iris said she realized that relationships don't have to be movie perfect to work. Ours isn't. We couldn't even get through prom without mayhem. We made all these rules so we wouldn't get hurt while faking dating, and yet walking her to class, working the case, and calling her pet names only made me want her more. I don't care if we don't work out. She's worth at least trying for something more. I don't want another second to pass without her knowing how I truly feel.

I race after her, and before I can talk myself out of it, I jump on the stage. My legs are shaking with nerves, and my hands are so sweaty I'm afraid I'm going to drop the mic when I grab it from the DJ.

"Hey!" the DJ complains, sparking a few boos from the crowd.

"Iris James," I belt into the mic.

The ballroom quiets, and a few heads turn. The crowd parts slightly to reveal the prettiest girl in school, the glittering gold dust on her rich brown skin rivaling the decorations. A dozen phones shoot into the air to capture the moment.

I clear my throat and try to remember what the hell I'm doing. As I stare at Iris with her crossed arms and pursed lips, words begin pouring out.

"Iris, I'm sorry I lied to you. I won't give you an excuse, but please know all I wanted to do was protect you." Her stance softens some, encouraging me to continue. "The last month has been one of the best of my life. I love that you're a hopeless romantic. I love that you document our dates and make me watch cheesy nineties rom-coms. I admire how determined and unafraid you are to go after what—or who—you want. I like you, Iris. For real. And I'm so sorry I hurt you."

By the end of my speech, Iris is fighting off tears. I take that as my cue. I tell the DJ to play "Kiss Me" by Sixpence None the Richer and jump off the stage as the guitar starts thrumming.

I jog over to Iris, whose eyes are shining. She tries to hide her face by turning away from me. I cup her chin and hold her gaze. "Can you forgive me?" I ask.

Iris nods. "I forgive you. And you were right. I was using you to get back at Anita, and it totally backfired. I'm sorry, too, Roe."

"It's okay." I swipe at the tears sliding down her cheeks and then pull her closer, so close that I feel her breath against my lips when she exhales. An intoxicating scent of lavender and vanilla fills my nose and makes my head swim.

Her perfect lips part slightly, and I use the opportunity to lean in and press my mouth against hers. My grip tightens on her waist to stay upright as her tongue sweeps across mine. The kiss is pure magic.

A chorus of hoots and hollers brings me back to myself. Iris giggles, peppers a few lingering kisses against my lips, and leans back to smile at me.

When she does, the dust stuck beneath her skin drifts to the ground. The charm's been broken!

"Iris," I whisper. "You're no longer charmed."

She opens her eyes. "Seriously? Oh my God. Why now? I've liked you for weeks," she says.

"You *have*?"

Iris rolls her eyes and throws her arms over my shoulders, looping her fingers behind my neck. She sways our bodies in time to the beat of the song. "You honestly didn't know I had a crush on you? I thought you didn't like me at first, and after the party, I thought you were only stringing me along because my mom promised to make you an agent."

"No. I've liked you since movie night at my house, probably before then."

The corners of her eyes crease when she smiles and tugs me closer. "So why am I just now losing the charm? Why the mishap in my bedroom?"

I think back to the other couples who've managed to break the charm. Daisy had liked Chloe for a while, not knowing Chloe felt the same. At some point, they finally gave in to their true emotions. Iris and I have been avoiding ours until tonight.

"It's not just mutual attraction that stops the charm, but having the courage to act on those feelings," I tell Iris as soon as the realization hits me.

"So what you're saying is, I should've kissed you weeks ago," Iris replies with a cheeky grin.

I pull her closer and whisper, "We can make up for lost time now, babe."

Iris doesn't even cringe at the pet name before she tugs me into a kiss. The sure press of her lips sends a tingling warmth spreading through my body.

"I didn't need some big romantic gesture, you know," she says when we part.

"I don't know; my texts went unanswered. I had to get your attention somehow," I reply.

"I'm sorry. That was before I knew you liked me back. I was

trying to figure out if I could be friends with you and not flirt or hint at my massive crush," she replies.

"Massive, huh?"

"It's the *worst.*" Iris giggles.

"No, it's perfect. Because so is mine."

When I lean in to kiss her, she puts one finger to my lips. "One sec."

The song ends, and Iris rushes back onstage and whispers to the DJ. She takes a folded card out of her purse and is all smiles while she says, "Sorry, not sorry for the interruption, friends." She winks at me. "Without further ado, your prom court is . . ." The DJ hits a drumroll sound. "Chloe Nguyen, Sean Ashton, and Kori Matthews! Congratulations to our queen, king, and sovereign!"

The crowd erupts in cheers. Iris jumps off the stage and finds me as "There She Goes," a song I've heard in most of Iris's favorite movies, plays. She wraps her arms around my neck, and I hold her close.

"Who are we making jealous next?" I ask.

We share one long, earth-shattering kiss before Iris pulls back and smiles.

"Everyone, Monroe. Everyone."

Thirty

The Director sits at the head of the conference table, her shoulders drooping tiredly as she prepares to address the junior recruits. According to Iris, she's had a busy weekend, conducting interviews, giving briefings to the rest of the Bureau, and talking to the press since a recruit stealing and selling contraband is a PR nightmare.

The Director and I haven't spoken since the hospital. I can't decipher her expression. I wish I could tell if she's still disappointed in me or not.

She clears her throat, and the room quiets.

"Good afternoon, recruits. By now, you all know that Taylor Evans has been apprehended in connection with selling contraband in violation of Bureau regulation 17.1. I spent yesterday collecting a formal statement from her and others involved. I want you to hear it from me first. Taylor is no longer a recruit. Her actions were not those of an agent, and she will be facing consequences. Students who used the charm on others are being reprimanded as well."

Whispers fly around the room. The Director silences us with a raised hand.

"I also want to commend you all for your hard work on this

first case. I will be assessing your performance, and you should hear back within the next week or so about your next case."

The Director gazes at me, and I want to read into it. Is she going to recommend me for the task force?

After the Director answers questions like how long it'll take to help the students still charmed now that R&D has found a suitable dissolver (a few days) and whether Taylor is being arrested (yes), we're dismissed.

"Monroe, can you stay a moment?" the Director asks.

My pulse kicks up a notch as I wait for the rest of the recruits to leave. Once they're gone, the Director says, "I want you to know that I'm impressed with your performance on this case. You were integral in apprehending Taylor. I'll be recommending you for the task force in the fall. It would be part-time so you can focus on college. I look forward to working with you."

My heart leaps into my throat. "Th-thank you, ma'am! I can't wait!"

My whole body is vibrating with excitement. Before I can do something foolish like hug her, the Director adds with a mischievous glint in her eye, "Oh, and when you see Iris, remind her that those dishes she left in the sink aren't going to wash themselves."

I'm sure my face would be bright red if that were possible. Sounds like Iris told her mom about us and the Director approves . . . ? "I—I will."

"Have fun," she says.

Drive Me Crazy is playing at Electric Dust tonight. It feels serendipitous, the perfect movie for my plan. Liz, Andie, and Noah text me different versions of "You got this."

"Hey, Jimmy! Two tickets," I say to the attendant as we drive up.

Jimmy takes the cash from me and gives me a discreet thumbs-up without Iris noticing.

"Your mom wants me to tell you to wash the dishes when you get home," I say to take my mind off things. I'm so nervous, even my knees are sweating. Iris assured me she doesn't need perfect dates and big romantic gestures, but I know she likes them, and it's okay to romance the person you're with.

Iris releases a bark of laughter. "She and I stayed up late watching *Dirty Dancing*."

"So that's why she seemed exhausted this morning. I guess things between the two of you are getting better?" I ask as I drive toward the front of the lot. I park the car in her favorite spot.

"I took your advice and talked to her. I think she missed spending time with me too," Iris replies. She snuggles against me as the movie screen flickers on and the speakers crackle to life.

I wrap my arm around her shoulder as the Electric Dust logo fades, hoping she doesn't notice my trembling hands. A single question pops up on the screen.

Iris James, will you be my girlfriend?

The gasp Iris lets out makes the stress on my nerves worth having.

"Oh my God." She starts giggling, and her hand tightens around mine. "Yes! I'll be your girlfriend," she squeals, and then promptly kisses me until my belly swoops.

"Good," I mumble against the soft curve of her lips. "Let's try this again. For real this time."

IRIS-APPROVED ROM-COM LIST

- *Breakin' All the Rules*
- *But I'm a Cheerleader*
- *Clueless*
- *Dirty Dancing*
- *Drive Me Crazy*
- *Get Over It*
- *Love & Basketball*
- *Love Don't Cost a Thing*
- *Pretty Woman*
- *She's All That*
- *10 Things I Hate About You*

- *Heartstopper* by Alice Oseman
- *Simon vs. the Homo Sapiens Agenda* by Becky Albertalli
- *They Both Die at the End* by Adam Silvera
- *The Summer I Turned Pretty* by Jenny Han
- *The Sun Is Also a Star* by Nicola Yoon

ACKNOWLEDGMENTS

The idea for *Charmed and Dangerous* centered on a love charm and mischievous garden gnomes running through traffic. From there, the story bloomed into the wonderful book it is today. As always, I had a lot of help getting it to this point.

Mom, thanks for always supporting and believing in me. You're the best. Toby, my road dog and furry assistant, who has a cameo in this book like in the last, thanks for making me smile, bud. I miss you. Alaya, you're the best sounding board and the ultimate creativity boost! You help me untangle all the plot threads in my head, and I'm eternally grateful.

To my editor, Bria Ragin, for helping shape an idea into a book and coming up with a killer title. Your editorial guidance is top tier. And to David and Nicola Yoon for their enthusiasm and support through two books! Thanks to the rest of the team at Penguin Random House, who helped make this book shine: Megan Shortt, Colleen Fellingham, Tamar Schwartz, Tracy Heydweiller, Gabriella Murdoch, and Jasmine Ferrufino.

Thank you to my cover artist, Roxie Vizcarra, for bringing my girls and the gnomes to life, and to Casey Moses for designing a whimsical cover for this book.

To my agent, Rebecca Podos, for being an advocate and champion of my stories. Thanks for prepping this pitch with me when all I had was a loose idea.

Jenna Miller, thank you for patiently waiting until book two to be acknowledged! You taught me the ins and outs of writing. Your advice, like your friendship, has been invaluable. Thank you for always being there to hype me up and answer questions, and for generally being the best.

To Shalini Abeysekara, who read the first draft of this book and didn't hate it: Your feedback was perfect. Thanks to Isabel Sterling, who helped me flesh out the magic system and come up with some fun charms. And to the rest of the DTW crew, who are always the first people I turn to for anything writing related.

To everyone who made my debut year for *Brewed with Love* a blast, especially my conversation partners: Jen St. Jude, Leanne Schwartz, Trinity Nguyen, and Christine Callela.

And finally, thanks to my friends and to the booksellers, librarians, and readers who have shown up to every book event, shared every post, and celebrated every win. Writing is so much better with you by my side.

Read on for a sneak peek at . . .

"Everything you could want from a contemporary sapphic romantasy."

—Rachael Lippincott, *New York Times* bestselling coauthor of *Five Feet Apart* and *She Gets the Girl*

Published by Joy Revolution, an imprint of Random House Children's Books,
a division of Penguin Random House LLC, New York.

1

My tonic is out for blood. Raucous green bubbles burst from the mixing pot, spilling over the sides and rushing at my feet like starving mice. Unruly fizz chomps at the toe of my high-top Converse, instantly melting the rubber with its searing heat.

In hindsight, adding the carnations to the pot *after* my magic was a bad idea. Magic brews are fickle, and this one doesn't have neatly printed instructions in my family grimoire for me to follow. I'm creating it from scratch, a feat only a witch as skilled as Nana manages to make look easy.

A smoky haze clouds the kitchen, and the scent of charred rubber fills the air as I lurch away from a particularly large bubble.

"Sage! What's that smell?" Nana yells from her study.

“Um . . .” My gaze whips around for a way to stop the foamy mess before it escapes into the rest of the house. I’m not supposed to brew at home. Most of my supplies are at our apothecary, but after spending all night tinkering with this blend, I thought I’d finally cracked it. Joke’s on me.

Nana’s heavy footsteps and her signature scent—rose oil and lemongrass—meet me before she does. A second later, she’s standing in the doorway, wiry bifocals sagging halfway down her broad nose. Her large gold earrings match her gold bangles. The green monstera hair clip I gave her last Mother’s Day holds her tiny gray afro in place. It complements her olive linen shift perfectly. If Nana was a succulent, she’d be aloe vera—nourishing and sweet, with a hardened exterior.

“I know you are not brewing in my— Oh! Not my rug!”

The poor rug she’s had for the last three decades is fighting for its life against the remnants of my failed tonic. Scorch marks decorate the patterned fabric. Nana’s stricken, and my most apologetic smile doesn’t help the situation.

“Which rug, Hazel?” Tiva hollers from the other room, though her footsteps are light and swift as she heads our way.

“The purple runner from Rugs R Us, but that’s hardly the point,” Nana replies sullenly.

Tiva pokes her head into the kitchen with our oldest pothos tucked under her arm like a baby. Her thick, waist-length hair frames cheekbones as sharp as blades.

Sizzling bubbles charge toward her on a mission to

destroy anything in their path, but Tiva's fast. She flicks her wrist, gathering magic in her palm, and extends her hand. Instantly, the angry bubbles turn into harmless puddles.

Misbrewed tonics can do anything from itch to burn if touched. They leave behind nasty stains that are nearly impossible to get out (RIP my rainbow cacti shirt), and if ingested, they can cause dizziness, fever, pain, or even memory loss.

The key to brewing the perfect tonic is not only the ingredients—all grown in the Hemwood, a redwood forest soaked with more magic than a fairy tale—but how and when you put them in the pot. If the grimoire says "toss in" an herb, you better toss it. If it says to add a burst of individual magic *after* the mixture, don't add it before. The order of operations, the attention to detail, and the witch's intentions are what make a brew glow. Brewing isn't a problem when I have guidance, but inventing something new is advanced magic requiring a deep understanding of herbal properties and the problem in need of remedying. I'm still trying to wrap my head around that.

"Explain yourself," Nana demands, her round face pinched with annoyance.

I turn to Tiva for a show of support, but she shakes her head and covers a smirk with her free hand. Her and Nana have been together longer than the rug has haunted our kitchen, long enough to be like a second grandparent to me—one who is all too amused by my predicament.

Nana levels her gaze. "Well?"

"I swear I thought I finally cracked this tonic. It's going to put Bishop Brews back on top."

"Ah yes. Your breakup cure."

"It's not a *breakup* cure. It's an emotional recovery tonic, not just for heartbreak but for anything emotionally difficult someone might experience. It's genius." All the tonics we sell are healing, and this one would mend the mind and the heart.

Nana hums noncommittally. "And this has nothing to do with Ximena Reyes starting at the shop today?"

Ugh. As if I needed reminding. I've been dreading today since Nana told me Ximena applied for the open cashier position two weeks ago. Back then I could pretend it wasn't happening. It was easy to imagine Ximena's full day of training with Nana last weekend as a fluke. Now I have no choice but to face the music, which is easier said than done, because I'd rather pull out my teeth than spend fifteen long hours a week alone with Ximena.

I skirt around the counter, stepping over the now harmless mess on the floor, and throw the residue floating at the bottom of the pot into the trash. "Of course not. I'm doing this for Bishop Brews."

It's not a total lie. I *am* creating the tonic for our family apothecary, but I'm also doing it for me. I just don't mention that part because it's embarrassing enough to admit to myself that I'm still not totally over Ximena, even though it's been four years since she ghosted me.

I dust my hands off on my jeans, blow a frizzy curl out

of my face, and add for good measure, "Something needs to be done about Bottled Wonders."

Bottled Wonders is an apothecary in the neighboring town of Crimson Grove, the only other town in Northern California with a reputation for magic. The store is a force to be reckoned with. Customers say their prices are lower than ours, and their tonics work faster. Nana's too tired from running Bishop Brews for the last thirty years to try to compete with them, but at the rate Bottled Wonders is growing, our business won't survive much longer. I can't let everything she's worked so hard for crumble.

Nana grabs the mop from the hall closet and starts sopping up the remainder of the fizz. "Don't you worry about the apothecary. Tiva and I will figure something out. You should be focusing on—"

"School. I know, Nana, but Bishop Brews is important too."

Nana shakes her head, probably because she knows I'm not giving up. "Actually, I take that back." She points at the charred remains of her precious runner. "If you want to worry about something, worry about getting me a new rug."

A car horn blares from outside. Perfect timing. "You needed to upgrade anyway. This thing is nearly as old as you," I tease.

Tiva covers a laugh. Nana scowls half-heartedly and pushes the mop in my direction. "I'll pretend you didn't just say that. Go on, or you'll be late. It looks unprofessional if Ximena gets there before you."

"Can't we switch shifts? You work Sunday mornings, and I'll work evenings." I don't even try to keep the desperation out of my voice. I wouldn't have stayed up half the night if I wasn't desperate for a fix to this Ximena-size predicament.

"Sage, we've been over this. You have to be eighteen to work the farmers market on Sundays. Tiva has her own stall to run. She can't manage Bishop Brews as well. It has to be me." Nana peers at me over the rim of her glasses. "Unless your birthday changed overnight?"

I'll be eighteen in four months, which is exactly how long Ximena and I will be stuck working at the store together until we go to college in August. The universe hates me.

The car horn shrieks again and my phone buzzes in my pocket, begging me to get a move on.

"I really don't want to do this," I announce, slinging my bag over my shoulder.

"Luckily, I'm the nana here."

I grunt and shuffle toward the door. The parlor palm and the hanging verbena in the hallway wilt from my mood.

Tiva follows me. "Keep your chin up, love. This helps your gran. And believe it or not, a little change can be good."

Change can also be bad, especially when it means spending time with the girl who broke your heart.

"Not," I mumble. "I wish there was another option."

"You love Bishop Brews, right? Since Tracy retired,

the store could use the extra hand, at least for the spring and summer while your gran and I work the farmers market. Ximena may not be your friend anymore, but she's a good kid and a qualified applicant. Hazel isn't doing this to hurt you. She just wants to see the two of you find common ground again."

Nana has always seen the best in people and couldn't hold a grudge against a murderer. When she overheard Ximena asking about job applications at the Forage Collective last week, she readily offered her a position at Bishop Brews despite knowing our history. She said it was "time we get over our differences," as if what happened was just a simple misunderstanding. Nothing short of a miracle would get me to forgive Ximena.

"That's not going to happen. I don't get why Ximena would accept this job in the first place. She wants nothing to do with me."

"Maybe she needed the money, or she wants to make things right. Or both. You could ask her."

"Pass. We're only talking when strictly necessary."

Tiva shakes her head amusedly. "Have it your way. I'll see you tonight."

She nudges me outside, where my best friend, Mercer Kim, is waiting for me in her mom's Prius. On Sundays, we carpool into town because we both have morning shifts: me at Bishop Brews and her at the Enchanted Emporium. As far as succulents go, she's a lipstick echeveria—bright around the edges and blooming in warm seasons.

ABOUT THE AUTHOR

SHELLY PAGE is a young adult contemporary fantasy romance and horror writer. By day, she's a practicing attorney representing unhoused LGBTQ+ youth. By night, she's writing stories about love, magic, and mystery—all with the hope of providing genuine representation for queer readers of color. Shelly lives in Los Angeles with a collection of half-dead plants. She is the author of *Brewed with Love* and *Charmed and Dangerous.*

SHELLYPAGE.COM

@SHELLY_P_WRITES

CHOOSE LOVE.

JOIN THE JOY REVOLUTION!

Swoony romances written by and starring people of color

Learn more at getunderlined.com

1626g